"That night lingers like a ghost in the night. I haven't spoken a word about it since. Shit, no one could change it, so what was the point in talking about it? Auntie had suggested therapy a few times but what good would that do? It damn sure wouldn't bring my dad back! I guess going to see Joyce would allow me to put it away, hopefully. Secretly, I sometimes wish Joyce could have been part of my life. When I see a mother and daughter on a shopping trip or just having lunch, enjoying each other's company, watching them laugh, I feel like I missed out on something. Then I say fuck that. You can't miss something you never had."

Sherrie,

Thank you for
your support

Traci

Wild Ivy
Publishing, LLC

Published 05/15/2016 by Wild Ivy Publishing, LLC, Norcross, GA.

Any people depicted in stock imagery provided by Thinkstock are models, and such images are being used for illustrative purposes only. Certain stock imagery, © Thinkstock.

Because of the dynamic nature of the internet, any web addresses or links contained in this book may have changed since publication and may no longer be valid. The views expressed in this work are solely those of the author and do not necessarily reflect the views of the publisher, and the publisher hereby disclaims any responsibility for them.

ISBN: 978-0-9968140-5-8
ISBN (eBook) 978-0-9968140-6-5

10 9 8 7 6 5 4 3 2

Wild Ivy
Publishing, LLC

www.wildivypublishing.com

Author's Acknowledgment

First and foremost, I dedicate my existence to my Father God, my Lord and Savior, who has planned my life awesomely. I am thankful for my adorable son Que'von. You are my life and joy. Words cannot express the gratitude that I feel when I look at you. My goals and dreams have never been bigger than you; they are you.

When I decided to pen this novel, I was skeptical about telling a story that would touch a lot of people. I felt that it would impact some far more than others. My expectation was that it would ultimately help. By no means were my intentions to disrespect anyone. It's just a story highlighting a pain that takes on a life of its own, leaving you searching for healing. Understand that the only way to truly heal is to recognize that the things that happen in your life, my life, our lives. They are all a learning experience, so that you may be able to help someone else.

To family and friends: thank you for being just who you are. To my Wild Ivy Publishing family: thank you for helping me give Chantal Laine to the world. Shalom!

Meet Chantal Laine, a triple threat: rich, bootylicious, and brilliant. She was raised by a pimp and birthed by a hoe. Since she was taught that a nigga wasn't shit at a very young age, she became a fierce, unemotional bitch. Her number one rule was to never get caught slipping. Knowing how and when to play the game enabled her to move in a way that was necessary to win. She was undeniable and demanded respect in every room she entered, and in every situation she found herself in. Her validation came from all the commas in her bank accounts.

Money was her motivation. It felt way better than any amount of love a bitch or a bitch-ass nigga could give her. Her father's teachings about never catching feelings and that shit called love created her hard exterior. The moment she lost sight of her goals or became weak to that emotional shit... well, it would be fatal! Love will have you thinking with emotions instead of your mind, which results in wrong choices and reckless circumstances. Here's her story.

Chapter 1

Joyce Oglavee Laine grew up the oldest of three children in a single parent home. She never knew her father, and her mother was the type of woman that sacrificed everything, including her own children to have a man around. She allowed men to come into their home and scar her children's lives forever. There were countless times her mother would watch, smoking cigarettes, as Joyce was being fucked by one trick or another. Joyce became numb to all the predators her mom let rape her. When she tried to fight them off, they would physically hurt her. One man went as far as taking out his switchblade and cutting her across the face, telling her to 'never fuck with him again' and that 'whenever he wanted that pussy it was his'. All the while, her mother watched, laughing, as her young daughter was being abused. She was only nine years old at the time.

After four continuous years of abuse, she got enough courage to tell someone, but the damage was done. The scars were there and she would never recover from the one on the left side of her face, which seemed to validate her worthlessness, or the one in her soul, which validated her pain. Her mother wasn't the least bit moved by what those men had done to her daughter. When the nigga left her, she blamed Joyce. Said it was her fault that the he left and she didn't want her in her house any longer. She kicked her out and Joyce, having nowhere else to go, moved in with her grandmother. She lived in a two-bedroom apartment on the east side with eight other muthafuckas. The Oglavee's were a bunch of dysfunctional-ass people. Joyce was hopeless. It was no better than where she had come from. Each of her uncles and cousins abused her in one way or another. She would leave for days only to return to the same sexual and verbal abuse that she tried running away from. She became addicted to sex and drugs at a young age and her grandmother didn't pay attention to anything but her daily liquor bottle.

By the age of fourteen, Joyce had dropped out of school and barley knew how to read. Making a living would prove to be tough, but she found ways to survive. She was a pro at clapping her booty and popping her pussy. She would have sex with anybody. Age, race or gender didn't matter. Being raped all those years had taught her a lot, especially how to please any and everyone. Her goal in life was to be the best hoe in the world. She fucked every mediocre-ass trick on the block for forty dollars a nut. At that rate, she would never get to the next level of her game. In order to get the type of money that would change her life, she needed representation.

And then one day she ran into the nigga that changed her whole life. Jermaine Laine. Everyone called him Maine. His daddy and granddaddy pimped until the day they died, so pimping was in his blood. He referred to his stable as the bunny ranch and he had hoes everywhere.

His motto was 'fuck all bitches; I'm in love with the game!' It was all about the money with him and the minor details didn't matter. Little details like, the reason why a hoe ain't where she supposed to be and all that unnecessary shit. It was a waste of his time. See, he was a no-nonsense pimp and the last mafucka you wanted to cross with some fantastic foolishness. You didn't get much conversation out of him because he didn't have much to say. The only words he had for a hoe was, 'Where my money, bitch?' He should have had that tattooed on his forehead!

He demanded loyalty and the right accessories: big booty, little waist, eatable titties and a fire-ass pussy. He didn't have time for anything else. Joyce jumped at the chance to be with this nigga, pimp or not. She put in so much work that she became the recruiter, the dick licker and the ass kicker for his organization. She was willing to do anything for Maine. He made sure she never lost sight of the fact that this was a business, and their business was pimping. Maine protected her from the tricks, her family and even herself. By the time she was seventeen, she was a thousand dollar an hour, well groomed hoe. He exposed her to shit she couldn't even pronounce. The little class she had, well Maine bought that shit from a store.

Maine moved Joyce into a four bedroom house in Ladera Heights. Her neighbors were doctors and lawyers. The big house and grand lifestyle was foreign to her, since she came from nothing. She was definitely out of her element. She had to learn how to conduct herself accordingly because this was a world she knew nothing about. Since she was so young and had no real understanding of life, let alone the game, she was like a needle in a haystack. But Maine gave her the knowledge she needed to get right. He even gave her the gift of loyalty by giving the bitch his last name! He made her his bottom but nothing he did for her was good enough. She was constantly giving the pimp game a black eye. He thought her loyalty was suspect and Joyce never could figure out why Maine kept putting hands on her. One must realize that if you continue to do the same shit, you will continue to get the same results. Hoes have to be accountable for the choices they make, and know that those choices have consequences. Soon her antics were going to catch up with her, and she had no idea of the price she would pay.

Macy, one of Maine's hoes, was the snitch bitch for opportunity. She was also the middleman between Joyce and all of her tricks. Whenever they wanted to meet up with Joyce, off the record, they would holla at Macy. But little did Joyce know, the messages always went to Maine first. See, in this game, loyalty is the ultimate form of respect. What's not respected is a snitch ass bitch with ulterior motives. Macy wanted to become the one hoe that mattered, but what she didn't know was that she was just a bitch Maine would bend until she broke. Maine dragged and pushed all his hoes.

If they weren't built for that shit, they were sure to blow. One thing and two for sure, Maine knew exactly what type of cloth Joyce was cut from and every other hoe at the bunny ranch couldn't match her. He had no trust for bitches. Their only purpose was to get that cake up as quickly as they could. He said, "A hoe is liable to blow, so get all you can out her ass." The fuck he needed with a bitch? He just needed what that hoe could contribute. He loved them all in a way, because he loved the game. They worked their asses off because they all loved him, too.

But shit didn't get past him. He started noticing Joyce's mood swings. Sometimes she got slapped in her mouth for it, and sometimes he let her attitude slide, charging it to the fact that females had hormonal shit going on. One evening, Joyce came in from shopping. No one else was allowed to go shopping but her. She was responsible for buying all the gear that the girls would need for the week. On this particular day, she walked in and didn't speak to anyone, just threw the bags on the sofa, grabbed her cell out of her purse and went into the bedroom. She called her best friend, Tiffany.

"Hello?"

"Hey Tiffany, this Joyce." Tiffany was one of Joyce's slutty friends and she hated Maine and everything he stood for.

"Hey Joyce. What's up witchu?"

"Girl, I really need to talk," Joyce said, her voice just a whisper.

"What's up? Girl, what's wrong?"

"Bitch, I'm pregnant."

Tiffany let out a long sigh and then said, "Pregnant! Does Maine know?"

"Naw, Tiff, not yet."

"What you mean, 'not yet'? You not thinking about keeping it, are you?" Tiffany could not believe what she was hearing.

"Yeah, Tiff. I'm already like six months gone. Ain't nothing I can do about it now."

"Six months! Bitch, why you just now telling me? And where you hiding that baby at?"

Joyce said, "I know right? I was in denial, trying to do any and everything to hide my stomach." She took deep breaths and willed herself not to cry.

"You want me to come over?"

"Naw, I'm good, Tiff. I gotta go to work, but if I need you, I'll call you."

"You going to work?" She couldn't believe Joyce was still turning tricks when she was that far gone.

"Yes I gotta go. Bad enough I'm pregnant, but missing work is unacceptable."

"Yea, right. One of Mr. Laine's rules, huh, Joyce? Okay. Call me if you need to talk. Later."

Joyce hung up the phone and opened the door. Maine was on the other side and had been listening to the whole conversation! He had noticed the weight gain months ago and all the cravings this bitch was having. He wasn't dumb by a long shot. Maine grabbed her by her hair and slung that bitch down the hallway, striking her with his fists, knocking out some of her teeth. The blood went everywhere! She cried out, "Maine, please stop!" She was scared. The way the he was kicking and beating her made her fear a miscarriage. She screamed again, "Please stop! I'm pregnant! Please!"

Maine said, "Yea, hoe. I know you are. That's why I'm beating your ass. I should kill you, bitch!" He kicked her in the stomach and walked away, saying under his breath, "Go clean yourself up, you fucking ungrateful ass bitch." She struggled to get off the floor while wiping blood from her face. She felt as she did when she was a young girl, knowing she was in strict violation, bringing a baby into the fold. All those childhood feelings resurfaced and threatened to drown her, but she regained her composure and did as she was told.

Since there was no bleeding from her vagina, she didn't go to the emergency room. Instead, she lay in the dark until it was time to go to work. Maine knew that what was done was done and there was nothing he could do about it. True, he expected all his hoes to use condoms, but you couldn't trust a hoe to do what she was told. Regardless of whether the baby was his or not, it was his duty to accept it. On April 7th, a beautiful baby girl arrived, weighing 6 pounds and 6 ounces. She was named Chantal Vivica Laine. Everyone came by to see the offspring of Jermaine and Joyce Laine. Although Maine wasn't happy when Joyce got pregnant, some say it changed him. He became more humble, however the pimping didn't stop. Joyce still had to suit up and get on the grind more than ever now. She didn't like how Maine cared for Chantal. He never showed her affection they way he did the baby. When the time came for baby Chan to go to daycare, he wasn't trying to hear that shit! He took care of baby Chan during the day.

Meanwhile, Joyce started seeing this trick by the name of Antonio Milton, unauthorized for about two years. Maine knew exactly what was up because he had dealt with this trick in the past. He had already warned him that this particular hoe was, to some extent, off limits. Nonetheless, she was still a hoe and he was a certified trick so an agreement was made. He could have an hour fuck two, maybe three times a week. Maine advised him of the consequences of going too far with this particular hoe, and if he tried him, there would be repercussions to deal with. Antonia didn't give a fuck about all that shit because he was in love. Maine's threats went in one ear and came out the other. Antonio was determined to get this hoe and he didn't care about no consequences. His lame ass lost sight of what was real and what was paid for. He was the type of trick that thought he could come into a bitch's life and save a hoe. Joyce thought he was all the things that Maine wasn't. What she failed to realize was that Maine was her pimp and this trick-ass nigga was nothing!

One beautiful Sunday afternoon around four thirty, Antonio sent a message that he wanted to take Joyce and baby Chan out for ice cream. By this time, Chantal was about three, maybe four years old. Even though Joyce had taken her on many outings with this trick, she made sure today was different. She groomed Chantal up with extra care, paying attention to every detail. When Maine got the information about the secret rendezvous, he was furious. But no one would have known it. He laid low to see just how far this bitch was gonna take this shit. When Joyce accepted Antonio's invitation, she lied to Maine about going to a doctor's appointment. He was so kosher with it! He even helped the bitch get ready, which was way out of the norm for him. All the while, he thought about the lies that this hoe had been telling him and the dishonorable shit that she was getting ready to do. He felt disrespected. He wanted to bust that bitch upside her head. But he decided to make it easy for her and even offered to let her use his car to drive to the appointment.

Joyce couldn't believe it. She said, "Are you serious, Maine?" He said, "Yeah, take the Beemer." Well, that made her happy because it showed that he cared and trusted her enough to give her that privilege. And it was a privilege, cause no one ever drove Maine's vehicles. He was being very helpful and attentive, which was way out of his character. Joyce, unaware that Macy had snitched, just thought it was love. Silly bitch. Maine waited for her to pull off and then Macy drove Maine in her car to follow her. Joyce was so excited that she never noticed them behind her.

When she arrived at the ice cream shop, Antonio was waiting for her outside. He helped her with the stroller and the baby bag and then they walked into that shop like a fuckin' family. Maine was parked across the street, watching it all. He waited maybe ten minutes and then got out of the car. Then, Macy drove right in front of the shop as Maine walked across the street. When Maine walked in, not too many words were said. Joyce couldn't believe her eyes when she saw him. Instead of trying to defuse the situation, she was acting as if Maine was wrong for stomping in that bitch the way he did! She jumped up from her seat and said, "Maine, what are you doing here?"

He looked at her with rage in his eyes and said, "What the fuck you mean, 'what I'm doing here', bitch? Whatchu doing here, hoe? Take my daughter and my car home right now!" As she was trying to pack up, looking stupid and caught in her act, she turned to Maine and before she could say another word, he backhanded that bitch in the face. "Bitch, you heard me." He grabbed her jaws and squeezing them as hard as he possibly could, looked her dead in her eyes and screamed, "NOW, BITCH!" Maine then turned to Antonio and said, "What up, nigga? You paying for this pussy today?" Antonio stood up and said, "Hold up, Maine. It ain't what you think!" Maine said, "What is it then, nigga?" He grabbed him by the neck and told him, "Nigga, I told you once and that was it." Maine pulled the forty out of his back and pointed it Antonio's chest. Joyce knew what was getting ready to happen. She ran out of that ice cream shop as fast as she could.

By the time she was in the car it, was done. Maine shoved Antonio by the throat and blasted two rounds of that hot lead in his chest before he could catch his balance. Antonio dropped right the fuck where he was standing. Maine turned around looked at all the scared ass people in that shop and said, "You mafuckas better not say nothing." He walked out that bitch like nothing happened.

What happened to Antonio Milton that day was his own fault. Maine definitely made good on his promise. One thing about him, if he said it once, no more conversation was needed on that subject. Antonio Milton had Jermaine Laine fucked up. He didn't play and he didn't take that shit off nobody. Afterwards, Maine laid low over at his twin sister, Jackie's house. He was only able to kick it there for a few hours. There was one thing she didn't play with and that was the law. She convinced him to turn himself in and he did. On the way to the jail, she called the best of the best attorneys and represented him like any boss sister would.

When they arrived at the jail, the police didn't treat him like an animal as they are known to do, especially with black men. Had it not been for his sister and the rest of the legal team she put together, the police would have beaten Maine's ass or killed him. After taking his statement, they booked him on a murder charge with no bail and it was all Joyce's fault!

Chapter 2

When my daddy got locked up for murder, Joyce let everything go, even herself. What little she was left with, she pawned, then fucked off the money on bullshit. She never learned how to maintain and be a boss bitch, it just wasn't in her. Her only option was to move us in with her mother, the same bitch that didn't give a fuck about her years ago. We lived there with nothing except welfare and food stamps until her mama got tired of us and kicked us out on the street. It was nothing for her to put us out cause she was a cold hearted bitch. Joyce's grandmother passed away about two years before Maine got locked up, so she couldn't go there. Her last hope was based on some trick she met at the club or on the corner somewhere.

When Maine got the news that we were homeless, he blew up! He reached out to his sister, my Aunt Jackie, to make sure that she went and handled that situation. But Joyce always ignored her and wouldn't accept any help, telling her that we were okay. That was a lie! We were damn near starving and homeless! She had me out in the streets for six years while she held onto the dream that Maine would be back in a minute and that our situation was temporary. She used to say, "We gonna be straight, Chan. Just give it a minute."

Finally, she moved us in a low income housing project, and let me tell you, it changed my life. At such a young age I had already been through a lot. Thank God I was never molested by any of the ratchet ass niggas she brought around. She wouldn't have cared if I was, but I cared and I wasn't letting no shit like that happen to me. I was eleven years old and I didn't play with or even look at her tricks. It was obvious that Joyce had no respect for me or herself because she was fucking these tricks with me in the same room. In a way, I'm glad she did, because I learned a lot from my hoe ass mama.

Quilla Jones, my BFF, my ride or die, we were eight months apart in age. We both had the body of grown women and the sense that most kids didn't have at our age. Unlike me, she had a motherly instinct that I didn't have or want. I met Quilla when she was hanging clothes on the line in the projects. She was doing her best, standing on top of a shopping cart to reach the clothesline. I noticed her struggle and asked if she needed help. She looked at me with the strangest expression and said, "No, and don't try being so nice. Around here it will only get you fucked up."

"Well, it just looked like you needed some help. My name is Chantal. Me and Joyce just moved into four twenty four." She started laughing and said, "What? Gay ass Larry's crib?" I really didn't know what was so funny but I said, "Yeah, I guess."

Quilla said, "So you his people?"

"Naw. He know Joyce, but I don't know him."

"So, who is Joyce?" she asked.

"The lady who birthed me."

Quilla looked at me as if I were slow. "What you mean? She your mama, right?"

"No. I don't have a mama."

"Girl you sound crazy! 'The lady that birthed you.' What the hell is that about?" Quilla thought that was the funniest thing she had ever heard. I thought she would never stop laughing, and when she did, she said, "Well, my name is Shyquilla, but you can call me Quilla. And yeah, you can help me."

I said, "And I ain't crazy, Quilla. My story is a long one."

"Shit, who's ain't? You got any sisters or brothers?"

"Nope, it's just me and my Auntie Joyce. My dad in prison."

She said, "Wow. I bet it is a long story, but at least you know where your daddy at. I never met mine." From that moment on, we felt we had something in common, and from that day until this one we have been best friends. I was timid and spoiled and she was rough and hard. I showed her how to be a girly girl and she showed me how to survive in this jungle. We clicked like the hands on a clock. We were always together. We were the flyy girls that always rocked the newest shit. My Auntie Joyce made sure of that. All I had to do was ask and I would get it and then I would share it with Quilla. I loved her and more importantly, I trusted her. Our friendship was genuine from day one. I spent the night with her and her family the first day I met her, and for the next two years, it was the same routine.

Ms. Bea was Quilla's mom. Actually, she was more like a guardian. She gave zero fucks about her kids, or anybody for that matter. As such, she gave Quilla all of her parental responsibilities and then she would micro-manage her. But Quilla handled the responsibility despite the problems and heartache that came with it. She dedicated her young life to her brothers. She cooked and cleaned, but her mom wasn't concerned with any of that. Ms. Bea worked all night and drank all day. If it wasn't for Quilla, they probably would have starved to death.

Her mom's career consisted of sliding up and down that pole and playing games with the welfare authorities. A damn stripper that never made enough money to do anything with. I never did understand it, but that seemed to be enough for her. She was just like most females that worked petty ass jobs trying to stay under the system's radar, living mediocre, becoming stagnate. However I must admit, Ms. Bea showed me consistency, cause she was constantly at that damn welfare office, begging them folks. You see, the system is designed to keep you down. A crumb is all they give you, and if they find out you done got enough crumbs to make a full loaf of bread, then your ass is through! You going down for fraud.

Ms Bea also showed me what I did not want to be, which was lazy. She stayed in a can of Schlitz. I don't know what kind of strip club she was working at, but I do know some bad bitches that live on the pole, and they getting it! As I said, some do and some don't. Maybe it was the fact that she was a functional alcoholic and only maintained for the next beverage. I could never understand why she went to the store at 11:00 in the morning to get two Schlitz malt liquor tall cans and then go back at 1:00 in afternoon, to get two more cans of the same shit. Why not get the whole fucking six pack at one time?

"Quilla!" As usual, she was screaming at the top of her lungs. She didn't have an inside voice.

Quilla answered, "Yeah ma?"

"Where you at? Come here!"

Quilla rolled her eyes and moved two steps closer. "Yes?"

"Listen, Quilla and listen damn good. I need you to go to the store and get dinner. Only get what I tell you. And clean this kitchen before you leave."

"Okay Ma. Can Chantal..." Before Quilla could finish, Ms. Bea knew what she was going to ask. She knew I wanted to spend yet another night. Shit, I had practically moved in already. "Yes, Quilla. Chantal can spend the night, but I know ya'll better keep this house clean." One thing about Ms. Bea, she didn't clean but she liked it clean.

I said, "Hi, Ms. Bea."

"Hello, Chantal. Did you hear what the fuck I told Quilla? Ya'll mess up my house, I'm gonna beat both ya'll ass."

"Yes, I heard you, Ms. Bea." As usual, I was unfazed by the threat.

"Then act like it, bitch. Come here. Let me see them earrings. Is them zicronics?" This lady didn't even know how to pronounce zircons so how would she know the difference from the real thing? I said, "They're diamonds, Ms. Bea." How dare her think I would wear something fake!

"Oh, them diamonds," she said in a sarcastic tone with a smirk on her face.

"Yea, my auntie gave them to me on my birthday last year."

"Quilla told me you got a rich aunt in Beverly Hills. Well why don't you go live with her, instead of running around here in the projects with diamonds in your ears? You ain't rich, Chantal!" She was such a negative person. She really got on my nerves, but I always respected her because she was my best friend's mom.

"Ms. Bea, she don't live in Beverly Hills, it's Bel Aire and I would love to live with her. It's just complicated."

"Umph. Whatever. Quilla, did you hear what the fuck I said?" She just brushed me off as if I wasn't even standing there talking to her. Quilla answered, "Yea, ma I did." Quilla could only mumble under her breath, "Sorry-ass." I could see the look on her face and I understood it immediately. It was 8:30 in the morning and her mother was already drunk and probably just coming in from the night before.

"Listen, take these foods stamps and go get some ground beef and the shit for the tacos. That's what you're cooking tonight, and chicken tomorrow night. I'll be out till Wednesday." Damn, it was Sunday and she didn't even care. Sometimes she would stay gone longer than that on holidays. "Get some juice and cookies. And get me some grapes. Don't spend all my fucking stamps either! Oh and get Man-Man some chips."

"What kind?" Quilla asked.

"Bitch, I don't give a damn! Just some of that bullshit he be eating all the time."

Being called a bitch by Ms. Bea was like a second name. She called everybody that. Quilla and I laughed at Ms. Bea all the way to the store. We kept mocking her, saying, "And get me some grapes." The way she talked was so hilarious. Growing up, our parents were the main characters in our lives. Instead of wishing they would change, we just accepted them for who they were and dealt with it.

Chapter 3

Quilla had two brothers. The younger one was named Jaquan Jones and we called him Man-Man. He was a scholar in school, young football star and very talented. He would always invite me to his games, but with all that was going on in my life, I could never make it. I promised him that one day I would go. I could tell he had a baby crush on me, because he was always picking me flowers and shit. Telling me how good I smelled. He definitely had the understanding of how to approach a lady. He said that he was a Mack like his older brother, Jah. His dreams were bigger than his situations. He had goals to get outta of this fucking hole and make a better life for his family. That's all he would talk about. How he was gonna be this famous football player, buy his momma a big house, and make his sister and brother rich.

Jaheim Jones was the older brother. He and Quilla were four years apart. Now this nigga right here had that shit from top to bottom! Pretty-ass hazel eyes, black silky straight hair, and the complexion of them Indian muthafuckas down at the 7-Eleven. You know, black but with a bronze coat. Yeah, Ms. Bea did her thang when she gave birth to him! That body was flexed. He was wonderful eye candy and loved to work out. We had a great relationship. He was my best friend's brother but we *played* with each other. He was funny and attractive so it was hard not to notice him. Besides, who doesn't *play* with their best friend's brother anyway? Quilla loved her brothers. She wasn't old enough to take care of herself at eleven years old and here it is she got two kids to look after. She grew up really fast.

The next morning it was raining, which never happened in Southern California. We were getting ready for school. Man-Man had already left because his bus came super early. Quilla was screaming from upstairs. "Jah, hurry up! You're going to be late for school."

Jah said, "I ain't going today, Qui."

"What you mean? You should have walked Man to the bus stop." She came from the stairs, trying to figure out what Jah was talking about.

"Ah, he cool sis. He with his lil homie."

"And why you ain't going to school, sir?" Quilla asked, assuming the mommy role, as usual.

"I ain't feeling that shit today, sis."

Tat tat tat. We all stopped to listen to gunfire outside. "Damn!" Quilla yelled. "They always shooting around here. I can't wait until we move. I'm going to get in the shower. Chan, you take yours already?"

"Yeah, I'm good."

"Well, did you make breakfast?"

"Yeah and I ate yo momma grapes!" She looked at me and we both laughed so hard. That was our inside joke of the day, "Yo mama grapes!" We forgot about the racket outside and Quilla went to take a shower. The gunshots were not uncommon in this neighborhood. Niggas shot in the hood every day. It was just normal. I focused my attention on Jah. "And why you not going to school, Jah?"

Grinning, he asked, "Why you ain't going, Chantal?"

"Oh, boo boo, I'm going to school. I gots to know how to count my money."

"Why don't you come over here and count these nuts." He started rubbing himself.

"Ugh, you get on my nerves, Jah!" I was pretending to be angry, but...

He said, "No I don't." This nigga was so fine I would do anything he told me to do, but...

"Yes you do! I can't stand you!"

He stopped teasing. "Let's go upstairs." Just by the way he was holding me, I knew I was going with him, but I didn't want him to stop trying to convince me.

"No, stop. Don't touch me!"

"What you mean, 'don't touch you?' Let me lick your pussy, Chan."

"You so nasty. Stop it!" *Please don't stop!*

"Come on girl. You know you want to and I know you want to, so come on. Why you gonna act like a little girl now?"

"Boy, I ain't no little girl!" I'm saying 'no' but my body is saying 'yes'. Jah and I were so young to, first of all, be doing what we were doing and, second, know how to do it. At 11 years old, I had seen and done more in my short life than most grown women. I was quite promiscuous, but I was still a virgin. I knew a lot about sex and wanted to have it, but I wasn't ready for it and that was my choice. Joyce used to fuck niggas in the room with me. She thought I was sleeping, but I saw everything she was doing. She was a slut, but I must give credit where it's due though, because she was good at what she did. Other than sucking on some nigga's dick or letting him fuck her in the ass, she had no other skills. She was another one that I didn't want to be like.

I decided to give in. "Okay, but we gotta be quiet and quick."

"Just shut up and go upstairs, Chantal."

"No. Down here in the bathroom, and don't tell me to shut up."

"Why? Let's go to my room." Jah wanted to get her in his bed.

"No, Jah. Downstairs bathroom. Look, you want to or not?"

"Fuck it, come on."

I've been touching myself since I was six years old. When he locked the door and leaned me over that sink, I knew what was in store for me. Jah taught me so much about having sex without the penetration. Yeah, he was fire with it! Every time I was at their house, this nigga was on me. That was the beginning of me and Jaheim Jones. We used to sit up for hours *playing* with each other. He appreciated the skills I had. He said I was so sensual and he loved that I loved to blow him. That was good enough for me. I literally had to stop this nigga or he would have kept going. "Okay Jah, I gotta go to school. That's enough."

"Okay Chan. Shit, my day ready now!" He slapped my ass and called me a 'bad bitch'. I liked the sound of that. I used to hear niggas tell Joyce that shit all the time. Now I got a nigga telling me I'm a bad bitch, too. He kissed me on the forehead and went to brush his teeth. As I was coming outta of the bathroom, I thought, "Damn, what if Qui catch us one day? What would I say?" I ran upstairs to see if she was ready to go.

"Quilla, how long you going to be in there? I don't wanna miss the bus."

"Okay, here I come."

Bam, bam, bam! The beating on the door made it seem as though an earthquake was about to erupt.

"Damn! Who the fuck is beating on the door like you crazy? Hold on!" Jah was hollering out the window of his mom's bathroom upstairs. His mouth was full of toothpaste. The water was running and Quilla was in the other bathroom screaming for Jah to shut, up thinking he was the cause of all the noise. Jah wiped his mouth and ran downstairs. He couldn't believe his eyes when he opened the door. There stood his homie, Bear, holding Man-Man in his arms, who was covered in blood... dead. Another homie had his feet, trying to get him in the door. All I heard was Bear screaming at the top of his lungs.

"Get the lil homie! Get the lil homie! They going to pay for this shit, believe that!"

As I came to the bottom of the stairs, I saw Jah laid out on the floor, passed out from the sight of his little brother's dead body. He was out cold! I guess shock was the first emotion that hit me. I didn't know what to do or say. I tried to compose myself. I asked, "What the fuck happened, Big Bear? Who did this?"

Jah was gaining consciousness and woke up in a rage, jumping and crying and screaming. Just hysterical, saying over and over again, "Who did this? Who did this? Not my muthafuckin' little brother! Who did this, Big Bear? Muthafucka, who did this?" Jah jumped in Bear's face and snatched Man from his arms. He fell to the floor again and began to rock back and forth. Big Bear said, "There was a police chase. I don't know if the punk-ass police or them buster-ass niggas fired the fatal shot. All I know is that I couldn't leave lil man at that bus stop. I had to bring him home." He kept repeating, "I had to bring him home, I had to..." Big Bear made a promise that he was "gonna get those niggas and they whole fucking family. That's on everything!" He angrily slammed out the back door.

I was calling the paramedics just as Quilla was coming down the stairs. "Jah, what's going on with all this damn noise?" As she hit the bottom stair, she saw one brother in a state of shock, covered in blood while he rocked the other brother in his arms. She yelled so loud. I think that the paramedics got the gist of the call just from her screams. It seemed as though Quilla had just stepped into a movie. Everyone was standing around in disbelief. Quilla managed to crawl over to the only two people that she had in this world. She grabbed both of them and held on. Those boys were her responsibility, the only real lifelines that she had. Quilla was devastated. I think she stopped breathing when she realized what was going on because she was still trying to gasp for air when the paramedics arrived. Jahquan Jones was pronounced dead on arrival.

This shit had definitely made the hood hot. Niggas was strapped up, just waiting and hoping for a fool to step outta line. If you didn't belong on the block, your ass was got, simple as that. Man, woman or child, it didn't matter. There were no passes. Niggas was suited and ready for war.

Ms. Bea didn't find out her baby boy was dead until two days later. At the time, she was nowhere to be found. When she finally did come back, she was broke and disgusted. My Aunt Joyce gave the funeral home six thousand dollars cash to bury Man-Man. She was more than happy to do it because she knew it meant a lot to me. The funeral was sad and short. No one was able to say anything at the service. It was very emotional. After the service, Ms. Bea partied her ass off. I never did see her cry. Later, everyone gathered at Quilla's house to offer their condolences. They didn't bring the normal food dishes that folks usually bring, not at Ms. Bea's house! These fools brought Jack Daniels, chicken, Bacardi, gin, chicken, Boone's Farm, more chicken, Schlitz malt liquor, and Jalapeno peppers for the chicken.

Ms. Bea kept saying "life goes on" and that "everybody was going to die eventually." I thought Quilla would slap the shit outta her mother for saying that. The fact that she didn't give a damn was evident, but disrespecting her baby boy on his burial day...well, she was a cold bitch!

The homies found out about the fools that smoked Man-Man and murdered them and four other muthafuckas that looked like them. Ms. Bea dealt with the death of her baby by staying in a bottle. That's how she dealt with everything. She just shut down. I guess the guilt of not raising him was taken a toll on her. She stopped stripping, stopped taking care of herself. She was just a good hoe gone to waste. Before, you couldn't pay Ms. Bea to walk out of the house without her 'face' on and her clothes coordinated.

There was a lot to deal with right after Man's death. Jah was brought in as a suspect in a criminal investigation and then arrested on a felony drug charge and some other charges that never made any sense, just mafuckas planting shit on him. The judge sentenced him to fifteen years on some bullshit ass charges.

Ms. Bea dealt with the loss in her own way. She had lost both of her boys: one to the grave and the other to the prison system. Jah's sentencing took a toll on Quilla and me. For me, it was just another example of not having the ones I care for with me. But those mafuckas that don't matter are in my face every day. Jah was only 16 and would spend most, if not all, of his prime years in a cage. With the boys gone, Quilla's house wasn't the same. It had become a dark place and we didn't feel comfortable kicking it there anymore. Everything had changed. Our weekends were mostly spent at my Auntie's house. She would drive down and get Quilla and me on Fridays. Hell, Ms. Bea didn't care. She wasn't there most of the time anyway, so Qui was always alone. Joyce asked Auntie if she could come with us on several occasions but Auntie Jackie always told her that it wasn't a good time. Then Joyce would see us picking Quilla up. She felt some type of way, but what could she do? It was as if I was Aunt Jackie's daughter and Joyce was nobody.

Chapter 4

Ms. Jackie Laine, Esq. was a Harvard law graduate and Maine's twin sister. She was his favorite girl on the planet besides me. She was a boss bitch. She had everything and could buy anything or anyone. I loved her so much! She took no bullshit from a man and absolutely nothing from a bitch. Jackie is a serious investor and her portfolio is very impressive. Her net worth is over fifty million dollars. She owns real estate in New York, Miami, and of course California. She even has land in Dubai. We're in Bora Bora twice a year because she loves it there. She has taken me on six cruises around the world and given me all the materialistic shit that I like.

Since Aunt Jackie never had any kids of her own, she spoils me. She said marriage didn't fit into her lifestyle so she felt she could do without a man and all that comes with keeping one. Said she only needed to get her grass watered from time to time. We do everything together. She has class and money, and those two things mixed like cornflakes and milk. I wanted to be just like her when I grew up. My aunt taught me things that I needed to know. She spends her money on things that make money. Aunt Jackie was the one that taught me how to be a lady. She even taught me how to use my first tampon. I will never forget when she drove over an hour to get me out of the bathroom. See, the first time I got my period, I wouldn't let Joyce touch me.

Auntie Jackie insisted that I move in with her when Joyce was about to move us yet again. This time we were going back to live with her mom in San Diego. Auntie Jackie and my daddy had had enough of moving me around. After four years of the same shit, they were tired of it. Daddy told Auntie Jackie to go and get me, by any means necessary. And that's exactly what she did. She was more than happy to look after her niece because she adored me. When my aunt pulled up in that convertible Bentley, all white everything, wearing red bottoms on her feet and Gucci this and Gucci that, them nothing ass hoes stopped in their tracks. See, they had never seen that shit in living color. She knocked on the door and told Joyce, "Send Chan out. I'm here to get her and don't worry about packing a bag cause she don't need nothing. I got everything she need so just send her out." She said that no niece of hers was going to be homeless or living in some San Diego trailer park. She wasn't having it. Joyce had no choice but to give me to her, and I was so happy.

She opened her split-level, five-bedroom home in Bellaire Estates to me and welcomed me home. She kept most of my dad's stuff when he went to prison. She made sure his cars stayed clean the way he liked them. His jewelry was in a safe deposit box. I felt very much at home there. Besides, my dad was on his way home. He was up for parole very soon. My auntie said, "In three years time, something positive might happen." I didn't know what that meant, but it sounded good. Honestly, I had no positive female role models in my life except for her, so I believed every single thing she said. The only problem with wanting to be like her was that it required way too much school. She studied her whole life to be a lawyer. All them books just ain't for me, but I could use the nurturing and that's exactly what she wanted to do, so I let her.

After Joyce seemed to have gotten herself together, she took up a roommate situation with a co-worker of hers and begged Auntie to let me come over for the weekend. Said that she missed me. My aunt would only let her visit me at her house and Joyce always said we lived too far, so she never came. My aunt never took the time to bring me down to see her, so almost three years had passed before we saw each other. When I got there, I didn't wanna stay. I remember telling my aunt not to leave me. She said Joyce wouldn't let anything happen to me and that I would be okay, so I stayed. After several hours in my own world, not talking to anybody and not moving from where I first sat down, Joyce called my auntie and she came got me.

Chapter 5

"Jermaine Laine, Inmate number 1020133, roll it up!" Today was the day that my dad, Mr. Jermaine Laine, was stepping back into the free world after doing time on the chain gang. When my dad was arrested, my auntie called in the best of the best as well as her own team. Between them, they brought half of them years that punk ass judge sentenced him back. He was sentenced to serve eighteen years, paroling out in ten. I was taught at a very early age that money talks. That fuck prosecutor wanted to kill my dad with the death penalty.

Uncle Black was an old lame ass nigga that loved slumming in the hood. He was very successful, one of those OB/GYN doctors. You know, them doctors that play with pussy all day. Shit, now that's worth going to college for, having knowledge on the pussy! That was a degree worth attaining. Anyway, he owned a mansion in Bel Aire and one in Beverly Hills. He had a drunk-ass wife and a fat-ass daughter who eats herself to death because she thinks her daddy doesn't love her. He also had a son that wants to be accepted by everyone when he don't even fucking know who he is. They're all just a bunch of dysfunctional mafuckas. Uncle Black was supposed to have my dad's back while he was down. Promised that he would take care of the family and shit. I don't know what that meant, since the only time I saw this muthafucka while my dad was locked up was at Joyce's birthday party two years ago. Sometimes I saw him around the projects, drunk as hell. He ain't shit! He had the nerve to insist that he have the honors of picking him up from prison since he was his best friend. Could this nigga be serious?

My dad was a hustling-ass muthafucka. When he got knocked, he had money, cars, and hoes. He was the envy of all these lame-ass niggas trying to be what they were not. Of course the hoes got gone and Joyce denies it all to this day. She's afraid of letting anyone know her past, but that's who she is. She ain't nothing but a hoe. That's all she know and that's all she ever gonna be.

By now, I was not that adorable little girl that dad had left all those years ago. Although still adorable, I was a teenager now. My dad got Joyce out that damn trailer park and brought the bitch with us to our new home. Things were great for a while. He said he would take care of me, take care of us. I really didn't give a fuck about Joyce because it was all about me. He said that his time down taught him to appreciate the things that mattered to him, and that was me and Joyce. I couldn't understand why he wanted Joyce in the picture, though. I guess it wasn't for me to understand at that time. I guess now I understand it.

He took good care of us. My dad was a hustla. It didn't take long for him to get back on his feet. Good old Uncle Black and my dad hit some fools up for a knot. I'd say it was about 6 million dollars. That, combined with the skill my dad had to flip that shit, bought us a whole lot of things. He moved us into a beautiful home a long way from the projects. Malibu and the Pacific Ocean was my backyard. The gated community we lived in offered all the amenities you could ever ask for. Dad decided on Malibu because he loved the water. He often said that water was the most abundant compound on earth and vital to the existence of life. He also believed that the fresh air helped his sinuses.

Our home was 5,200 square feet of beautiful living space. It had six bedrooms and seven bathrooms. The state-of-the art kitchen had European cabinets and top-of-the-line appliances. The entire estate had a wraparound patio that offered a 360 degree view of the ocean. It was valued at 3.6 million dollars and had security inside and out. I may have left the hood, but the experience and best friend that I gained from that part of my life were priceless. Believe me, the hood will always be a part of me, but that house was heaven on earth. My dad's car of choice was the BMW. He felt it was the ultimate driving experience, so much so that he purchased two in one day. He was a firm believer in paying cash for his shit. He gave Joyce anything she wanted. The only thing that low budget-ass bitch asked for was a Honda. Imagine that! Dad made sure all the cars were detailed or at least wiped down every morning. Moe, the crack head, was the best car detailer in the hood and Dad made sure to find him when he got out so he could give him back his job. Moe was dedicated to Dad and made sure he was there at 7 a.m. sharp every morning. Taking care of those cars was his job and he was very proud of it. For me, living like a princess came naturally. I was royalty. My dad was a king. My hoe-ass mama was a queen but she didn't know how to shine her crown.

You couldn't tell me shit! I rocked my tiara with attitude. I was chauffeured to school every day and the door to my chariot was always open, awaiting my arrival. My driver, a big and tall masculine man that adored me, would bring me to school every day. When he picked me up, he would lean on the hood of the car with swag and a sexy pose. He always treated me with the utmost respect and to this day, I won't accept a man not opening doors for me and treating me like the lady my daddy groomed me to be. See, my dad was the prototype of my perfect gentleman. I had all the girls in my high school jealous because he kept me in the most expensive things. I loved him very much. I was his girl, no doubt. We were living large, wearing the best, and eating at the finest restaurants. Life was good.

Chapter 6

Since my dad has been home things have changed all for the better. My Auntie Jackie hated for me to move out. Said her house was gonna be lonely without me. I promised her I would spend the night as often as I could. Christmas was my favorite holiday and dad went all out. He piled presents under the tree. I couldn't wait to open them all. It seemed as though all of them had my name on them. Joyce was always jealous. She tried putting her touch to things by decorating. This bitch went to the local supermarket to get a tree and bought some dollar store decorations. She was so tacky, but dad let her do her thing and Christmas was lovely.

That year I got diamonds and my first Rolex watch among other things. I could not wait to show off at school. My dad was very generous. He wanted to spend the New Year in Miami. I loved Miami and that was home away from home. My Aunt Jackie owned a seven million dollar, four bedroom, six bathroom mansion in Devon Court, which was a secluded community just south of Miami. She often said that her retirement dream was to move to Florida. We all appreciated the culture of Miami. Dad said that he wanted to retire there as well. I guess it was the true retirement capital of the world.

Every great city has a secret jewel, a tucked-away treasure. Miami was no different. For me, I loved Coconut Grove the most. I enjoyed dining beneath the full moon and strolling past street musicians along the brick walkways beside the shimmering blue waters of Biscayne Bay. I guess I could retire in Florida, too. My phone rang.

"Hello, this is Chantal."

"Hey, girl. What you doing?" It was Quilla.

"Hey Qui. Girl I'm in Miami with the family."

"For real, Chan? I wanted to go." I detected pouting from her friend.

"I'm sorry. I promise, on the next trip your coming."

"Yea, right."

"For real, Qui. The next vacay we take, your coming with us."

"I got a letter from Jah," Qui said, changing the subject.

"Oh yea? How he doing?" To this day, Jah was still my boo.

"He asking how you doing."

I said, "That's my boo. I'm gonna write him as soon as I get back. Tell him to look for a letter from me."

"Ok, well I'm gonna let you go and finish doing Miami, bitch."

"Okay girl. Love you."

"Love you, too." Quilla sounded kinda depressed. Maybe I should not have rushed her off the phone. On this particular vacation, Aunt Jackie came along for the ride. She wanted to spend time with her Bubby – that's what she called my dad. She adored him. She said she wanted to catch up with him and it would give her a chance to spend time with her good friend, Mr. Carl. He was an old flame from college that she kept in contact with over the years. She wasn't comfortable with the fact that Joyce was on the trip with us and neither was I. Aunt Jackie's politeness was forced. She tried to show respect because of her brother and niece, but it wasn't easy. Everyone knew how she felt and she never played as if things were kosher between the two of them.

I loved being in my dad's presence, especially when he would reminisce about the old days, dropping subtle hints about the game. Teaching me that I was cut from a different cloth. He said only those of same cloth can recognize one another, and he stressed that only loyalty was important. He told me to never stop getting money and to always be a classy, independent, and confident woman. He always wanted me to make sure that I let no one compromise the value of my worth. My dad's words were as smooth as liquid gold.

Because of those types of conversations, I was able to build a wealth of self-esteem that no one could fuck with. A muthafucka couldn't brainwash me, couldn't give me what they thought I wanted or tell me what they thought I needed to hear. I was tight, as solid as they come. I wasn't gonna get money for nobody but me. No nothing-ass nigga was gonna pimp me. Not Chantal Laine! I knew I had 'it'. I had the game locked in my head. With the knowledge my dad gave me on the game and the killer genes that Joyce gave me on the body frame, I could have anything and anyone I wanted.

Auntie Jackie decided to leave early the next morning to do some shopping before joining Mr. Carl for lunch. Joyce wanted to go with her. Said she wanted to get some souvenirs. Aunt Jackie didn't want any part of Joyce in her space. No one wanted her around so I don't know why she even came. As for me, this was one of those adventures that I didn't want to go on. I didn't know Mr. Carl and I hated doing anything with Joyce. Me and dad decided to have a day at the beach, so they left without me. It was a good day. Spending time with my dad always made me happy. After returning from a full day on the water, we decided to go back to the house and order some takeout. We agreed on Chinese food and we ordered everything on the menu. Dad was in the family room, rolling up one. I said, "Daddy, I'm gonna get in the shower."

"Okay, baby I'll call you when the food get here."

While I was in the bathroom, I started looking in the mirror at my naked body, acting very sexy. I was caressing my frame and I noticed that my body was changing. I was filling out and getting curves and oh how, I loved me! I felt like a woman, even though I was just a young girl. I wondered what it would be like to have sex. I thought I was ready for that next step but honestly, no one was worthy enough to get my virgin body. I needed to wait for the right person that would respect and adore it. I really wanted to masturbate cause I was turning myself on, but I didn't wanna be embarrassed if I got caught, so I just got in the shower. Apparently the food arrived and dad had called out to me, but I guess I was taking too long to answer, because he knocked on the door.

"Yeah?"

"The food is here. Let me in so I can use the bathroom. I gotta pee like a racehorse, Chaney. Open the door!" I couldn't understand why he needed to use this bathroom when there were six other bathrooms that he could use. "Uh, okay. Just a minute!" It surprised me that my dad wasn't embarrassed to use the bathroom right in front of me. Although the shower door was made of frosted glass, it provided little privacy. Dad knocked on the door again.

"Let me in, Chaney, damn! I'm your daddy! You ain't got nothing I haven't seen before. Hurry up!"

"Okay, just a minute!" I grabbed a towel, wrapped it around my naked, wet body, and let him in. I tried to run back to the shower before he came in. The towel fell to the floor as he came through the door. He must have been aware of my curiosity, since I left a small opening in the shower door so that I could see my dad. To be honest, I wanted to see him pull out his dick. I wanted to see how it looked, how big it was. I can't help it, I was curious. And it was just as I had imagined, long and black with a slight upward curve, very smooth. The sight of his dick stimulated the muscles in my vagina. He must've felt me watching, because he turned around in full swing and just stared back at me and asked, "What you doing?"

I was so shocked that I could only stand there looking at him, trying to answer his question. But the main attraction had all my attention, slightly hooked and hanging to the left. Yeah, his dick had my full attention. All I could do was stare for what seemed like an hour, but was probably like six seconds. He glanced down at his dick, looked me in my eyes, and said, "You want it, baby girl?"

I was frozen. I couldn't move or speak. Before I could come to reality with what was getting ready to happen, it was happening. Before I knew it, he was standing there licking those juicy lips. A chill went through my entire body. He had lust in his eyes. He said, "If you want it, here it is, baby."

I couldn't reply. God help me, I wanted it! This felt wrong. I didn't know those words had left my mouth for him to hear. In total embarrassment, I closed the shower door so hard I thought it would shatter from the impact of it. I could hear my dad leaving the bathroom in laughter. Why was he laughing? Ain't nothing funny! I wasn't the same little girl that dad had greeted in his arms when he was released from prison two years ago. My body was changing, and he was noticing it. So was I.

I tried to avoid my dad for the rest of day. I could feel him staring at me. I caught myself looking at the imprint pressing through his pants at different times. Something had definitely changed between us after fateful that day in Miami. When I sat on his lap, there was a different feeling than before. At times, I could feel the muscle in his dick flexing through my dress, tapping on my ass. I must admit, I was curious. After all, I was almost fifteen and I thought I was ready for the penetration. I knew that he would never make the first move. I would have to choose him, and if there was a man to give my virginity to, it might as well have been him. I started noticing that when I was in my dad's presence, I wanted to be ladylike and sexy. The way he looked at me was definitely not a fatherly look. It was more like a hunger, a thirst on his lips and lust in his catty, bedroom eyes.

The way that he licked his lips when he looked at me! I wanted to run from the desire in my heart, the desire of wanting my daddy. I knew that he loved me more than any smooth-talking, trick-ass nigga in the streets and that he would never hurt me. He had taken care of me my whole life, nevertheless, I wanted him and he wanted me. I don't know if it was by accident or hope that he would come in, but I started leaving the bathroom door unlocked. One day, Joyce was away at Mama Oglavee's house in San Diego for a weekend, so the perfect opportunity finally presented itself. Joyce begged me to go with her, but I refused, and dad didn't want me to go either. Mama Oglavee was very sick. She was a hypochondriac as well, so you never knew when she was telling the truth. She was also a fault finder, you know, one of those types that were always certain about what you should do, but could never seem to take care of their own situations. She was my grandmother by birth, but I felt nothing for her. Actually, I didn't like her complicated ass. I was happy that Dad had insisted that I stay behind. I didn't respect any of Joyce's side of the family and I would never accept them as family. They were broke-ass phony people.

Later that night, me and Dad rented movies and popped popcorn. He was always smoking on his weed. He lit a fat blunt and smoked half of it to the head. After he got high, he wanted to play pool. We loved playing games together. Pool, Xbox, dominoes, you name it. We were serious with the wordplay on Scrabble. We really enjoyed spending time quality time together. After a long night, it was bedtime. He was on the couch, high and stuck on stupid as they say. It was kinda funny. I kissed him on his forehead and went upstairs. As I was getting in the shower, I could hear the music blasting from the family room. Dad was awake and started partying again, singing and dancing and yelling my name. He was lit. As the water was getting hot in the shower, I wrapped my hair. I could hear dad calling me.

"Chaney, where you at?"

"I'm getting in the shower. I'll be out in a minute!" Right as I got in the shower, I heard the door open and immediately shut. I could hear my dad locking the door behind him. Above the beating of the water on my body and the radio in the background, I could hear my dad getting undressed. His pants and belt hit the floor, then all of the change that was in his pocket fell to the floor and they sounded like emergency sirens. I stood there in shock. I felt as though I was having an out-of-body experience. The anticipation of what he was getting ready to do made me feel uneasy. Was he actually going to get in the shower with me? Was this really happening? I was confused. I knew that I wanted him...or maybe I didn't.

As the shower door opened, he stepped one foot in, looked in my eyes, and softly asked, "Can I join you?"

My dad was so suave and debonair. He had been a gentleman all my life, showing me how I'm supposed to be treated, and now he was getting ready to give me something that was priceless. All I could do was turn towards the shower head and close my eyes. He was waiting for an answer. "Chaney, choose me," he said quietly as his body came closer and closer.

"Yeah, Daddy. You're the one I choose." The words were coming out my mouth so faintly that I didn't hear myself say them, but that was enough for him. As I stood under the running water, he stepped in and leaned into me. He didn't say another word after that. He just stood there behind me. It seemed like an eternity. I could feel his breathing on my neck as the water was streaming down on both of us. We were becoming one, my flesh to his flesh. He rubbed my back and bent me over slightly. His body heat and the seductiveness of his loins made me burn with desire. My flesh was weak, and he was being very gentle. He followed the water trickling down my back with his finger, down, down, down.

Oh, the chills that electrified my soul! He came closer and closer, hard as a rock and straight ahead. He took his time, loving me slowly. After all, I was a virgin and his princess. There was no form of abuse or foul play. My body literally sank into his body. All I could hear was his heart beating. I was totally numb and very consenting. He continued, ever so gently, and then, he thrust his body into mine and popped my cherry. The whole time he was stroking my body with his big masculine hands.

He definitely started something that day and I knew that he was going to nurture it into a beautiful, exotic existence. Scooby was priceless and I wasn't giving him up for nothing or no one. I knew Joyce and no one else would approve, but that was their business. We would just fuck right over them – literally. From that point on, I loved and adored Scooby, my dad. I was gonna be faithful and loyal till the death of me, and dared anyone to call him Scooby because that name belonged to me.

What I had for him, no other man would ever receive. We fucked passionately every chance we got, in the wee hours of the morning, in the afternoon. We would even go to the store and end up at this spot overlooking the ocean, fucking in the car. Scooby became my everything. He taught me everything. How to smoke weed, clean it, roll it, buy it, and hold it. He taught me how to hold my liquor, taught me the game on these bullshit-ass niggas in the streets. He even taught me how to control the gag reflex in my throat when I sucked his dick. No one knew our secret, and no one needed to. Fuck the world. It was all about us. And most of all, fuck Joyce!

Each time we were together, I tried to make sure that I was better than Joyce. I wanted to do everything that she wouldn't or couldn't do. I wanted to take her place. I let him do things to me that no other nigga would ever have the pleasure of experiencing. I had to face reality, I was addicted. Addicted to my dad. I think that was the day he became addicted to Chaney and we fell in love with each other. We had sex and partied every night for the next two years. I had a healthy appetite for sex, and I loved letting Scooby feed me.

Chapter 7

"Happy birthday to you! Happy birthday to you! Happy birthday, Chantal. Happy birthday to you!" Everybody sang and then Joyce said, "Blow out the candles, baby girl!" Joyce knew I hated for her to call me that baby girl shit. She was in her usual mode, pretending she had done everything when she hadn't done shit. She was so fake with her broke ass. I hated her. Angrily, I said, "What the fuck, Joyce? Don't call me that!"

"Watch your mouth Chantal." This chick was trying to correct me?

"Ah shut up, bitch."

Joyce said, "Jermaine, you better get her before I whoop her ass. She think she grown cause she sixteen today. I'm still your mama, little girl." Little did she know, I was grown and fucking her man. We stayed at each other's throats. Scooby was the one to diffuse situations between us all the time, and this time was no different.

He said, "Come on, Chaney. Cut the cake."

"Ok daddy." Everyone was surprised at the way I talked to Joyce, but in my book, she wasn't shit but a cock blocker. It was my sixteenth birthday. I was grown. Couldn't no body tell me shit. I was getting more dick and money than any bitch at my party. And I didn't give a fuck who knew it.

Aunt Jackie said, "Come on, Chaney. Cut this cake so I can get a piece, princess, okay?" Auntie Jackie provided the cake. She knows this really great Beverly Hills bakery on Rodeo Drive that she loves. She had some samples delivered to us two weeks prior to my birthday. We sampled at least fourteen different pastry delights, and my top three favorites are what my dad surprised me with. The dedication read, "For my girl who can't make up her mind. I love you. Daddy." It was a three-tier, delectable delight that fed up to 100 people. The pedestal that it sat on was a gold wired cage housing sixteen white doves.

"Here I come," I said. Before I cut the cake, he was supposed to release the doves. When I said, "here I come," he raised an eyebrow and he licked them fine-ass lips. I knew that tonight would be special as hell. I didn't know if he was gonna take me out and get a room, which is what I really wanted. If not, that was okay too. We fucked right over Joyce on any given night, so tonight would be no different. A familiar voice shouted, "Happy birthday, Chan!" Oh damn! My girl arrived, looking awesome. "Thank you, Qui. Come on. You're just in time for the toast and the cutting of the cake."

I paused to address my guests. "Hello, everyone. Thank you for coming and blessing my day with your presence! I would like to give a special thanks to my dad. If it weren't for my daddy, I don't know where I would be. You're everything to me. Cheers!" I could hear Joyce in the background talking about, "What about me?"

"Joyce. Yeah, thank you. And to my best friend for life, Quilla, thanks for being my bestie. Auntie Jackie, you already know how much I adore you. Thank you. I love you! So now that that's out the way, let's cut this cake and continue to do the damn thing!"

"Hold up, I got a few words to say too. My baby..." Joyce paused to dab her eyes. No she didn't! Here she go with all that phony shit! "You've become a beautiful, young lady in your own right. I'm your mother, and I love you. Sixteen years ago, I gave birth to you and that was the happiest day of my life. Please, let's continue to be friends and honest with each other." Bitch sounded like Charlie Brown – whomp, whomp, whomp. I was angry. I turned to Quilla and said loudly, "What the fuck is her drunk ass talking about, Quilla? That bitch ain't never been my fucking friend! And a mother? She can't even spell that shit!"

Me and Qui were laughing in the middle of her speech. "Yeah, yeah, Joyce. Cheers!" I cut the cake and couldn't wait to open my gifts. I knew that I could depend on two major gifts on birthdays and holidays, and that was from my Auntie Jackie and Scooby. No one else mattered. Quilla always gave me nice cards and whatever she could afford. The birthday card this year was especially nice. It read, "We ain't no broke bitches and we ain't no gold diggers. Just paper chasers."

My home girl, Quilla saw the potential in me years ago. I was definitely a paper chaser. Auntie Jackie gave me a sixteen thousand dollar American Express gift card to buy whatever the fuck I wanted and a pair of Prada thigh-high black leather boots. Scooby always showed out, giving the best gift of all. This year it was four carat pink diamond earrings. He had them made especially for me, his princess. Joyce did the cooking and decorations to the best of her low-class-ass ability.

The only thing I ate was the cake because my dad had ordered it. I didn't trust Joyce's cooking. That bitch might try to sabotage me. I always felt that she was jealous of me. She was real salty about my gift from my dad. She said that I didn't need a gift like that at my age and that he had wasted his money. He looked at that bitch like a stranger. I guess all the bullshit along the way had changed his feelings toward her, or maybe it was the fact that I was pussy whipping his ass. He had begun disrespecting her, like calling her a bitch in front of the family. But he wouldn't give her any money to buy anything. He was only taking care of the necessities for her ass, which were lights, water, and sometimes food. He and I would go out to dinner, come home with our stomachs full and go to bed.

He really didn't give two flying fucks about her anymore, and that's where the line was drawn. If it didn't have shit to do with the house or me, she was ass out. I got all the love, respect, dick, and money. For my birthday, Scooby hired a band that played the classic Isn't She Lovely by the great Stevie Wonder as we danced ballroom style – something we learned on one of the many cruises we enjoyed. Me and daddy loved to dance close in each other's arms. The passion between us on the dance floor, well I know it was visible to the crowd, but I couldn't contain myself. He held me close, as if we were the only two people in the room.

It was a beautiful thing to watch, and so was my dad. He was wearing a white linen suit by Gucci, cream colored Gucci gators, and a diamond-encrusted platinum Rolex. He had six carat stones in each ear and the scent of Dolce and Gabbana followed wherever he went. I made sure he stayed heavily supplied with expensive colognes. He never had to buy any of that kinda stuff. I remember Joyce had asked me one day why I bought all those different colognes for him. I just looked at that bitch, and said "Cause he's my dad and I like him to smell good."

Whenever I went shopping, Scooby was sure to get something back: a shirt, tie, shoes, cologne, silk boxers, whatever I thought he would like. We had the same taste, and he loved silk. He said that your shit needed to breathe, and only silk allowed that to happen. He never allowed me to wear cotton near my pussy. He said it dried a pussy out and he hated the lint that got on his dick. I never bought Joyce shit. Oh, I did buy her something one Christmas. Scooby had asked me to get her something while I was out, so I picked that bitch up some of that cheap Bath and Body Works shit and some cotton drawers. That shit was so funny on Christmas morning. She thought that was so nice of me. She was so dumb! I wouldn't even share my mall candy with that bitch! She never seemed jealous of our relationship, though if she was, she was too passive too show it. I guess sharing him with all those women all her life was second nature. But I wasn't one of his hoes. I was his princess, and if it came down to it, he would leave that bitch in a heartbeat to be with me.

As the party came to a close, I saw everyone out. "Thank you, Joyce." I never did get used to calling her Mom, so we both agreed one day that Joyce would be fine. After all, that's her name, right?

"Oh, you're welcome, Chaney. I love you, and congratulations on turning sweet sixteen, baby."

"Yeah, and by the way, from this moment on, call me Chantal, okay Joyce? Only Scooby can call me Chaney."

"Who's Scooby?"

"My daddy." I think that's when she knew. I think she felt it at that moment, but she dared not say anything. The hired help finished cleaning the kitchen. I paid them and let them out. Joyce had went to bed over an hour ago. All the guests were gone. My auntie was the last to go. She was in the den, enjoying a blunt with my dad. She would only hit that shit with her bubby on special occasions, and tonight was special. The moment I smelled it, I wanted to hit it, but I didn't dare disrespect my aunt like that. I could wait until she left.

I let auntie out and joined Scooby. As I sat there with my dad getting high, while Joyce was sound asleep and deep in her dreams, I played with his dick, just caressing it and massaging his balls. I acquired a special skill that drove him crazy. It's the juncture where the two ends join the shaft of the head. It's the most sensitive spot on the penis, and if you follow this ridge with your tongue to the underside of the penis, it will drive a muthafucka crazy! He will have no choice but to skeet all over your face and mouth.

Scooby taught me very well and I loved him. Every chance I got, I showed my appreciation. I regard oral sex as the highest expression of love that can be exchanged between two people. He told me that no hoe ever showed as much appreciation as I do for the little things. He said he loved me very much and that he would always be here for me. He told me he was teaching me to be somebody that could take care of herself. He slapped my booty. I knew exactly what that meant. I wish I could have sat on his shit right there. He pointed towards my bedroom.

He squeezed my left ass cheek and told me to go get ready in that voice. You know, when a nigga get horny, his voice goes down one, maybe two octaves. At that point, he ain't on no bitch shit. It sounded masculine and sexy. So I got up, went into my bedroom, took off all my clothes, and got in the bed naked. He didn't wanna waste time undressing me. He said he wanted to get right down to it. The thunderstorm made the evening more seductive. It seemed that the rain and the beat of my heart were jelling in rhythmic unison. The potency of the high that I was on had me feeling horny.

After I lay there and played with my clit for what seemed like ten minutes, the door opened. I could feel my dad in the darkness, watching me. A tall, nude silhouette, rubbing on his dick, watching me rub my clit. I felt his eyes piercing through the darkness into my soul. Ever since my dad came home from prison, I've been able to have privacy in my room, so if Joyce ever heard anything, she would assume it was me and one of my friends. She never invaded my privacy. She knew the boundaries, and if she had something to talk about, she had better wait until my company was gone. Disrespect in front of company in this house wasn't allowed, that's just how it was and the way Scooby said it was gonna be.

He climbed into the bed next to me. He began to caress my body as if he was sculpting a piece of art. It felt like heaven. Just the touch of his hands made me melt as he drenched my body in oil, massaging me from head to toe. I could feel him as he lay there, teasing me with all ten of his fingers. He would always talk me through it. He leaned my head back and sucked my tongue, then told me to relax and arch my back as he massaged the oil all over my booty. He said, "Easy, baby. Arch your back." I tensed slightly. "Shhh," he whispered in my ear. "Easy, baby. You know daddy loves you, right?"

"Yes, Daddy, I love you, too."

"This is gonna feel a little different, but I promise, you're gonna love it." All the while he was talking, he was sucking on my ear, neck, and lips, assuring me that this is what he wanted and it was something that I needed in order to go to the next level. He slapped my ass as he spread my cheeks open and said, "Whose is it, baby?"

"It's yours, Daddy."

"Then give it to me, princess. Do it like I like it. Give it to me like I taught you. God, I love you, Chaney." He squeezed my entire body. I wanted to please him by any means. I relaxed all of my muscles and let him in, whether I liked it or not. After the head entered and the burning stopped, it was something that I thoroughly enjoyed. To this day, it's my favorite and one of the most intimate positions, but you gotta be a special nigga for me to go there. It is definitely an acquired feeling, just like escargot is an acquired taste.

He made love to me as if it were my first time, gently, until I was submissive to the things that he was doing with my body. All I could do was lie there in total relaxation, letting him have his way with all of me. He was whispering in my ear the whole time, telling me that I had what a man needed, and that as long as I stayed true to Daddy, I could have the world.

We washed up afterwards and took a blunt break. As I rolled the blunt under candlelight, he played with me, almost as if he was the doctor and I was the patient. It was time for round two. The one thing that I appreciated about Scooby is that he was like a porn king. He was ready at the drop of a dime. Most niggas I know get one nut and then the lame-ass muthafucka would have to rest or wait hours before he got hard again.

But not my Scooby. He turned me over with the sweetest pearl necklace that I ever tasted. I climbed on his face. We were in this land of fantasy, pleasing each other for three, maybe four hours. I guess Joyce missed him in her sleep, which I don't think was at all possible, since he wasn't sleeping with her lately. After he left my room, he would retire to the den and play that damn game until he fell asleep on the couch. But this night, she must have smelled the sex in the air. Scooby and I continued on like we were the only people in the house. "Oh, baby girl, you taste delicious!" As I climbed on top of Scooby, the door swung open. I heard a loud scream coming from the doorway.

"What the fuck is going on in here? Jermaine, you muthafucka!" I looked over my shoulder. You see, I was sitting on my dad's face. He had his hands around my waist with an unconcerned look on his face. He let out a sigh as if to say, "Damn, she finally caught us." Although I was somewhat in awe, I was relieved that she had finally caught us. I knew that one day it would happen, but just didn't quite know how it would go down. Maine always had a wary look in his eyes. He didn't trust nothing and no one. With all the shit he had seen and been through in his lifetime, everything and everybody was suspect. Haters were always trying to destroy him. But he knew that I was his and in his corner through thick and muthafucking thin. I was his girl.

Joyce was standing there screaming and yelling at the top of her fucking lungs. I thought, "This bitch is tripping!" Scooby kissed me on my shoulder and said, "Watch out, baby girl. Let Daddy up." After I climbed off of him, we both sat there in the bed, looking at her dumb ass like what?

"Jermaine, you muthafucka, I hate you!"
Scooby began putting on his pants and in a moment, he was right beside her, yelling back. "Joyce, get the fuck out my face! What the fuck you talking about, anyway?"

I said, "Daddy, close my door, please."

"Okay, precious, I love you."

"I love you, too." I didn't know that would be the last time that I would get my wink and a smile.

Joyce said, "I'm talking bout you fucking my daughter!" Scooby was smooth. He said, "I wasn't fucking her, Joyce. I was teaching her how to do what she needs to do."

"And what's that, Maine? Huh? How to be a hoe and fuck her Daddy? What the fuck is that?"

"Joyce, you tripping! You need to calm your ass down!"

"Calm down or what, Maine? You gonna hit me? Yeah, hit me, muthafuckas! Make it that much easier!"

"Bitch, calm your ass down, hoe! I done told you, I was teaching my fucking daughter to be a woman. Teaching her how to get her money and not depend on no trifling-ass niggas. The same shit I did for your sorry ass, bitch! And if you don't stop yelling in my muthafucking house, I'm gonna bust your fucking head open! Where my cigarettes at, Joyce?"

"You muthafucka! Sitting here asking me for some muthafucking cigarettes and I just caught you fucking my daughter.

"Why you keep talking about your daughter? She mine!" I had been in the hallway listening as they fought over me. When I heard my dad say those things to her, it didn't seem like he was talking about his baby girl. He was loyalty to me. I knew it, and she knew it too. What could she expect? Anything you fucking, you loving. If a man constantly sticking you, he gonna fall in love with the pussy, if nothing else.

All I could hear was the yelling back and forth. It went on for hours. I could see my dad sitting there, playing Madden and smoking a blunt. As he sat there, Joyce was ranting and raving all through the house, breaking shit and cursing. All my dad did was sit there and ignore her. I went to bed cause I knew she was gonna go on all night. She knew just how far to go, though, because at the end of the day, she wasn't gonna do shit about it. But this night was different. She wasn't letting up. She spoke up about all the things that Maine had done to her throughout her life. How she was tired and wanted to leave. That bitch never spoke on how good he was. She kept going on and on and finally my dad had enough.

That's when the shit hit the fan. Maine jumped up and started throwing her shit out the front door, yelling, "Leave, bitch! Leave! Take all this materialistic shit that you love so fucking much and leave, bitch!"

"Yeah, all right, muthafucka, but I'm taking my daughter!"

"Oh no, bitch. She stays!"

"Maine, you got me fucked up! I'm not leaving my daughter for you to trick her the fuck out! I'll call the police on your ass!" Oops! That was the wrong thing to say! He jumped up and slapped the shit outta Joyce. Blood was everywhere. I never saw my dad so angry that he actually put his hands on Joyce. I've seen him slap another bitch like it was nothing, but not Joyce. This was serious! When she said she would call the police, I think the rage from all those ass whippings she deserved in the past came with one blow.

As Joyce ran to the bathroom with blood dripping down her face, all I could do was get out of her way. She looked at me with something in her eyes, and I should have known that it was hate. When I looked at my dad sitting there, smoking his blunt, I saw a different man. Joyce came back into the living room with a towel on her face and a .25 caliber pistol in her hand. By the time I realized what she was getting ready to do, it was done.

Pop! The first bullet hit Scooby in the back of the neck. My dad jumped up and turned around, and went in on that bitch. I don't think he knew what had hit him. As he got closer to her, she unloaded the rest of the bullets into my dad's chest in a violent rage. Pop, pop, pop! With each bullet, I died. All I could do was run and hide. The kitchen table was my only refuge. There I hid, waiting for my destiny. I knew that she was gonna kill me, too. When I saw my dad hit the floor, drenched with blood, I unraveled from the fetal position because the fear of what Joyce might do was gone. I crawled from underneath the kitchen table and I held my daddy in my arms. His body was riddled with bullets. He looked into my eyes and with his last breath he told me, "Get that bitch." I promised him I would.

Totally in shock over what she had done, Joyce just stood there. She dropped the pistol and fell to the floor. It was over. She had killed the only somebody that I really loved. I grabbed that bitch and tried to strangle her fucking lungs out of her throat. If the nosey ass neighbor hadn't heard all the commotion and called the police, I would have killed Joyce. The neighbor said he had come over to see what was happening. Said he had knocked the door down when he heard the chaos. That bitch, Joyce, would have gone with Scooby that night had it not been for the neighbor! I crawled back to my dad after the neighbor pulled us apart. I sat there with my daddy in my arms until the paramedics arrived. He was already gone but I just wanted to hold him. Jermaine Laine was pronounced dead at the scene. My daddy left me that rainy night in April, the day I turned sixteen. My life would never be the same. He had only been home three years and now he was gone forever.

When the police arrived that night, they arrested Joyce for the murder of my dad. Waiting on the trial seemed like another funeral waiting to happen. Even though she was the woman that birthed me, I wanted her to die! The trial had taken 16 months and finally the verdict was in. Hell, I was the only witness and I threw her ass so far under the bus, she was going to get life in prison, if not a death sentence. My aunt and I were there every day. Mama Laine, my dad's mother, was with us, too. She never left her house, so today was obviously a very important day.

"Joyce Oglavee Laine, please stand. Do you wish to say anything at this time?" The judge motioned for her to stand.

"Yeah, I would just like to say to Chaney that I'm sorry. Sorry for not being there for you. Jackie and Mama Laine... I am sorry." We just looked at the bitch as if she was a stranger. She said that shit with no remorse, no feeling.

"Joyce Oglavee Laine, you have been found guilty of voluntary manslaughter for the death of Jermaine Laine. You are hereby ordered to the Women's State Correctional Facility for a maximum of ten years, with the possibility..." All I heard was with the possibility! I went the fuck off. I started yelling and screaming at the top of my shit. The judge was trying to get order, but I didn't give a fuck about none of that.

"What the fuck are you talking about, 'possibility'? The only reason I came here today was to make sure that bitch dies!" I was livid. "She deserves nothing less. Kill that bitch! You raggedy ass hoe! He gave you everything! Everything, you selfish bitch!" I heard the judge ordering the bailiff to remove me. I kept screaming and kicking the air cause I was surely in contempt of court, but this bitch had destroyed my life beyond repair. And now she gets a possibility! I wasn't having it! "I hate you, Joyce. I hate you, Joyce. Fuck you, Joyce! I hate you!" I kept repeating myself as though I were in a trance.

"Order in the court! Order in the court!" The judge was trying to get control of his courtroom. "Order in the court!" The judge kept banging his gavel as the bailiff took me out of the courtroom. Joyce tried to scream over the chaos. "I'm sorry, Chan! I'm sorry for not being there when you needed me! I'm sorry! Please forgive me!"

"Fuck you, bitch! My life is over!" I was screaming at the top of my lungs. I didn't hear shit and couldn't nobody tell me shit. They took me out of the courtroom screaming and crying. The judge was red as fire. The entire courtroom was chaotic. I could see the look in my Auntie Jackie's and granny's face. They were hurt as much as I was. They were looking at Joyce and they hated her as much as I did! I wish my aunt had been able to be the opposing council. She would have made sure that bitch died in the gas chamber. No one knew the truth about that night. They heard all my testimony, but none of it added up to the real truth. My dad was dead and that skank bitch killed him, bottom line. I wasn't worried about no contempt of court. I tried to get at that bitch. "Fuck that hoe! Lock me up. I don't give a fuck!" That's all I remember saying.

My aunt got me out of that fuck shit as soon as court was over. When I got in the car, all I wanted to know was if auntie could do anything about the sentencing. After all, she was a lawyer. "Auntie can't you do something about it?"

"No baby. She got her sentence. She pled self defense. That's what saved her from the death penalty."

"Self defense, my ass. My dad wasn't hurting her. She was the one acting stupid that night."

Auntie Jackie looked at me for longer than a moment and then said, "Chan, tell me what did happen that night." Now one thing I know, and that is my aunt is sharp when it come to that law shit. And reading people.

"What you mean, auntie?" I asked innocently.

"Answer the question."

"What you mean, what happen that night?"

At that moment, my grandmother turned around to look into my eyes. My auntie asked, "Did Maine rape you?"

"Of course not, auntie! My dad loved me, and I loved him."

"I was just asking. There was a lot said during the trial and I want to know the truth."

"Well auntie, that is the truth. My daddy would never do anything to hurt me." When I was done speaking, my granny turned back around and looked out the window.

"I can't believe the time that she got for murdering my child. After all Maine did for her, she sat there like some old stupid idiot talking like the victim." My granny was in tears.

I said, "Justice ain't shit. Excuse me, granny. I mean it ain't nothing."

"Chile, you didn't care about excusing yourself in that courthouse. You got a bad mouth, girl. That's not ladylike, Chantal."

"I know, granny, and I'm trying to do better with my profanity. It's just hard sometimes, but I didn't mean to disrespect you and auntie. For that I'm sorry, but Joyce will get hers. If it's the last thing I do, she will get hers."

"Chile, leave that alone. The law got her now."

"Yeah, you right, granny." I was just telling my grandmother what she wanted to hear. I hated Joyce Oglavee and my spirit was vindictive.

Chapter 8

Getting back to school was the hardest thing I've ever had to do. My days were spent crying in the bathroom, or at the graveside. My auntie and Quilla were very worried about me. I wouldn't eat and I stayed in the dark. Auntie Jackie saw the need to hire a tutor for me. I was in my junior year of high school. She couldn't see me failing anything, most of all high school. She would say, "Not on my watch." She was real big on education. I wasn't focused on anything but my dad. I just wanted to die with him. I wanted to be with him.

"Good morning, honey."

"Good morning, auntie." Of course moving back in with my aunt was a requirement after Scooby's death. He would turn over in his grave twice, if he knew I was with the Oglavee's. She also shared my animosity and resentment towards Joyce, so all was well with she and I. Living with her was gonna happen, even if it took me getting emancipated to do what the fuck I wanted to do, so be it. I was my dad's angel, and everybody knew it. Besides, his spirit was there with my aunt and she loved her brother just as much as I did. She kept pictures and old memorabilia from his life all around the house. I was at his gravesite once a week, changing the flowers or trimming the weeds, just talking to him.

In my dad's will, he left all of his belongings to his first born, his only born, me! My aunt matched that shit 100%. My portfolio consisted of investment property, stocks, bonds, and mutual funds. My net worth was six million dollars at the age of seventeen. Who needed college or a nigga? I own a three bedroom high rise condo in Buckhead, a very prominent area in Atlanta, Georgia. I also have a condo in Miami, which I use as rental property, a timeshare in the Turks and Caicos Islands. I own the house Scooby, Joyce and I lived in out in Malibu, but it's just sitting there. I can't seem to do anything with it. Although Aunt Jackie doesn't share those not going to college thoughts with me, she expects me to at least think about attending. Yeah right! With my money, this body and the skills of a seasoned pro, fuck College! If all else fails, I'll open my own business. Maybe something like Pandora's Box, where you can experience different fantasies in different settings, with any mafucka you choose. That would be the shit! I'd call it Chantal's Box. And what happens at Chantal's Box stays at Chantal's Box.

The last year of high school gave me a sense of independence and I felt reassured that the rest of my life was going to be awesome. As I sat in class, wondering how we could have changed that night, which always threw me into a zone of unhappiness, I came to the same conclusion as always. It was already written to be that way, and there was nothing that I or anybody else could do about it. The only thing that I can do now is to honor my father by being exactly who he raised me to be. One thing's for sure, I ain't gonna be like the hoe that birthed me.

Over my thoughts, I could hear, Mr. Reid my English teacher saying, "Ms. Laine, can you please read paragraph three on the next page?" He had noticed that I was in another world. I asked what page we were on, or more importantly, what book. The class erupted in laughter. He became agitated, and responded like a knife cutting through paper.

"Ms. Laine, I'm gonna need you to pay attention. Stop daydreaming and pay attention. Thank you." I thought to myself, "No this muthafucka didn't! He gonna put me on blast like that after all the free pussy and mike checks that I've given him? I'm charging his ass from here on out! I'm so not ready for this shit. "Can you give me a moment, Mr. Reid? Call the next person."

The last time that I serviced this muthafucka was at the football game last Thursday. I really wanted to see this particular game because I was checking for the quarterback from the opposing school. So I made sure I was there. My BMW was in the shop for weeks, waiting on a part. It seemed that old car gave me more problems than it was worth. I could have gotten any vehicle I wanted straight off the showroom floor. When your paper is right, you can have shit delivered on the same day. You don't have to go in the fucking sun and listen to a lame-ass car salesman trying to sell you some shit that you don't want. But I couldn't bring myself to getting rid of that old BMW, no matter the cost. It belonged to Scooby, and now it was a part of me. I didn't wanna ask auntie Jackie if I could drive one of her whips, but I knew she'd let me. All I had to do was ask, but there's one thing about aunt Jackie, she don't play. All that love shit goes completely out the window when you fall out pocket with her. If you're gonna use one of her cars, you better go where you say you're going and come right back. I didn't have time for that tonight. Besides, Qui wanted to go too, so I would just ride with my bestie.

After the game Meachie, our team's quarterback, wanted me to go with them to celebrate. Although I wanted to, he was the wrong quarterback. He was still cute, though and he wasn't a stranger. We had fun before, but it was just too many niggas in his car, so I passed on the offer. I liked to fuck, but no one was gonna run a train on me, that wasn't going to happen. Had it just been him, and his homeboy, cool. We could have had a little fun. I could have sucked his dick while his homeboy licked or dicked my pussy. I let Quilla leave over thirty minutes ago, playing with this nigga, and now I really did need a ride. Then, who do I see in the cut? Good ole, trick-ass, limp-dick Mr. Reid, my English teacher.

"Um, I ain't fucking with you tonight, Meachie. I'm straight." I started walking briskly over to Mr. Reid.

"Need a ride Chantal? I'm here to oblige."

"I'm sure you are. Let's go, with your old ass. And why you try me today in class? That was some fuck shit." Everyone knew I was on top of my game with this school shit. No one could figure out why I always had detention in Mr. Reid's class. After all, English was one of my strongest subjects. Shit was funny! He would always use that detention bullshit just to get me alone.

He said, "You know we gottta keep it on the low, Chantal. I'm sorry."

"Don't go fooling yourself. I don't like being disrespected, Mr. Reid."

"Okay, I said sorry. What you want me to do, baby?"

I said, "Don't call me baby." He was getting on my nerves.

"Listen Chantal, I'm gonna be straight up with you. I want you to suck my dick tonight. is that cool?"

"You got some money, nigga?"

"Naw, but I can bring it to class tomorrow."

He got me fucked up! "Tomorrow? Shit, when you bring me the money, that's when I do it."

"Okay, so what I get tonight for giving you a ride?"

"A thank you. Oh, don't get it fucked up. A ride is something I don't need."

He started back peddling. "No, Chantal! I didn't mean it like that." This mafucka sure is being super nice, but when we're in class, he treats me like I'm the enemy. I said, "Ok, Mr. Reid, you can suck on my pussy for the ride home."

"Suck your pussy? Naw, if you want a ride, you gonna do what I ask." I thought about it, then said, "Fuck it. Come on, cause I'm tired of going back and forth with you on this bullshit. It's cold out here." As we were riding home, he pulled out his old, shriveled-ass dick and motioned for me to slob on it. Fuck it. I tried to suck his shit dry. I worked it, sliding my tongue up and down, swirling it in and out of my mouth, spitting globs of saliva on his dick. Jacking it made him weak. I know this mafucka better not wreck this car, with his stupid ass!

I said, "Don't wreck the car."

"Ah, shit. I won't, now shut the fuck up and suck that dick." With one hand, he was holding my head down on his dick and kept the other hand on the steering wheel. I never sucked anyone's dick like Scooby's. You had to pay out your ass to get treatment like that. The way I sucked a dick was like dope. I jerked his dick until this mafucka almost crashed, with his simple ass. All I could do was laugh at this old trick-ass mafucka, while thinking how fucking amazing I was. I jacked that dick, until it skeeted all over his fucking windshield. Stupid ass. Now explain that to wifey!

Since Scooby and Jah were taken away from me, I was numb to feelings or any other type of affection. It was just about my money, and sometimes the fuck. I was tired as hell, and I really needed to talk to Quilla, but it was late, so I'd catch up with her tomorrow. The next morning, I woke up very excited. Today I was getting my graduation cap and gown. I called Quilla. "What's up, boo?"

"What's up, Chan?"

"I'm down here at the office, paying my graduation fees. What's your receipt number for your cap and gown, bitch? I'll just pay your balance off, too."

"That's what's up, Chan. Girl, I love you and I'm gonna pay you back."

"Don't worry bout it, Qui. I got you!" She knew she didn't have to thank me. "Oh yeah, while I got you on the phone... I know that you're not trying to think about it, but we're gonna roll in the Bentley to the graduation, so don't worry about transportation. It's auntie. You know how she do it."

"I'm with that, Chan. Thank you again, Chantal! I love you, girl."

"I know you do, Quilla. I love you, too. Bye, bitch!"

Quilla was still dealing with the loss of her brothers. No matter what she needed, I would be there for her. Hell, I was dealing with my own loss and I felt like no one was there for me, but I never dwell on that. I just keep it moving. That's all I can do. I've never been like everyone else. I have to be supportive because she was my friend.

Quilla never cared too much for my dad, although she never let me know that. But I could feel the tension whenever they were in a room together. I never asked her if there was a problem because it didn't matter. He had taken her place as best friend in my life. Maybe that was the problem. And she knew she couldn't change that. Hell, he had taken everyone's position in my life. He was my father, mother, friend, lover, everything. If I wasn't with my dad, I was thinking about him or on the phone with him. I don't know, maybe it was the fact that when he came home, I didn't see her that often. I spent all my time with my dad. Then again, my dad might have tried Quilla. After all, Jermaine Laine was a pimp, so he was always pimping. That was a possibility. One day I'm gonna ask her, but not now. She was barely making ends meet, working part time at that cheap-ass clothing store. She was trying to get a scholarship for college, which meant long hours in the books. I guess that's fine for some, but not Chantal Laine!

Quilla studied her ass off. She read all the law books in the library and any other book she could to prepare for her future. She was driven to graduate and go straight to law school. That was her number one priority. I couldn't be mad at her for that. She was a strong, young lady. Quilla was so much a part of my family that when my aunt introduced us to people, it was as her two nieces, not her niece and a friend. Quilla would come to Bel Air during the week for school and go home on the weekends. When she asked auntie Jackie if she could use our address to enroll in a better school zone, my aunt was more than happy to help. Quilla thought the education was better in rich neighborhoods, and she just might be right. During the years I attended schools in the low income section of town, I didn't learn shit.

Graduation weekend was awesome! Auntie Jackie was ready more than we were. "Wake up, graduates. Get up, sleepy heads!" Auntie insisted that Quilla spend the weekend with us. She called it "the bonding of young girls becoming young ladies" weekend. Sometimes I would catch Quilla trying to sit like her or move as she did, preparing herself to one day become a partner in a very prestigious law firm herself.

My aunt went in to business mode. "First things first, ladies. The graduation ceremony is at 4:00 p.m. tomorrow. That gives us enough time for a pampering session today and a party tonight." We went over the agenda as if it was one of her board meetings, very organized. "So ladies, should we have breakfast before the spa, or brunch afterwards?" After completing a two hour aromatherapy spa treatment, we brunched at Mr. Chow's restaurant. That's where she presented each of us a beautifully gift-wrapped box from Tiffany's.

"Ooh, auntie! Tiffany's! My favorite! Thank you!"

Quilla was too happy. "Thank you, Auntie Jackie. I never had Tiffany anything!"

"You ladies are most welcome. I'm very proud of both of you. Job well done and you both deserve it." Inside each box were two carat platinum tennis bracelets. Quilla was emotional.

She said, "Wow, Auntie Jackie, this is beautiful. Thank you so much. The only diamond I own is the heart pendant Chan gave me on my birthday. Thank you. I love it." Quilla looked at me and I could see the tears in her eyes. She whispered, "Damn, bitch. Put it on for me."

I thanked Auntie Jackie, even though I already had three that were very similar. Even though Quilla never had much, she wasn't jealous of anything that I had, and that's been since day one. A long time ago, we made a promise to never let jealousy, money, or a man come between us. Back at the house, auntie was preparing for our party. She hired the best people to do what they do. I think she needed all of this relaxation more than we did, since all she ever did was work. She invited all of our friends and some of hers to the party. What I liked most about the guest list was that there would be more men than ladies. My aunt's philosophy was not to keep too many bitches around because you couldn't trust them.

The cake was awesome! It fed 150 people. It had a two-sided stairway in the middle. One side was made with Quilla's favorite, which was chocolate. The other side was my favorite, red velvet. Twelve stairs led to the top of the cake, which displayed the word SUCCESS. It was beautifully decorated in magnolia petals and neon lights, very unique. My aunt was very creative when it came to things like that. She made sure that if she put her name on it, the details were perfect. There were two figurines in the likeness of

Quilla and me, perched on each staircase. Each stair represented a milestone in life. The first one was GOD, and then there was LOVE, LIFE, FAMILY, LOYALTY, RESPECT, CONFIDENCE, KNOWLEDGE, INDEPENDENCE INTEGRITY, and finally, CREATIVITY.

I stood there wondering if I had what it took to achieve all twelve steps, beginning with GOD. I knew that if nothing else mattered in this world, at least I had a personal relationship with God, and with that belief, I was saved. Love? Yeah, I knew of it, heard about it, and if it's anything like the feeling that I had for Scooby, then yea, I felt it. Life... I was definitely living that in full color! Family... Well, I had my Aunt Jackie, Quilla, and Jah. They filled a void. They were all the family I had. The fourth stair represented loyalty, which I considered to be one of my strong points. Respect... Let's just say that I respect those that respect themselves, and that's as far as that goes.

I thought about the next stair, Confidence. Our figurines occupied this step and I knew I had confidence, if nothing else. I was wearing a silk-blend pink dress by Roberto Cavalli, got the ass popping and the titties perky. Pink Gucci stilettos were on my feet and pink framed Gucci glasses on the cheeks. Four carat pink diamond studs in each ear and eight carats around the neck....priceless. Oh, I was very confident! My body made a nigga pay to play and beg to stay. As the dicks got bigger, so did my pockets. Oh, don't get it twisted.

I love to fuck, but ain't no nigga running up in this pussy for free!

The next set of stairs represented my levels to reach. Personally, I felt like I was already at the top of my game. Auntie Jackie felt that we had to be college graduates, executive-level employees, always stressed out and all that bullshit that comes with that type of success. I am my definition of success. I know how to get my money, and that was my only mission. All the other shit fell into place.

"Chantal Vivica Laine! Come here, baby! Give your uncle a hug!" This mafucka disappeared six months after Scooby was sent to prison. Said he was out of town on business and how sorry he was. All that weak shit you don't want to hear. I know why they called him Black. He wasn't just black, he was purple. He was a character too, always wanting to give hugs. Hugged so much that his dick got hard while he was sweating and feeling me up. He wasn't slick. Hell, he wasn't even my uncle. I could see straight through his ass. He was a hater, and I had to watch his ratchet ass up close.

"Come here, baby. Hug your Uncle Black. Umm, you smell good, girl. Make a nigga wanna commit a crime! I wanna do something freaky with you!" He sounded like a knock-off Bobby Brown and looked like a broke-ass Rick James. "Look at you, Chantal," he said, spinning me around with a thirst on his lips. "You sure have grown up and out, girl!" I could feel his dick getting hard as he grinded on my pelvis. He whispered, "A thousand dollars, baby, right now, for me to stick this long, black dick in that sweet-smelling pussy, with your fine ass. Meet me in the bathroom."

Shit, all I remember is that mafucka saying a thousand dollars. His stanking-ass was wearing knockoff cologne and thought he was balling. Niggas kill me with that shit! They think cause they paid $30 on a bottle of some toilet water from Ross, he doing it. This trick ain't shit. The mafucka had clout though, so he was definitely one to keep on speed dial. My relationships with tricks were profitable. It was all about my money and the networking. I had skills in more ways than one. I could get anything you needed before it hit the streets. You need Social Security numbers, birth certificates, Section 8 vouchers, tags for your car, driver's license, I got you. A bitch don't play! I even got some real killas in my pocket. I've been called everything in the book, I still get my money, so fuck 'em. Call me what you wanna, but it won't be broke, bitch.

I went to the bathroom. "What's up, Black? Sitting there playing with your dick, huh?" I entered the bathroom just in time to see him trying to wake that limp mafucka up. "What you doing, praying that shit get hard? Let me help you 'cause I ain't got all night. Run me my money first." I got my money, then I lifted my dress up, slid my G-string halfway down my booty and slid a condom on his limp dick. Shit! That mafucka started leaking! I only needed to show this nigga my juicy-ass booty and he was cummin'.

He started panting and said, "Damn, baby, you make me a happy man!"

"Yeah, I've heard that before. Come on, time is money."

"Sit right here on this big dick and make that ass clap!"

Fuck that. I had things to do. "You get no tricks tonight, nigga. All you paid for was a nut, so let's get it." As I bounced on his dick like the true thoroughbred that I am, my mind was on my money. Fuck a party and I don't give a fuck who party it is. The price was right and the fuck always felt good no matter whose dick it was. I didn't give a fuck. Niggas treat you like shit, anyway. What I need a nigga all up in my daily for, getting on my nerves, laying around, fucking and eating for free? That shit wasn't for me. I controlled everything about me, including my pussy, and from the look in Black's eyes, I knew that I had a client for life. The way I bounced on his old dick made him go into convulsions. He begged me to suck it, damn near cried for me to. The nut was busted so it was time to go.

"Chantal, at least kiss it!" He was actually whining. I climbed off his dick and told him, "The fuck was all you paid for." He held me so tight I couldn't breathe. "Nigga, let me go!"

"Damn, girl, you is bad! Marry me!"

"Marry you? Nigga, is you crazy? Let me go."

"I'm just playing, Chantal. But can I propose something to you? If you visit me just like that once a week, I'll pay you a thousand dollars, baby."

"Nigga, please! You got me fucked up! Make it fifteen hundred and we got a deal." This old mafucka was good for it. If I could make his old shrivel dick pop once a week for fifteen hundred, run it. Now that's a check, and how could he refuse this pussy? It had Scooby's mojo on it. He was still taking care of me from the other side. He taught me everything I knew about riding a nigga's dick and sucking muscle out that shit. I remember how he used to massage my ass for hours. He would say that he was shaping it into a perfect little bubble. I appreciated him for that, 'cause my shit is like an onion now. It makes a nigga cry. He loved to jack off on my booty. He cured and molded this ass from a very young age, massaging it with oil and shit - that drove me crazy!

I said, "I'm gonna fuck wit' you, Black, but let's make this perfectly clear. I make that dick pop, you run me my fifteen hundred. I'll be at the office on Wednesdays. You betta let them hating ass bitches you got working up in there know that I'm coming cause I ain't got time to be sitting there like I'm some fucking patient. As, I was wiping out the pussy and getting back fresh, this nigga still laying on the floor begging! "Black! Get up and put your shit together, mafucka!"

"Don't I get a kiss, Chantal?"

I was done. "What? Nigga, let's get one thing straight right now. All we gonna do is fuck, that's it. No feelings, no dates, no nothing! I make the dick pop, you run me my money. That's it! Understood?"

"Yea, baby I got it."

"And don't call me baby! Shit, you act like you need flash cards for this shit."

"Yeah, baby, I got it."

"Don't fuck with me, Black!"

"Anything you say. It's your world, with your fine ass! Just let me kiss the booty one more time, please?" I love for a nigga to beg for my shit, so being the freak I am, I bent that ass over for a kiss, lifted my dress halfway, then clapped the cheeks a few times. And damn, before I knew it, this nigga had slipped his finger in my pussy. It only took two bangs on it, and this mafucka made me skeet in a matter of seconds. He had a hand full of cum. I don't know what happened. I guess he knew the exact spot. He was an OB/GYN doctor, after all. I guess when you playing with pussies all day long, you acquire very prominent skills concerning the vagina. This nigga lay back on the floor and accepted my juices as if he had just milked a cow. That shit felt so good, it took everything in me not to give this nigga some more pussy, but that would have been for free and that's a no-no. He better be glad he got a free milkshake!

"Move, Black. Get out my fucking way." This nigga was thirsty! I grabbed a wet wipe and wiped my pussy, and then I dropped it on his face. I left his ass right there on the floor. I stepped over him and went out to the terrace to get some air. There was Quilla, surrounded by niggas, as usual. She said, "Where you been, bitch?" She was drunk as hell. "Auntie Jackie looking for you. We're getting ready to do the toast."

"Well let's go, bitch. Wait. Is somebody out here smoking a blunt? Let me hit that shit real quick."

Quilla said, "Oh, you smoking tonight, bitch?"

"Why not? We're graduating tomorrow, and it's all good, right? You're my best friend and we paid." I pulled the stack out of my bra, and she went crazy.

"Oh Chantal, where you get that? Bitch, give me some!"

"Qui, don't play. You know I gets mine. And I'm done with that school shit, so it's all about the money, college girl."

"Yep, that's right. I'm going to college and what?"

Changing the subject, I said, "This shit good, Qui. I ain't got high in a minute. Where you get this from?" Somebody I never met before said, "Me, shawty. Roll with me and I can get you some more. You the flyest bitch in here. What's up with you? The name is Freeno. Nice to meet you."

Who the fuck was this broke ass nigga holling at. talking bout 'nice to meet you'? "Who you calling a bitch?" I turned to Quilla and asked, "Who the fuck is this nigga, Qui?" He said, "Come over here and give me some conversation, with your bad ass and find out."

Now I was hot. "Quilla, who the fuck is this broke-ass mafucka? Talking 'bout roll with him for some weed? He got me fucked up!" I turned back to that nigga and said, "You must be mistaking me for a broke bitch. Easily handled, huh? I don't know who the fuck that nigga came with, but it's time for him to go."

Quilla said, "He came with Black."

"Ain't no need in asking somebody else who I am, lil mama. I told you, I'm Freeno."

"Who the fuck ever. You and your lame ass friend need to go." I was heated for real now.

Quilla said, "Come on, Chantal. Fuck this nigga."

Freeno said, "Hold up! So I get no conversation?"

"Right. I don't talk to broke-ass niggas. Let's go, Qui."

He said, "Okay. Oh, I'll see you again, Miss Lady. I will see you again."

I was done. "Nigga, fuck you!" I pulled Quilla's arm and said, "Come on, Quilla. Let's go get our toast on. Girl, we graduating. Fuck this nigga!" The party was a blast. I ended up drunk and passed out. We had so much fun. I could hardly wake up the next morning. The good thing about this morning though is that I woke up to a letter from Jah. A wonderful surprise. I loved hearing from him. It read:

Sup Chan,

How you doing, love of my life? I'm missing on you something terrible girl. When you coming to see me? I'm so proud of you. Congrats to you, ma. You and sis doing ya'll thang. On another note, I'm so ready to come home. This shit ain't no walk in the park, baby. It's hard as a mafucka in here. NE way, fuck all that. You know, I was thinking the other day how when we was young we used to "play". Lol, yea I used to eat that pussy up, girl. Shidd, you know Chan I'm getting old. I been in this shit since I was seventeen. It is what it is, though. I got some good news. You gonna be proud of me. I got my diploma! Yea, it took a while cause I was really fighting the fact that these mafuckas was making me do it, whether I wanted to or not, but I'm glad I did. Gave me a since of accomplishment, you know? So yea, I did that! You proud of me? So, moving on. What's wrong with your pen? What, you don't love me no more? You better write me, chump.

I love you - One.

Jah really understood me. He was very special. I made a choice to stick by him, no matter what. I cared for him a lot.

Today is the day that Quilla and I graduate. I'm so happy we got to this day. It was a hard and long road, but we made it. The graduation was definitely one to remember. The ceremony itself was long as fuck, with all the boring speeches and songs. This person or another speaking on whatever. They called each person to receive their diploma. There was excitement and joy from the audience. The commencement lasted about two hours. A few homies from the hood even showed up. Said they were very proud of Quilla and I for making it and wanted to show their support. They were more so proud of Quilla. Through all of her adversity, she still made it and was gonna go on to great things.

Mr. Carl even flew down for the ceremony. I wasn't no fool. Mr. Carl came to get my Auntie pussy. Said he had flown in for the graduation. Yea right! His ass didn't even bring a gift. Big Mama Laine, auntie Jackie and of course Ms. Bea, who had managed to pull some dress from the bottom of her closet with shoes on that needed a heel, and a style replacement. Had I known she was coming looking like that, I would have offered her something from my own closet or took the bitch shopping. They were all there to share in our graduation. It was a good day. This was my circle, my family. All I had and all I knew.

After the graduation, Auntie Jackie insisted we go celebrate at Benihana for dinner. She even invited the homies. She also invited Ms. Bea to join us, but she refused. She said she was through with all this celebrating shit and she was going get a beer. She kept it real, though. I think deep inside, she felt as though she didn't fit in and truth be told, she didn't. I could see the sigh of relief in Quilla's eyes after she refused the invite. She was embarrassed by her mom, always has been. Dinner was quite the experience, as most occasions my aunt put together are. She always goes the extra mile to make sure everything is five star. We enjoyed not one, but three knife-wielding, joke telling chefs for our dining experience.

After the feast, we made sure to present Auntie Jackie a gift for all she had done, not only for me, but the guidance and support she had given Quilla as well. She was appreciated and well respected and we wanted her to know that. We presented her with a bouquet of her favorite flowers along with an eighteen carat gold charm bracelet with gavels. She was so overjoyed, tears flowed down her face. This had to be the second time I could remember my aunt crying. She said no one had ever did anything for her like that. Said she was just doing what was right by us girls and that she loved us very much. She promised to never take it off.

Quilla gave me an identical bracelet with a Chanel charm and I gave her one with a dictionary. We all thought that was a unique and personal thing, so we made it a tradition. On birthdays, we would give each other a charm of love, life and happiness. That was the bond that Quilla, auntie and myself established that day. In the words of TeTe it was the grandest of gestures for a sisterhood bond. In the middle of the tears and happiness, she put the focus back on Qui and I. She gave us special gifts as well. Even with all she had done for us, she still had more love to give.

To Quilla's surprise, Auntie Jackie gave her ten thousand dollars cash. Said that it was for her first year of college and told her to use it wisely on her education. Qui was speechless and ran to auntie with the biggest hug. I've never seen her so excited. Qui really needed that money and it would help a lot. As far as I was concerned, she had already given everything except life itself, so there was nothing in this world that she could give me. But being the lady of class that she is, she surprised me with an all-expense paid cruise-land excursion for seven days to the lands of Egypt, India and Peru. That should be very exciting. These were places I hadn't experienced yet. My only problem was who to take with me to places of that magnitude. Or should I just go alone? There's a whole lot of business on that side of the world and I was very good at meeting new people. I had an open ticket so maybe I would wait for Jah to come home. Who knows?

The evening turned out to be a memorable one. Me and my bestie were done with that school shit. Well, I was, anyway. She had dreams of continuing on that path of education and I will be there for her in support only. I ain't sitting in another class room, period. When we made it home, it was well into the night. Auntie Jackie and of course Mr. Carl, who decided to catch a later flight, arrived home and we were all exhausted. It had been a long day.

The bacon and French toast smelling in the air was a pleasant aroma to wake up to. Mr. Carl was in the kitchen, getting it right. The only time food was actually cooked in this house was when Auntie had a dinner party or some occasion that I would throw together. And almost always it would be a hired chef in the kitchen doing all the work. However Mr. Carl had managed to stop at Starbucks and get the morning Java. He brought my favorite, Macchiato. How did he know I loved a large cup of this shit so early in the morning? That was a point for him. It was good to have someone in the house who knew how to cook and be quiet at the same time. Mr. Carl was a keeper. He was an older gentleman, nice physique and well spoken. He was still a man, though. I could tell by the way he watches me. I'm sure he would pay dearly for this pussy cause he no doubt wanted it, and he could afford it.

Auntie Jackie was still in the bed or in the mirror. She never came out of her bedroom without looking poised and professional, even if we were just gonna hang around the house. Maybe this was because of the fact that her wardrobe mainly consisted of business attire and that's what she was most comfortable in. I toned her down a lot though, had her experiencing more sporty, casual attire.

I walked into the kitchen. "Good morning, Mr. Carl."

"Hello Chantal. So how does it feel to be a graduate? No more school, huh?"

"Right. Don't have to think about that anymore." As I walked toward him, he wasn't looking at my face. He was more so focused on the belly button and downward. I pretended not to notice and said, "Oh, this fruit looks so fresh, Mr.

Carl." I bit into a peach and the juices were spilling out of my mouth, oozing down the cleavage of my breast. You could see the lust in his eyes as he watched me effortlessly wipe the mess. "This peach is so juicy! Where did you get these from, Mr. Carl?" I could tell he was excited by the way he was licking his lips, and my innocent little girl role didn't hurt.

"Let me get you a napkin, Chantal. Yeah, let me help you with that." When he reached over to hand me the napkin, I knew that he would much rather wipe it himself. So, you know me, I leaned over to give him the pleasure. In a helpless manner, I used my baby girl voice to say, "Oh yeah, Mr. Carl! Thank you so much. That feels wonderful." I exposed half a breast, made sure all the juices were wiped up, and then shook the titties a little. His old-ass dick was leaking as we were standing there, I'm sure. I could see his erection through his shorts.

"Damn, girl! You need another napkin?"

"No, I'm good. It's just that this is the juiciest fruit I've had in a while." I had him on the ropes. "Yeah, it does look good, Chantal. I-I mean it tastes good. I-I mean it looks like it tastes good. Damn, Chantal. I got those over at the farmer's market this morning, okay?"

"Okay, Mr. Carl." I knew the effects I had on a nigga. It was cute to see it in action, especially with the older men. I giggled. He was still wanting a bitch. I said, "So, Mr. Carl, you got up super early this morning. You already went to the market and cooked breakfast. Oh and by the way, thanks for the Starbucks. It's my favorite. How did you know?"

"Your Aunt Jackie told me." I took another bite. He was gazing at my body as if I were the peach and he was hungry. He could barely finish preparing breakfast with all the distraction. He couldn't take his eyes off me. "Well, thank you for this great breakfast, Mr. Carl. I'm very impressed, and that's not easy for most folks."

He looked at me, almost flirting and asked, "What does it take to impress you?"

"A lot."

"Well I think it's because you're so damn sexy. You're intimidating to a guy."

"Thank you, Mr. Carl. I woke up like this." He didn't have to tell me my worth. I knew it from a very young age.

"No, thank you for the wonderful view this morning. You're definitely a breath of fresh air." He also should have thanked me for that small drip he had in his pants. I walked out with my plate of breakfast, which consisted of two pieces of French toast and two pieces of turkey bacon with fruit and an egg white. It's more than I normally eat, but I was gonna live a little this morning. I was going to take advantage of this live-in chef for this moment, cause soon he would be gone. I'll make it up at the gym or on some nigga's dick later, so no worries.

Auntie Jackie bent the corner, looking exquisite at 9:30 in the morning. She was beautiful. The only difference between me and her was that I had that natural shit and she needed a lot of Mac products to pull hers off. Nonetheless, she did it well.

"Good morning, Chan. What ya'll got going on in here?"

"Oh, nothing, auntie. Mr. Carl got some amazing fruit over there. You should try the peaches. They're really fresh."

"Ok, I'll make smoothies. You want one?"

"Oh no, thank you. I have French toast and bacon."

Auntie Jackie looked surprised. She said, "What? You eating carbs, Chan?"

"Yes, today I'm living a little."

She frowned and said, "I call it fat, Chan."

"I know auntie, but it's just for today." One thing about Auntie Jackie is that she didn't play that fat shit. She would spend all her fortune to look good. Looking good and being healthy was her quest in life. She was also a vegetarian. Said if it had a mother, she couldn't put it in her mouth. I respected that. My dad had similar eating habits, but he occasionally had a piece of fish or turkey. Aunt Jackie said, "Chan, you wanna go shopping? Mr. Carl is gonna take us out today."

"Most definitely, Auntie. Shopping? Don't ask me twice. Give me an hour and I'm ready." The look on Mr. Carl face let me know that he didn't know he was taking us shopping. I guess that was the charge for the pussy he got last night. He just stood there with a smile on his face, looking dumb. I teased him and said, "Well I hope you got your wallet, Mr. Carl."

"Oh I'll be okay, Chantal."

Shopping on Rodeo Drive was total bliss for me. I wanted to go in all the shops, but my favorites were Chanel and Gucci. My Aunt was more inclined to Prada and Fendi, so the choices were always in abundance. By the time we settled in at 208 Rodeo Drive to get a bite to eat, Mr. Carl was sweating and tired. A shopping spree with the Laine ladies was exhausting and financially draining. We knew high fashion and we had class, so the day was rewarding for any man to be in the presence of ladies doing what they do best. On the way home, we made an unexpected detour to the airport. Mr. Carl was headed back to Miami. Damn, I thought it was rather abrupt and bittersweet, but I like the way Auntie handled that one. Give him a little quality time, spend his money, then drop his ass off.

Me and auntie rode all the way home laughing at the way he was sweating each time he had to pull that credit card out his pocket. Shidd, at one point, I told him to wear it around his neck for easy access. He was a trick and didn't even know it. The time spent with my aunt had valuable lessons in it.

Chapter 9

Time sure does fly! It has been two years since I graduated high school and the celebration has come to an end for the most part. I've been on my grind harder and more consistent than ever before. My ass is better than it ever was. It's got a nice jiggle to it that makes niggas bark and holla. I'm all about my money, though. No bullshit. And free pussy? Those days are long gone. Living with aunt Jackie has been quite the experience. She has taught me so much as far as how to keep my money growing.

My phone rang. "Hello, Chantal speaking." Ever since my Aunt Jackie explained the importance and gracefulness of answering your phone with your identity, it has become second nature.

"Ugh, wake up bitch." It was my girl.

"Sup, Qui?"

"Girl, it's eleven in the morning. Get up!"

"For what, school girl? I don't have classes at eight o'clock in the damn morning like you. Besides, I had a late night."

"Whatever. I'm on my way. Bye." I absolutely hate to be awakened by a ringing phone and this bitch just rung it off the hook. Since I've graduated, it's been leisure time. I don't' punch nobody's clock, and I don't do that school shit. I'm done with that. Can't say the same for my girl, though. College is her life. She's in that bitch all day, every day. She's very serious about becoming a lawyer and her academic achievements prove it. She's at the top of her game, always being recognized as an outstanding something or another. I'm very proud of her.

Me on the other hand, well I guess you can call me a spoiled rich kid. I've lived here with Auntie Jackie for almost five years, bill free, stress free. Letting me be the adult that I am. There are boundaries of course, as with anyone when you're in their space. We get along and we make it work. She has made my life here very comfortable, from the early years to this time right now.

My day normally starts with having breakfast, which is the most important meal of the day, right? Most times, my aunt is juicing and other times a chef prepares anything you could ever want. How could you not take advantage of that? Then I go to the gym. I'm there four times a week, keeping it tight. That's where most of my clients are. After that, there's hair, nails, spa and facial, shopping. Let's not forget shopping. That's about eighty percent of my time. In the middle of all that, I have clients to serve, so there's lunch and dinner appointments, secret rendezvous, and my sky mile club is awesome, mostly on private jets. So yea, I'm very busy. Haters hate my lifestyle, and I love haters, so do the math!

Looking from my bedroom window, it seems like it's a nice day. The sun is out, birds are chirping, not too hot, not too cold. I love California weather, although I prefer to be in my condo that overlooks Atlanta at this time of year. There, you're able to identify the seasons by the many colors of the trees. It's beautiful. It only lasts for a brief period, but the colors are amazing. Red-orange, yellow-gold, red-purple, which is my favorite. That's from the sweet gum and scarlet oak.

I love nature and all its wonders. Just because I chose not to go to college doesn't mean my appetite for knowledge is not thirsty. I'm connected with professors, doctors, lawyers, and other professionals. Although I'm not sitting in a classroom, it doesn't mean I'm not educated and well informed. It's one of the requirements of my profession. Being able to fluently engage in an intellectual conversation is mandatory!

Today seems like a Uggs kind of day. I donned Victoria Secret sweats, a tank top, diamond studs, hair in a bun. Yea, I have these kind of days sometimes, although not often. I'm utterly fabulous, but I'm still human. I'm really missing my dad today. There's not a day that goes by that I don't miss Scooby and our life. While it will never be okay, I can honestly say it gets better. When you lose a parent, a piece of you goes with them. You learn not to live without them but how to live with the spirit of them. The loss leaves a sense of homelessness, especially when there's no siblings to share the pain with you. I constantly pray for strength.

"Ms. Chantal, Shiqulla is here, ma'am."

"Thank you, Rosa." Rosa is auntie's maid. She has been in the family for over a decade. Very nice lady from the Dominican Republic. She has such a warm spirit and takes very good care of me and my auntie. "Hey Qui." I gave her peck on the cheek. "Mwah. What are you doing over here so early? Don't you have class?"

"Not until later. I want you to go look at this condo with me."

Now that was unexpected. "Condo? What, you're gonna leave Ms. Bea all by herself?" Ms. Bea had moved out of the projects when she received the money from Victim Services for Man's death. She had a nice little place in a good neighborhood. Qui thought it was too far from her college and she spent most nights here or at the dorm. She decided it would be best to get something closer, and besides, her relationship with her mother was always filled with drama. That's one of the reasons I don't' fuck with my own mother. Too much work. But Quilla always wanted more for her mom, and although the effort was one sided, she tried. She said, "Chan, at some point I gotta move on, right?"

"Yea, okay. Let me get dressed, bitch."

"Get dressed? You look good, Chan. Ain't nobody got time for you to do all you do when you get dressed."

"Qui, are you serious? You want me to go out the house like this? I got on some damn sweats and a tank top! Let me put on some jeans or something, damn."

"Okay, but hurry up. I got a class at four o'clock."

"I got you. Give me six minutes at the most." Looking this good required work but when it was time to put it all together, it didn't take long. I was done in a flash. I said, "Okay let's go!"

"Damn, Chan. You said you were putting on some jeans."

"What is this, bitch? Jeans, right?" I had Religions on my bottom, Hermes around my waist, Jimmy Choo on my feet, and a Birkin bag on my arm, all with a beat face. "I'm ready. Let's go look at condos." We rode around the San Fernando Valley area, looking at one place after the other. I said, "Quilla, this is a task. Looking for a place to live is serious business."

"Yeah, Chan, what you think?"

"Well I didn't think it took all this."

"Well I guess when you got money you can just pick up the phone, but I'm on a budget, so shopping for the right place is what I gotta do."

"I guess you right." We must have seen four different floor plans in four different locations, and none of them were up to my standard, but it did get me thinking that maybe I should get my own crib. And then Quila asked, "Chan, what you think about getting a place together?" I don't know about that, but I said, "Yea, that would be nice, Qui."

"You think so?"

"Yeah, I mean why not? We both so different when it comes to our space, though. I'm used to a lot of square footage and that condo we just saw is the size of my closet. Now, if we're talking about the presidential penthouse, we can discuss further." Laughing, we made our way back to the house so that she could go to class. Although we jokingly spoke about it, it was definitely something to think about. Maybe it's time to become more independent.

After several weeks, Quilla finally found something she could afford. A quarter of a million dollars sure don't get you much in real property in the San Fernando Valley of Southern California. Certainly not my location preference, just to dry for me. She settled on a 1,900 square foot, three bedroom, three bath condo in North Hollywood Hills. It was a nice space, to say the least. Many of the upgrades were of high quality and it had stainless steel appliances. Hell, she didn't care. It was her very first spot and she was happy. I offered to buy her a house and work out the mortgage but she wanted the independence of doing it for herself. I told her the least I could do was buy her a couple of furniture pieces for her new space. She appreciated the offer and immediately made a date for us to go shopping. The very next day! I thought that was really quick, but she was excited, so... Just then, we drove into a parking lot of some strange store. I had no idea where we were.

Quilla said, "Chan, I wanna get a couple of items out of here."

"What is this place, Qui?"

"It's IKEA. Come on."

"What the hell is IKEA?"

Quilla laughed and said, "Come on, girl."
When I tell you my girl went in this warehouse and
decorated her entire crib from front to back, I was
shocked! Everything from the bedroom to the
bathroom, to the kitchen in one stop. This was
some of the funniest bargain basement shopping
shit I had ever seen. So to be clear, you walk
around this tin can and shop for bulk items
wrapped in plastic on a shelf. You take a ticket for
the large items, along with your other items in a
grocery cart to a cashier. Then you pay and bag
your own things with brown tissue paper and carry
them out to your car. They don't even offer any
kind of delivery options or valet service! I had
never been shopping in that fashion before. It was
my honor to pay the bill, being that it was only
$1,600 for everything. Quilla was very happy. She
had a handyman on speed dial to pick up the
bigger items. She was on her own for that task. I
had a client to meet, so she dropped me off.

When I got home, there was a gorgeous
assortment of roses in the most exquisite vase
waiting on me in the foyer. The card read, "I can't
wait to see you. I've been thinking of you all day.
See you soon, Mr. NBA." I loved my clients. They
were so classy and thoughtful. Even though it was
all about the pleasure I gave them, whenever they
got a chance to show their appreciation, it was
wonderful. I've gotten cars, jewelry, exotic trips
and of course, that mean cash. I loved my job!

I packed my fuck bag. The contents were limited. All that was needed were two pair of thongs, some creams for the body and the booty, and an outfit to tease. That stuff, along with a tight pussy, which was mandatory, and some red lipstick was all that was needed. See, you had to cater to each client as an individual. This particular client loved for me to suck his dick with red lipstick on, the redder the better.

I'd meet my three o'clock at the Four Seasons in Beverly Hills. None of them meant much to me. This was strictly business, so getting on a personal level was not an option. I never addressed them by name, always by title, status or appointment time. They were just a check. Like any job where one has to clock in and out, this was mine. When I arrived at the hotel, I retrieved the keys to the executive suite from the concierge, who let me know that she would be at my disposal if there was anything I needed. She assured me that my guest was an hour and a half away. I was then escorted to the suite, where I made myself at home. It had all the bells and whistles. Five star everything, just how I liked it.

I was lying across the bed in a G string and stilettos, ready for the thrill and the money, when the door opened. There stood my client, Mr. NBA himself, very talented and rich. For the last seven years, he drove that ball straight into a successful career with the Los Angeles Lakers. He was married with three children. A very humble person, but a freak to the core.

The moment the door closed, this nigga ripped that string out of my ass and sucked my pussy 'til the lining fell out. He often acted as if he was teaching me something, which was cute. Oftentimes, he would tell me how to massage his dick or how to suck it, positioning my booty just right so that he could suck the crack. I would let him think he was in control. It was a part of the fantasy. The pussy was tight and stayed fresh, and the fantasy was real, that's why they kept coming back.

See, there's an art to this shit. You can't just jump up and down on dick all day and think you're not putting miles on it. Just as with any profession, it takes hard work and dedication. You gotta keep your game tight. You can never go back to being a virgin, but keeping the pussy tight is the goal. It's all about having skills. You see, the pussy is a muscle. You have to tone and tighten it, as with any muscle in your body. Exercising the pussy is essential to a woman's maintenance plan. You must take the time to care for it. If not, the miles begin to wear and tear on it. Kegel exercises are the best because they strengthen your pubococcygeus muscles. You can do those anywhere, any time of day. Thanks to Scooby, I knew the importance of cherishing the body.

Shit, I think my dad had a PHD in pussyology. He would say that a bitch gotta know what she was worth in order to acquire the assets that she needs. Every chance I get, I tighten up. See, you can suck on a nigga's dick all day with your mouth, but you milk a nigga's shit with your pussy. Now that's the key to breaking his ass. You can control that nigga without him even knowing it, just by using the pussy. Of course all niggas are different, but they're all the same.

This particular client liked for me to suck his dick sideways, meaning he wanted to see the head poking from my jaw. He wanted me to spit on it, then he wanted me to let him stick his dick in my ear. He told me his wife didn't play that ear shit, and that's why he over here in my ear. He took my cum juices and massaged the crack of my ass as he licked my pussy. He was a freak! He liked to try a lot of shit and I was down for it all. I mean, shit, it's a check and it felt good. He was so in love with this shit. I didn't get it fucked up. I knew he love his wife and his life, but I was his flavor of the month, every month.

He begged me to stay all night and said it would be worth my while, but I had too many things on the agenda for tomorrow. He offered to fly me to Miami, where his next game was in two days. I accepted his offer. I could get paid, take a mini vacay and take care of some of my real estate business, so it was a great idea. I sucked his dick one last time and got the hell outta there with $6,000 in a large, powder blue Chanel handbag as a token of his appreciation. Not bad for twelve hours of work. The dick was awesome and the tongue was even more special.

Chapter 10

"Scorpios are fiercely independent. They are able to accomplish anything they put their minds to and they won't ever give up. They are perfectly suited to being on their own." I thought this spoke volumes to my girl's character. It was the perfect inscription for her birthday charm. Quilla was turning twenty three years old, and she had accomplished just what she set out to. After completing her studies early, she sat for the state bar and passed on her first try. I was proud of her. Her mind, body and soul were in tune with her success. Today was her day and nothing was gonna stop her from celebrating.

We were having a girls only dinner because that's what she wanted for this occasion. She insisted that no men be allowed. It wasn't my type of gathering and she knew it, but it was her day. This should be interesting. Most of the ladies were from her new firm or the courthouse.

It had been my privilege to have it catered and decorated. I ordered appetizers of salmon and cream cheese puffs, Saucy Asian Meatballs and cucumber feta rolls. Everything was delicious. Quilla loved shell fish so there couldn't have been enough lobster, mussels, clams, and every other swimming species in the ocean. The chef made sure to stem, stew, and fry all of them. The decorations were beautiful, fall colors and baskets full of nuts and fruits. The thrifty items she had selected at IKEA went well in the space.

My Auntie Jackie took the liberty of ordering the pastries and the champagne, Moet Rose Imperial at a thousand dollars a case. She spared no expense and ordered three cases. The birthday cake was specially made with blackberries, raspberries and strawberries on vanilla bean custard with little red velvet cupcakes surrounding it. There were mini pastries, lemon meringue tarts, berry chocolate mousse cups, and the miniature chocolate cannoli was to die for.

Everything was superb. Quilla was very happy. She even took pictures with her mom, so she was definitely feeling the Moet. She was even being cordial to her mother. After the party, she wanted me to spend the night, but I was tired and needed to meet with clients in the morning, so I got ready to leave. "I love you, girl. I had a great time, but I got business in the morning."

"Thank you so much, for everything. Girl, I love you."

"Girl, you welcome. I'll call you when I get home. I love you, too." On the ride home, I must say that I was jealous that my bestie was in her own space. It made me wanna really get the ball rolling.

As I lay in the bed, my mind wouldn't let my body relax into sleep. So I laid there, thinking of all the things that my life represented to this point. First, my best friend was awesome and she had really come into her own. All that she had strived for, she had attained it. Second, my Aunt Jackie was a wonderful influence in my life and so was Big Mama Laine, although I rarely saw her. Riverside was too damn far to see her as often as I would have liked. Third, I was rich as fuck. Everything I needed or wanted, I could have. Life was good.

The cars that I drive are a reflection of me. I have a black G500 SUV Mercedes Benz. I drive that car daily. Last year, Auntie J gave me a BMW 760LI, all black everything, and she said that if my dad was here, he would have loved this model. She had it customized with "Scooby" stitched on the leather headrest. It had wood grain everything and $20,000 chrome custom wheels. It was the greatest birthday gift I've ever received. When I'm stunting, as Jah calls it, I'll pull out the Bentley. That's my material joy. I purchased the white pearl, drop-top Bentley coupe, with pink and white leather interior for $186,000 on my twenty first birthday. Actually, it was a steal. Let's just say, if you ride the right dick, you can get basically whatever you want, whenever you want it.

Now, at the age of twenty three, my portfolio is three times what it was when I was sixteen years old. I bought and own everything I got. I don't owe a muthafucka for nothing. And eight times out of nine, I get shit waived or reduced. I'll let a serviceman eat this pussy. He more than considered paid, and if the services are superior, he might get his dick sucked. Don't fuck with me! I got it and I will use it. The things Scooby taught me and the way I was seasoned to pop that pussy, pretty much helped me get anything or anybody's man that I wanted. If a nigga got heart to check for me in front of his broad, I'll snatch his ass from her at a fucking red light. If it looks like he's on a level that I could get paid, fuck it, I'm gonna snatch his ass right in front of his bitch! It can be whenever, wherever, and most times we might cause a scene 'cause a bitch know that I'm a triple threat. I'm rich, bootylicious, and brilliant. I'm undeniable. Been this way since yay high. I am who I am. Fuck those that don't approve.

For the last year and a half, I have dreaded the thought of moving out of this lavish abode that is my Auntie's mansion. The thought of being responsible for all that adult shit that comes with living on your own is something that I'm not looking forward to, but it's time to move into my own space! Quilla had been in her condo for over a year now, and I was getting a bit jealous of all the freedom she had. I was ready. After looking for more than a year, considering several deals and always disengaging at the last moment, I decided to make a move. It seemed that no house was worthy of being called my home. My realtor called with a pocket listing one day and insisted that I go see it. Said it had everything that I wanted and I should drive down immediately.

Well, he was right. The home is valued at $4.4 million. 6000 square feet, full of charm and character, nestled in the hills of Malibu on a private estate in a gated community. It has six bedrooms and seven and a half bathrooms. The interior featured bamboo floors, stainless-steel appliances and walls of glass that offered stunning views. It was the perfect estate with an office, and a separate maid's quarters, space with a second living area and three fireplaces. Truly an exquisite architectural masterpiece. I made a cash offer and closed in five days. I couldn't resist it.

I loved my master bathroom, the one place where you can be totally naked inside and out, your entire being, vulnerable in the flesh. No jewelry, no makeup, just you. I demanded that this space be very luxurious and roomy. That's the best place to love yourself for a few hours and reflect on what you got. If my Scooby could see my place, he would be pleased. His class and style rubbed off on me in a grand way. My home is rather large for just me, but I couldn't pass up the great deal. Shit, it was damn near given to me! I'll sell in a couple years, depending on the market. Shit, at twenty-three years old, I can't complain! I'm proud of everything that I got, and I'm very proud of who I've become.

Designing every room and the meticulous details of planning and decorating was something I enjoyed. I was a delegator at heart and gave orders quiet well. Having a very eclectic style, I was looking for a designer for my new home that would be creative in marrying the many pieces that I've collected throughout my travels with other high end pieces. My taste is impeccable and I needed that same quality in my designer. I decided to go with contemporary old school glam, the more bling the better. I've interviewed over twenty designers, looked at a million swatches of patterns and textures. You name it, I've seen it. Some were good at *their* vision for my home but one designer stood out when he realized *my* vision, which was why he got the job. And he did the job quite well. The entire house was amazing and I was impressed.

"Damn, Quilla, it's early as fuck. Where's the 'Bucks at?"

"We're gonna stop on the way, Chan."

"Damn, I thought you had it already! My mouth was ready for it! Bitch, you know I ain't shit without that fix!" Today, we were going to see Jah. It seemed that in order to get my day started, I needed steamed milk and an intense hit of espresso roast with a buttery caramel drizzle, known as the caramel macchiato, large please. And until I got it, I didn't wanna be fucked with. I was hooked. Dad had me feenin' on that Starbucks shit at the age of thirteen. He would send Molo every morning before he started to detail the cars.

We entered the prison compound and we noticed that the surroundings were beautiful. Checkerboards of brilliant flowerbeds were situated close to the sea between San Luis Obispo and Santa Barbara. It was not the view one would imagine on a prison campus. As we arrived at the main entrance of the Jail, there were lockers for purses, coats, wallets, keys, cell phones, and anything else that got on the police's nerves. I gave my ID to the officer and he was definitely eye candy. All the ladies flirted with him. I don't fuck with the police so he had none of my attention.

Officer Eye Candy said, "Visitors, form a line to the right of the wall and quiet down. If I say it again, you lose your visit. Listen up, and when your inmate's name is called, go to the red line and wait. I hated coming here, It brought back all those childhood memories when we visited my dad. The fuck police always treated visitors as if we were in this muthafucka doing time, too. Did they hate the inmates that much that they hated the visitors, too? Or was it that this low-paying-ass job that they hated stressed them out? They began to call names. The list went on forever. Finally, we heard, "Jaheim Jones."

Jah entered the room in a white prison jumpsuit with Gucci's on his feet and Cartier on his eyes. He was very sexy and well taken care of. He wasn't wanting for shit in this hellhole. He was a jewel, even under the circumstances. I smiled and said, "Hey, boo."

"'Sup, ma. How you doing?"

"Good. Happy to see you."

"Likewise, sweetheart. You dipped by yourself? Where Quilla?"

"Oh, she's coming. She down there flirting with some nigga. You know your sister." We made some small talk and then he asked me what I been up to. I told him, "Oh, nothing. I'm finally settled in the house. I'm gonna have a little dinner party."

"Oh yeah? How did the crib turn out?"

"Ah, Jah, it's nice. I'm loving the space. It's a little large, but it's peaceful."

He said, "That's what's up. I can't wait to come home." What? I was quiet for a minute, then I said, "Yea." For the first time, I realized that he was planning on being with me. Talking about living together. Damn!

"Chan, I wrote you a letter. I want you to read it and let me know what you think, ok?"

"Okay Jah." This sounded like another one of those jailhouse dreams a nigga be having, and trying to sell it to a bitch. Je said, "You should be getting your letter in the mail this week. I mailed it yesterday. Oh yea, that last poem you wrote me was on point! Spit it for me, baby!"

"Please, not now, Jah." My mind was on this letter and what was in it that he couldn't tell me about now. He asked me again, "Yes, baby, come on now."

"Not now, Jah," I snapped.

"Dang! What's wrong, Chan?"

"What's in the letter?"

"You'll see." He tried to laugh it off, but shit wasn't funny. I wanted to know what he was talking about and he wanted a fucking poem. Normally I don't share my poetry with anyone, just a part of me that no one has ever known, but somehow I shared with him and it has become a gift to this nigga. Always insisting that I share it. I appreciated the love sometimes. Quilla's loud-ass mouth interrupted the awkward silence. "Jah, what's up, baby! How's my man doing?" Quilla was just as loud as her mama. You never would have believed she was an attorney. She would strike you as one of the flyy girls. You know, the gold diggers of this society. The only difference is that she was 100% authentic. She took care of herself and called her own shots. I guess that's why we clicked. The only difference between us is that she is highly educated and I'm highly fabricated, but we're both very private. If you didn't already know something about Chantal Laine or Quilla Jones, you didn't need to know.

"Chaney, there's this fly-ass muthafucka over there! He rolled up here with his homeboys on a visit. He said after the visit we and his homey can get a bite to eat. They ballers, girl! Dropping money to a loved one. Girl, we gonna see what's up and shit!" Quilla was going on and on, just rambling about hooking me up with this nigga right in front of Jah. I had to bring this bitch back quick. She saw the expression on my face and then looked at Jah and said, "Oh shit, my bad, baby. I ain't gonna let Chan do shit. She loves you too much, anyway."

Quilla didn't find out her brother and I was as close as we were until he went to jail. I finally told her one day. I started at the beginning and went to the present. I wasn't sure if I would lose my best friend for keeping something like that from her. Didn't know if she would view that as a form of dishonesty because withholding information is the same as a lie. She took it quite well, to say the least. I don't think to this day she believes that it's based on love, truth, and respect though. She probably thinks it's more lust or a debt owed. The day I told her, she had tears in her eyes. The joy in her heart was acceptance enough. She loved me as much as I loved her, and we had many things in common and Jah was the most important.

Jah looked at me, then asked his sister, "So wassup with you, sis? How's Ma?"

"Drunk. You know your mama. Ain't shit changed her way." Quilla has taken care of him as a mother would, since their own was nowhere to be found. Ms. Bea has seen her firstborn son twice in seven years. She wrote a letter once a year and never sent any packages. Where they do that at? But he had Quilla and he had me, and we gave Jah whatever he needed and wanted. It didn't matter the price or the size.

Quilla said, "I got good news, bruh."

"I need to hear some real talk right now, Sis. These hardheaded muthafuckas in here stay talking that same shit every day."

Quilla continued, "Apparently the crooked ass detective that was on your case, got caught up. His shady ass was stealing and lying and now all of his cases are under investigation. I'm gonna roll up here Wednesday on my lawyer shit with my colleague, Bryant Wookens. You remember him from the trial, right?"

Jah was on full alert. "Right."

"Well, we gonna come and give you the details on where your case stands in all of this, but baby I'm sure it's gonna be in our favor."

"Oh yea? So what that mean?"

"That means your time gonna get cut short and you coming home. And if there's any fault in this punk ass system, we gonna sue they ass. But enough with all that. Today I'm on sister-brother shit so how you doing?"

"Shit, I'm better now! That's what's up, sis." While Quilla was spilling the good news, I was surprised and, to be honest, a little angry. She must have noticed, because she turned to me and said, "Chan, I'm sorry, but I been knowing this since Friday. I just wanted to wait and tell you both together."

"Yea, I know bitch. What up with that?" But I couldn't be mad. Shit, this was real good news! Jah had been in here for ten years.

"I'm sorry, Chan." The happiness on Jah's face warmed my heart and made my clit flutter. I thought a cold, black heart like mine never would feel anything again, but at that very moment, seeing his face light up like that... I felt love. Jah grabbed the both of us and squeezed so tight I could feel his and Quilla's heartbeats.

"You coming home, baby," Quilla said tearfully.

Jah was so happy. All he keep saying was, "I'm coming home." He spun us around so much that I felt as though I was on a merry go round. I was dizzy as hell! The guard had to tell him to sit down. It was a good day. Eye Candy said, "Final call. Sixteen minutes. Wrap up your visit!" Jah and I strolled away from the crowd and said our goodbyes.

The very first thing I wanted to do, since the house was complete, was have a dinner party. It would be great to invite some business acquaintances to share the success and solidify some projects. That would surely take me to the next level in my career. And I love a good party! I could have just rented out some elegant venue, but I wanted this party to be special and the first of many. So hosting it at my new home was a must. Because it was short notice, the planning and details were quite stressful! This would be more networking than actual partying, so it had to be professional and sexy at the same time.

The guests were money men: my financial advisor, the CEO of Trust Holdings, and three self-made millionaires. My assistant, Keshia, was there to take minutes throughout the evening, and of course my lawyer and best friend, Quilla was present. She loved my networking parties. She said that one day she's gonna get one of these millionaires that I had in the rolodex. I told her that there was a variety to choose from, so take your mafuckin pick. I would be able to supply her with personal notes and characteristics for each one. I'm gonna surprise her for her birthday next year and have the top ten over for drinks so that she can play stay-or-lay. Yeah, just give her ten billion on a silver platter and see how she like that gift. Shit, she might find what she's looking for, whatever the fuck that is!

I decided to call a few after dinner "mints" for the gentlemen, for pleasure purposes only. One thing about me, I liked to make sure everyone was happy. Whatever you like, you're sure to have it at one of my parties. I called my girl. "Hey Monica, can you pull a couple of girls and come over to the house around 9:00 p.m.? And don't bring that nasty-ass Nicole. I can't stand that dumb bitch!"

She was down like I knew she would be. "Okay, Chantal. I'll be there at 9 sharp. We just dancing or what?"

"No, Monica. It's full service tonight, baby."

"Okay, I'm with that, Chan."

"Good. See you then." Well, that was settled. The gentlemen always looked forward to the entertainment, which was the highlight of the evening. Pussy always eases the tension after major business deals, if you know what I mean. I was always looking to make more money. Investing was my niche, and I had players that were willing to invest not only *in* but *with* a boss bitch. I glanced through my daily planner, realizing that I had a laundry list of things to do and not enough time to do them. I'm so in need of a massage, so I put that on the list too. Next, I called Rosa.

"Hola."

"Rosa, Chantal Laine. I know it's your day off, but I need you desperately for tonight. I'm having a dinner party."

In a heavy accent, she said, "Oh yes, ma'am. You have dinner, Miss Laine. What you need?" Rosa was like family. When I moved into my own place, Aunt J had insisted that I have her to clean and take care of me. She wouldn't have it any other way. She paid for it and made the schedule. Gave Rosa all the instructions on how to clean and what not to clean. She always took control like that. I appreciated her for it.

I told her, "The place is a mess and I have less than nine hours to get it together. I need you to come over now."

"Oh yes, Ma'am. I on the way." Rosa's normal schedule to clean and cook are Mondays, Wednesdays, and Fridays. Shit, I'm gonna have to pay her some kind of extra Sunday tip. I'm sure she can use it, with all them damn kids she got. She shouldn't have a problem with making extra money. "Okay Rosa, I need everything in place. Can you do that?"

"Yes ma'am, no problem. Do you mind if I bring my two daughters with me? They can help, and I don't want to leave them alone."

"No, Rosa. You know the rule: no kids in the house."

"Okay, Ms. Laine, but I don't' have a baby sitter." Well, damn.

"Okay fine, but you better make sure they behave themselves. Put them in the separate quarters and keep them quiet. I'll see you in an hour. Don't be late."

"Si, Ms. Laine."

The nerve of her! Can she bring her daughters? She knows I don't allow kids or animals in my house! She got me fucked up! I've worked too hard for my things. I have furnishings and artifacts from places all around the world that I've collected during my travels. Priceless items that are very cherished and irreplaceable. I have memorabilia of Scooby throughout and I don't want no irresponsible children breaking up my shit and fucking up my floors. Made another phone call.

"Roth, Mayer, and Jones, this is Sheila. How may I help you?"

"Chantal Laine calling for Ms. Jones."

"Oh hi, Ms. Laine. Ms. Jones is out of the office. Let me page her for you. It won't take but a minute. Do you mind holding?"

"Yes, Sheila, I do. Page her with my number, okay?" What I look like on hold?

"Yes, sure, Ms. Laine, I shall."

Damn, it's 2:30 already! I'm seriously stressed out. The caterers are late and this fucking Rosa got every glass in my fucking house streaked. I don't believe this shit! I got eight people coming to my house at 9 p.m. and I'm not seeing any progress from these people that are making my life so fucked up right now. You would think they weren't getting paid. I thought I hired the best that could pull it off in a timely fashion but these guys that I hired? Fucking incompetent! *Okay Chaney, calm down...* My phone rang.

"Chantal Laine. Who's calling?"

"Hey, sexy."

"Who the fuck is this?"

" It's Black, baby. What's wrong?"

Shit. "I just got a million things to do. What's up, Black?"

"Tonight is my night, Chantal. What time can I come over?"

"Oh shit! I overbooked your ass, Black! Sorry, I gotta cancel. I got some real important shit going down tonight."

He got angry and said, "Hell naw! I need you, bitch. Don't do this to me."

"Look Black, I can't get with you tonight. Gotta do that shit some other time, ok?"

"What you mean some other time? Look, Chan. I'll pay double, ok?"

"It ain't happening, Black." Hold up! Let me slow my ass down. "Wait, you said double?"

"Chantal, I need to suck on your pussy tonight, baby. I need it like a fat kid need cake. Don't do me like that!"

"Hold on, mafucka." I looked over my planner and I just didn't see it working. Damn. I got a list of shit to do before 9:00. Hair and makeup will be here at 6:30, but my money is very important to me and it usually comes first. "Okay, I'll tell you what. You gotta be at my house by 5:30 sharp, and you got a thirties minutes. That's the best I can do."

"No, fuck that! I need my hour. I can't enjoy that pussy in no thirty minutes, baby."

"Black, you gonna have to work that out with your dick. I told you, I'm pressed for time. I'm trying to give you options and shit and you still crying. 5:30 or this shit ain't gonna happen today. And thirty minutes total or we postpone this shit altogether."

"Okay, okay. I'll be there."

"If you're even a minute late, the shit is off, Black."

"All right, all right, I'm there!" Oh, this nigga really gets on my fuckin' nerves! Was he really worth it? He's a pest, but hell yea, his money was worth it. Seven o'clock and the bells chimed. I could hear Rosa's voice inviting the very early first guests. Oh, hell naw! It was that nigga, Black. I told this mafucka to do one thing but he gonna do what the fuck he wanna do. I barely got to the door fast enough and here this ratchet-ass mafucka walking in with some grimy-looking ass nigga!

I said, "Excuse me, Rosa. I got this." I stepped in front of my door and blasted him. "What the fuck, Black? I thought I told you the time that I was gonna accommodate you, mafucka!"

"Damn, girl! You look good. You having a party? Shit, I'm right on time. Why you so mad?"

"I ain't mad, but you need to leave from in front of my door!"

"Damn, you ain't got no manners, Ms. Lady! Remember me?" I turned on that broke ass nigga and said, "Hell naw, and I don't wanna remember your ass! Both you niggas get off my doorstep!"

"Girl, you grew up nice. Don't act like that, Chantal."

"Yeah, yeah, I done heard it all before. Now get the fuck off my doorstep!"

"You not gonna let us in?"

"Hell naw, Black! And who this muthafucka with you? You know the fucking rules, Black!'

"Rules? Damn, Ms. Lady, you hard, ain't you?"

"Nigga stop acting like you know me and get the fuck off my property." I looked this dude dead in his mafucking eyes with anger and disgust. I said clearly, pronouncing each word, each syllable, "Get the fuck off my doorstep and this the last time I'm gonna say it." I wanted to slap this nigga dead in his shit, but I held back. I didn't need that kind of drama, not tonight. "Look, Black, you know I don't take kindly to strangers, and I don't like it when tricks break the rules. I'm gonna give you a pass and let you exit this muthafucka stage left with no problems or repercussions, cause I got too much going on tonight."

"What you mean strangers? You know me! I'm Freeno, hoe! I ain't no stranger, bitch!"

"Chill, Freeno." Black tried to calm his homeboy down. It didn't matter to me, I just wanted these mafuckas of my property. I said, "Yeah, chill! Whoever the fuck you is, don't turn this shit into something you don't want!"

"Okay, Chantal... high-price-ass hoe!"

Now I was heated. "Oh no! See, it's time for you and this broke-ass nigga to really get the fuck on! I don't give a fuck where you going, just get the fuck off my property! You gonna show up late and bring some broke-ass nigga to my crib being disrespectful and shit? You outta pocket! Get the fuck from in front my door, like now! You know better than to come with this shit, Black!"

"Chill, Freeno!" As Black tried to check his friend, I started slamming my door in this nigga's face. You could hear him cursing bitch this and bitch that at the top of his lungs from the other side of the door. You would think Black, being a doctor, would have some class and decorum about his ratchet ass. But he's just another stupid mafucka with a degree! I said, "Rosa, they're not welcome, and if they come back, call security." As I regrouped, the bells chimed throughout the house. That's my girl, Quilla. She was the only one that rang the doorbell like twenty times. Rosa answered the door and said, "Hello, Ms. Jones. Welcome. Can I take your coat?"

"Yes, Rosa, thank you."

"Enjoy your evening, Ms. Jones"

"Chan, where you at bitch?" I could hear her throughout the house, screaming as she normally did.

"Hey, sis." We embraced each other and shared compliments of each other's outfits. "Quilla, you look cute! Is that Gucci?"

"No, Louis Vuitton, bitch!"

"Oh, you changing designers in the middle of the season, hoe? So unlike you!"

She said, "I kinda feel like some chocolate tonight."

I knew what she meant! "Well, I got Teron and Orlon coming tonight."

"Bitch, I said chocolate, not mud! And ain't they name Ta-mo and Ta-co or some shit like that?"

"That's their African names, and you're a rude bitch. Come on, we're starting the evening outside." By eight thirty, most of the guests had arrived. When I entered the room, you could see the lust in their eyes. I was in my element. "Hello guys. You're all looking quite debonair. Extra wealthy, healthy, and wise. Thank you for coming. We're waiting for Teron and Orlon of Congo Industries, so enjoy and we'll begin shortly. I heard Quilla mumble under her breath, "Yeah right, the billionaire twins." I continued, "So relax and be comfortable. Please enjoy the hors d'oeuvres. We have Scampi Stuffed Roasted Shrimp, Almas Caviar soaked in champagne, and Moet to quench your palette, so again, enjoy. It'll just be a few more minutes." I turned to Quilla. "Quilla, let me speak to you for a moment." I pulled Quilla to the side and asked, "Why do you always call them the billionaire twins?"

"Because, they look just alike, talk alike, walk alike, smell alike, think alike...it's sickening! You wouldn't even know they were billionaires, they're so fucking frugal!"

"That's why they're billionaires, bitch! And their culture keeps them grounded. They're brothers, but not twins. They're as close as they are cause family is very important to them."

"I can dig that on the family thing, Chan, but this ain't Africa, it's California, bitch. They need to adapt to this culture!"

"Quilla, how vain are you? It's very attractive that they believe in some other shit besides the Rodeo Drive shopping lifestyle. They're self-made billionaires with assets of over 260 billion dollars collectively. They don't need your approval. As a matter of fact, they don't need shit from you, bitch!"

"I don't give a fuck Chan, they don't impress me."

"Quilla, Africa is a beautiful place. You know, when I was young, we vacationed in West Africa one year. We were introduced to the pygmy tribe. They have an amazing culture." I was so impressed with their beliefs that they were governed by. Whenever I travel, I try to adapt to the culture of the land. I enjoy the way other cultures live, eat, work, and maintain their daily agendas without all the modern conveniences of what we know as necessities. Those things are indulgences to them. "Can you imagine living in the African rainforest? It's one of the most beautiful places on this earth."

Quilla wrinkled her nose and said, "Hell no, Chan, and I didn't know that you were so passionate about this Africa shit."

"It's educational, Qui."

"Yeah, right! What the fuck you know about education, Chan? I thought it was all about your money and the game."

"It is, bitch, but I'm not as vain as one might think. Still waters run deep."

Scooby always told me to feed my brain just as I fed the rest of my body, because it's my temple. Intellectual stimulation is something that I can't get from a trick. I miss my dad a lot and all those priceless conversations we used to share.

"Okay Chan, tell me how you understand what the fuck they saying? Their English is so broken."

"You crazy, Quilla! That's the sexiest part, bitch, their accent!"

"Fuck that, Chan! Them niggas will slit your throat and eat your fucking tonsils! I don't care how much money they got."

"So tell me, Shyquilla Jones, why wouldn't you want that kind of mafucka on speed dial? It's called networking, baby."

"Wasn't their great-great-grandfather Shaka Zulu or some shit?"

"Yes Quilla, they're descendants of the Zulu tribe, kings of kings. Do you know anything about the legend of Shaka Zulu?"

"Not much, but what I do know is that their only intention is to conquer or die, and their grandfather was thought of as a brutal tyrant. His warriors had to run to the enemy and stab 'em, and if they came back stabbed in their back, then he would kill 'em."

"Yea, that's some of it, but understand that he only did that because a coward runs, and if he is stabbed in the back, then that's a sign of weakness. Weakness has no place in a king's existence." Some have called the tactics that Shaka used for his military conquests ruthless and brutal. But, through his leadership and teaching, he instilled in his tribe that failure is never an option. They had to be fearless. You should take some interest in the culture of African tribes and the Zulus in particular. You might learn something other than the hottest designer and that law shit."

"Bitch that's all I need. Besides, don't they practice that voodoo shit? Cause if I didn't know you better, I would say that African mafucka put a curse on you. You're just as materialistic as I am, bitch. Trying to talk about something other than Prada and Gucci. You would die without them Louboutin's, so sell the dream to somebody else, ole Beverly Hillbilly bitch!"

"Fuck you, Qui." We shared a laugh. "But we really need to take a trip to the motherland, for real."

"Shit, I ain't built for no bamboo tree-living shit! I'm from South Central LA. I don't need that type of experience, and if that's what you're trying to bring me to, I'm not interested, bitch."

"Qui, to be able to see the difference makes you appreciate what you have, like shoes on your feet."

"But remember, not just any shoes, fifteen hundred dollar Louboutin's, bitch. Get it right."

"Quilla, it's going to be wonderful. I'll take care of all the planning."

Quilla seemed a little unsure. She said, "I don't know. We'll see."

My assistant, Keshia had arrived, ready and on point. I hired her about three weeks ago, and I've been testing her ability to take care of me the way that I required. I needed her to do that with little or no resistance. And no hater tendencies. She had to have knowledge of the latest fashion, know how to shop, and where to look for the most unattainable pieces. She had to have clerical skills and she needed some class. The compensation that I pay her ass to do frivolous shit should be more than enough for her to not come around me or my team looking like she had no money for the cleaners. And if I ever smelled her ass, she would be gone as soon as the funk hit my nose. That's one thing I didn't play and that's body odor. I've even went that extra step in making sure that all my clients showered before I touched they ass. I must say tonight Keisha had stepped her game up. Hair done nice. Her makeup, well it wasn't flawless but she did her best working with local pharmacy cosmetics. Her ensemble was coordinated nicely, even though it was all low end pieces. She did well. She came across as a bookworm, no life, no style, real nerdy. That's one of the reasons I hired her. I saw the potential, and now that the layers were peeling off, it was a good look. I said, "Hey, Keshia. Are you ready for minutes? Do you have the recorder queued, copies ready?"

"Yes, Ms. Laine. I also have your dry cleaning. I'll put it in the hall closet."

"Wonderful. Just give it to Rosa. Let's go. First thing first, put on the to-do list a trip to Durban, Africa. Sometime in August, more details to follow."

"Got it. That sounds exciting, Ms. Laine. Am I going too?"

"Of course not, Keshia, but that was cute." As we entered the meeting room, Keisha began to set it up, conference style. I told Quilla, "I just gave Keshia a tentative date for Africa, and trust me, you're gonna enjoy it. It'll be sometime around August and everything's on me, Sis."

"Well, damn. I can't argue with free. What you think, Keshia?"

"Ms. Jones, I would go if I were you. Ms. Laine seems to know all about the land as if it was her backyard. It sounds like a fun trip."

"I know Keshia. Look Chan, I would love to experience it with you, but I'm not sure. We are talking about South Africa. I'll tell you what. Have Keshia call Sheila to match our calendars and we'll take it from there, cool?"

"Cool , sis. Your gonna love it, I promise. Keshia, you got that?"

"Yes, Ms. Laine. I'll get on that first thing."

I put my arm around Qui and said, "With billionaires as tour guides, this should be an awesome African safari. First class all the way baby! Teron's a great communicator. He enjoys talking about the richness of his culture, his beliefs, how a King is supposed to treat his Queen. They are fearless warriors, Quilla. So much more than billionaire boys. They have substance and generational bonds that constitute their worth, not their billions." Just as I was speaking highly of them, Rosa confirmed their arrival. "Get it together, bitch they're here."

Quilla rolled her eyes and said, "You say that like kings have arrived."

"Shit, they have! Let's go, ladies." I rushed out to greet them. "Welcome, Teron and Orlon. Nice to see you again." I hugged Orlon and he spun me around to examine me. His look was a form of approval, as always.

He said, "You're most extraordinary, Ms. Chantal." He executed a graceful bow, then kissed my hand. His accent was very sexy. "And who is the other lovely queen that is in my presence?" When he mentioned Quilla, she extended her hand and made her own introduction. I had to look at her twice. She was actually being courteous. That was a first.

"I'm Shyquilla Jones." He kissed her hand and bowed. She looked at me and gasped. I nodded, knowingly. She whispered respectfully, "Nice to meet you, Orlon."

"No, precious jewel, the pleasure is all mine." He continued in his African drawl, "I'm honored to be in your presence, Queen Quilla." Orlon gracefully extended his arm as he escorted her into the dining area where the rest of the guests had convened. Teron and I shared a laugh at Orlon's attraction to Quilla. And I was surprised by her attraction to him. If the night goes well, she gonna make time on the calendar for that Safari! Orlon was the shy type, but it was as if he and Quilla had arrived that night together. They were inseparable, from that moment on.

Teron felt it necessary to always be the composed, smarter one. The reserved type. He was the elder of the two. From the stories that Teron has shared of their childhood, he has protected his baby brother from life, which was a task within itself. Teron is a very strong-willed person, and he has had his share of life's pains trying to shelter Orlon from the same mistakes he has made. Everyone knows that doesn't work. A person is going have to go through life to learn their own mistakes, but you couldn't tell that to Teron. So growing up, there was always a battle within Orlon to challenge his brother, which is what he was taught to do. At the same time, he tried to live his own life from under that scope. Orlon was a remarkable 27-year-old businessman. Given the circumstances, the structure is very different from the normal life of an American.

I introduced the brothers to the other guests and we each took our places around the table. "Gentlemen, the final guests have arrived. Again, welcome. If you don't mind, go around the room and introduce yourselves. We're all here for the same reason, and that reason is to make money. Would you agree?" All confirmed with nods and toasts. "So we're gonna let that be the reason." I glanced over at Teron. He was so impressed with my business intelligence. He often told me that I was a champion. I thought that was cute. "I'll start. As all of you know, I'm Chantal Laine, your hostess for the evening." The other guests began to introduce themselves.

"Hello, I'm Dominic Willis, CEO of Trust Holdings financial."

"I'm Jartz Mouskit, founder of Mouskit Diamonds, Inc."

"Good evening, gentlemen. I'm Shyquilla Jones, Esq. of Roth, Mayer, and Jones."

"I am Teron Congo."

"And I'm Orlon Congo, of Congo Industries."

"Hello, everyone. I'm Laurence Goldmine, investment banker and financial advisor for Ms. Laine."

And in her best impersonation of a British noblewoman, my assistant said, "And I'm Keshia, the queen's lady-in-waiting." Laughter filled the room. She added,
"Or better known as the personal assistant to Ms. Laine. Nice to meet you all. I'll be taking notes and if there's anything you need, please let me know."

"Thank you, everyone, and Ms. Keshia, that was most amusing and definitely eased the tension in the room. I would like to extend my gratitude that you all could be present tonight. I know how extremely busy your lives can be. We have a lot to cover, so let's get to it. The first order of business is the main course." Everyone thought that was funny, since we were all hungry. A full belly was way better for business than an empty stomach.

"I'm starving, and I'm sure all of you are as well. At this time, I'll let the Chef give us the menu."

The chef entered the room to explain what was to be expected of the evening. Everyone was in full attention. "Good evening. I'm Chef Thomas, the executive chef of Thomas and Laine restaurant. For starters, I've prepared line-caught river salmon in a shiro miso ginger glaze, pan-seared Kobe beef, braised artichokes in their broth, asparagus, and chocolate mousse truffles, Ms. Chantal's favorite and special request of the evening. For dessert, a red velvet cream cheese pecan-frosted triple-layer cake. I hope you enjoy it. There are bottles of Krug Brut 1986 for your sipping enjoyment, compliments of the Congo brothers. Thank you and enjoy your meal."

Chef Thomas and my Aunt Jackie were very close. She paid his way through culinary school and became his partner in the restaurant venture, Thomas and Laine of West Hollywood. Actually, my aunt put in all the money and Chef Thomas does all the work. It's a successful business and a very quiet relationship. As the waiters began the first course, everyone in the room had their own personal conversations going. Everyone was strategically seated. I had to take advantage of that opportunity. I sat my financial advisor between Mouskit and Mr. Dominic Willis. He knew damn well whose payroll he was on. He knew the game. I wouldn't even be fucking with him if he didn't get that information.

Quilla seemed all giddy and impressed by Orlon. She was also impressed with the case of Krug that he and his brother had brought tonight. That could set you back $40,000. She was definitely impressed at that point. Maybe they weren't so frugal after all huh, sis?

As we finished the first course, the conversation in the room became minimal. It was refreshing to see Quilla and Orlon entertaining each other in a most comfortable manner. The last course was settling in our stomachs and it was time to convene in the library for the business portion of the evening. Each seat was equipped with a pad, pen, and either a champagne glass or coffee cup. Nice job Keshia. She's really setting the tone for a good track record. We all sat and went into business mode immediately. The cigars were in the air and the champagne was flowing. This meeting should be a piece of cake. We should have this done by the time the pussy started poppin.

"Well, gentlemen, I don't know about you all, but I'm feeling on the heavy side. That meal was delicious. The first portfolio of current investments on the table will be the commercial land for the mall in southeast Georgia, which I think will be very profitable. It's in a rural area, which would mean more jobs and more revenue." As the PowerPoint presentation was rolling, here comes the bullshit, of course.

"Chantal, the foot traffic in those areas is nothing but bad news."

"Well, Dominic, I look at it like this: Why do you give a fuck? Cause it sounds to me as though you're on the prejudiced side of the fence with that statement. So tell me, why does it matter what kind of traffic flows through, as long as your money is securely invested if it's black folks, which is what you're talkin' about, right? As long as those black folks don't fuck up your money or come to your side of town, it matters not, correct? A shootout could occur right there in the food court for all that matters to you as long as you get your money, right?"

"Well, yeah, but..."

"But what? We're all listening, Dominic. Tell us what you meant." I was not letting up on this bitch.

"Let's just move on and strike that from the record, Chantal."

"Yeah, that sounds about right, Dominic." He knew there was a fine line between us, and he better not cross it. Hell, he was only there for his money, not his fucking opinion. This muthafucka knew I had his face on my left booty cheek. All I had to do was shake it and his ass would get in check. He was a trick and he knew it, and so did Agnes, his bitch at home. "As I was saying, it would generate a lot of foot traffic. The next order of business will be the upscale nightclub and spa in Westwood. How's that, Dominic? That's on your side of the globe."

"It's okay, Chantal. Just give me the numbers."

"Keshia is passing out the final draft. If we all agree, we can ink the deal on both before the weekend and in six months, begin phase 1. It's an investment dream. Remember, the early bird catches the worm." The conversation around the room discussed the deal. All the numbers and the legal ramifications were in place. I asked, "Do we have a deal?" The majority agreed and we were officially in business. I'm very proud of this particular venture. Another door opened for success. Preparation prevents poor performance. All the legal documents were ready to sign that night. There was no need to think about it overnight. I don't believe in sleeping on shit but a dick. My dad always told me to get the money right then and there or you have a chance of losing it. Paperwork got signed, notarized, and sealed. *Another stair, Auntie*, I thought. Achieving the impossible.

The business of the evening was coming to a close. I noticed that Quilla and Orlon were on the lanai, sharing conversation and more of the Krug champagne. I thought that bitch said she couldn't understand his African drawl? I see his money does matter. Good for her, cause that celibacy thing she's been crying for the last four years is getting on my fuckin' nerves! She might as well get some dick and be happy. Now it was time for the entertainment since all the business was completed. I'm sure the guys were ready. Besides, it's the least I can do with the millions that were just put on the table. "Monica, are the girls in the entertainment area? You know I have to approve the bitches first. Where them hoes at? Not no ghetto-ass bitches, right?"

Monica said, "Come on now, Chantal. You know how I roll. These bitches is fancy! I got this, trust me." I knew Monica from back in the day. She used to strip at the spot where I used to scout for tricks. She was cool when I first met her, so we clicked. I hired her for this stripping shit whenever I threw a party. She's my go-to girl. "I trust you, Monica. Now hurry up and get ready. I'll let the guys know that you're here." I went back to the library and announced, "Gentlemen, I have some after-dinner mints for you. If you could join me in the entertainment area, please."

My entertainment room was something like a strip club. It had the bar, the stage, the pole, mirrors everywhere, and a really dark area where one could literally go and disappear until the lights came on. The girls came out and I was impressed. Monica had pulled together two money-making bitches, bodies right and ass tight. They was turnt! She always seemed to come through like that. I don't know why I doubted her. I must give her some gratitude, maybe send her on this business trip that's on the calendar. I could solidify the transaction with her pussy instead of mine. I'd let her think it was a pleasure trip. Yeah, that sounds about right.

If Scooby taught me anything, he taught me to use any and everything to get to where I needed to be. Those that are in the way need to get out of the way!

The music started playing and it became a freak show. Shit, these bitches were bending over, dropping down, spreading they pussy, doing the rabbit in a hat trick. It was going down, they was turned up! Monica bent over and let Jahrtz look inside the pussy. That muthafucka fell out the chair! She popped that pussy and pulled the hood back on his ass. That Indian muthafucka fell in love with that bitch on the spot! She was dropping it and shaking it to the floor. These hoes had my guests mesmerized, and I was loving it.

As the night was winding down and the dicks were harder, I noticed that one of the girls, Lisa, was on the lanai with my financial advisor, sucking his dick dry. The hostess in me wanted to give them their privacy, but the freak in me wanted to watch when this nigga busted in her mouth. My pussy wanted to join in, but again, it wouldn't have been a good look. I had company.

The night came to a close and Rosa retrieved everyone's coats. Monica and Jahrtz decided to take it to his mansion. You might as well say Monica was now officially in the diamond business. Well done, Ms. Mo! Some appreciate the easy sex a hoe gives. I appreciate the hustle in that bitch. Ms. Lisa and LG were continuing on the lanai at this point. She was riding this nigga's dick faster than the bull ride at the carnival. She was hitting this nigga's shit so hard, that bitch broke my patio furniture. Tore a hole straight through that shit! Both they asses landed on the concrete. Oh, that's gonna cost that bitch! They were enjoying that shit though, so who was I to spoil the moment? I'm sure it was gonna be a laugh when I look back at it. See, I got my shit on record constantly, 24/7, 360 degrees all around the property and inside from all angles. I got very high tech, expensive equipment. Besides this house is too damn big for me to see it without the videos, so yeah, their little escapade is on tape.

As usual, there's always a strike at the party. Mr. Married Willis took his dick home to wifey, Agnes. Lame-ass trick! All wasn't lost, though. Lisa invited the other girl to wherever her and Laurence were headed. The night was young. So that left the Congo brothers. Quilla, the brothers and I had decided to hang around for more conversation and champagne. It was what I wanted. I was horny as hell, but I knew that I wasn't gonna be able to get any dick, so that feeling passed. Quilla knew my card but she never pulled it, and I respected her for that. I wanted to fuck this nigga tonight! He was the only nigga in my Rolodex that I hadn't fucked. I was overdue on that dick. He was high on respect, though. I wanted the fuck, he wanted the feelings. I just wanted to suck that Mandingo dick. I knew that shit was like thunder, and I wanted it from the day that I met him about two years ago.

I was in the Santa Monica municipal court building paying a traffic ticket for running a fucking red light. That almost turned into a bribery charge.

I was trying to give a look, a smell, or some brains, whatever the officer wanted. He was either a fag or a lame-ass muthafucka turning down this pussy. That bitch still wrote me the ticket. So there I was, paying this ticket cause I waited till the last minute and I'm glad I did, cause there he was in all his gracefulness. I noticed him the moment I entered the clerk's office. His smell lit the room, Dolce and Gabbana. I could detect that shit from the mountains.

Everything about him was attractive. His presence was regal, very sexy and confident. From that moment on, I've been finessed by his intellect, his courage, his body, all of him. He enlightens me and he gives me an understanding as to how it's supposed to be. How two people can become one, how growth and development is for the betterment of family, not just self. The total opposite of what my dad taught me. He told me that he takes care of his mother and sisters, and that he would like to have a family of his own. Be a father to a young prince and teach him the principles and morals that separate Kings from ordinary men. He wants to teach him all the things that have made him the wonderful, remarkable, loving man that he is, and that is why I'm very attracted to him.

The night seemed to go exceptionally well. After I approved the restoral of my house, I paid the staff and let them leave for the evening. So there we were, myself, Teron, Quilla, and Orlon as if we were in high school, courting on the couch. Laughing and enjoying one another. Quilla noticed my attraction to Teron but she was so giddy with Orlon she just passed it off. I'm sure I'll hear about it at another time. For now, we would just enjoy the rest of the evening.

Chapter 11

On the way home from seeing Jah, all I could think about was the good news Quilla announced, and why she didn't tell me first. I guess she just wanted it to be a surprise for the both of us. I did think it was a little strange, though. We decided to stop to get a bite to eat at one of the local restaurants in the area, Ketchup. It had a nice ring to it and they served a variety of foods so decided on a salad and a cold ice tea. At the exit, who do we see the so-called ballers. More like scrubs at the bus stop. We laughed all the way into the restaurant.

"Hello. Welcome to Ketchup, ladies. How many dining today?" The hostess had a Mexican dialect. We laughed under our breath because we could barely understand the bitch. "Two please, preferably a booth."

Quilla said, "The visit was great, don't you think so, Chan?"

"Yeah. I wish I could've fucked or just tasted the dick!"

She said, "Damn, girl! Is that all you think about?"

I said, "Uh, yeah. Besides my money, pretty much!"

Quilla laughed and said, "You a mess, Chan!"

"I know, but I am a rich mess, bitch!"

"Hello. I'm Marisha and I'll be your server. Can I offer you ladies something to drink?" The waitress looked at us hard and then said, "Hold up! Chantal Laine? Shyquilla Jones? That's ya'll, ain't it?" She was very loud and ghetto as she screamed in excitement. She said, "Damn! I haven't seen you two since high school! Ya'll still tight, huh?"

I immediately became irritated with her voice. I said, "And who the fuck are you?" Quilla always said that I spoke down to people that I didn't know or didn't care about. Why should I respect nobodies? The waitress got an attitude and said, "Marisha Deveaux, Down Jordan High school." As if we should remember her. She fixed her face and said, "Dang, ya'll looking good. It's been a minute. Ya'll all fly and shit. Weave all done up. What's up? Put a bitch on!"

"Who the fuck is this broke bitch, Quilla?" I looked at Quilla with disgust. Quilla rolled her neck and answered, "Girl, that's the hoe that they caught in the principal's office, eating the secretary's pussy. Bitch, you remember."

"Oh yeah. Tony's hoe. Ratchet bitch. I didn't even recognize her." I turned to girl and said, "You look different without all those bruises and black eyes. Tony used to whoop your ass, girl."

"Hold up! Who you think you talking to?"

I wasn't even phased. I said, "You. You know it's the truth, bitch."

"But damn! Why it gotta be like that, Chantal? I ain't never been nobody hoe."

"Yea and that may be where you went wrong. Did not have a fucking clue how get to this money!"

Quilla laughed. "Chan, you crazy but you telling her the truth. Let the bitch do her job. I'm hungry."

Broke-ass waitress said, "Quilla, that's disrespectful. Don't call me no bitch."

Quilla replied, "Oh honey, that's just a word. Let me order."

I had to laugh because I knew Quilla was getting ready to bust ole girl in the fucking mouth. "Just bring us two chef salads with iced tea."

"Okay, It'll be out in a minute."

I said, "Qui, she better get her fuckin' mind right and do her damn job."

"Chan, I know you're not letting this nothing-ass bitch get under your skin! That bitch stank anyway. She ain't worth it! I'm in a good mood and that raggedy ass bitch is not gonna take my joy. Fuck her!" She came back.

"Here is your ice tea, ladies. I didn't mean any harm. It's just that in high school, you had that rich-ass auntie so you always acted boogie, Chan. But not you, Quilla. So how you making yours? You gotta work to eat, right?"

Now that pissed Quilla of for real. She had to let her know, so she said, "First of all, hoe, you don't know me like that. And it ain't your business. Your business is to take my order and serve me." I couldn't take it anymore. I burst into laughter and damn near choked off the iced tea. "Excuse me, Mary."

"It's Marisha."

"What the fuck ever. I know you making what, minimum wage in this grease spot?"

Now the girl was feeling some type a way. "I make more than minimum wage, Quilla," she pouted.

"Look, what Qui is trying to say is, all that pussy you used to eat in high school, you would think you would have something to show for your skills. So please stop harassing the patrons. That will be all." Quilla was ready to tell a muthafucka off and it wouldn't be a pretty sight. I knew it was time to go. This bitch had pushed the limit. Quilla never let anyone, under no circumstances, bring out Shyquilla Jones from the 'hood. She had class and money now, and that was beneath her. But this bitch was out of line. Qui threw money on the table, looked at me and said, "Chan let's go, before this bitch get knocked the fuck out." She grabbed her bag and left all that shit on the table. She said, "I ain't getting ready to eat nothing from this thug bitch.

As we were leaving, Marisha asked what was wrong. What she do that for? Qui lit into her ass! "Let me offer you some advice, Mar whatever the fuck your name is. Get some self-esteem and maybe wash that shit on your head, take a douche, with yo stanking ass, and your shit might start looking better. Thank you, and have a nice day. Oh yeah... fuck you!"

On the way home, Quilla was so mad that she had let this bitch fuck up her day. I said, "Don't sweat it, Quilla. That was one of our haters, and you know we respect our haters 'cause they have an advantage over us."

"What's that?"

"They can kiss our ass and we can't!" We laughed at that shit all the way home. When I arrived back home, the mysterious letter from Jah, was waiting for me in the mailbox. It read,

Hey ma, what's good with you? I miss you, girl. I want you to think about something. Will you marry me? I know, right? I thought it would be better to ask you in this letter, that way it gives you time to marinate. Then, when I really pop the question, you won't give me some fake ass answer. Sound bout right?

Moving on, I got this play that I been working on. This bitch named Yolanda gonna hit you up sometime this week. Chan, I know how you are, baby, but please sit with this bitch and hear her out. She gonna give you the playbook. When you come see me next weekend, we can finalize everything then. Well, ma, I'm gonna get out this letter. Just wanted to say that and tell you that I love you and I miss you.

Your one and only.....Jah

Well, I must say that letter was quite interesting. The fact that he wanna marry me is flattering, just not to sure if it would be logical to do. I'm glad that he gave me a heads up so that I could think about it, though. So some bitch will be reaching out to me on a play. I wonder what Jah got going on this time. It's always something with him. I'm sure it's some fuckery. This jail shit is fucking draining me. I got another visit with Joyce in the morning. This seems like a job. My phone rings and there's that call, just like clockwork.

"Chantal Laine. May I help you?"

"Hi, Chantal. How are you?"

"Fine. Who's asking?"

"This is Yolanda. Yolanda Price."

This was the bitch Jah was talking about in the letter. "Oh yes, Yolanda. How may I help you?"

"Well, I really don't want this to be considered just business, so it's not a point how you can help me. It's more like how we can help each other. I was thinking that maybe we could relax and have a nice conversation about that. I know this great spot where we can chill."

Huh? This bitch don't even know me. How could she possibly know my lifestyle and how I liked to chill? But what the hell. Jah set this up and I'm gonna see it through. "Okay, sounds good."

"So I guess we can set it up at the end of this week, say Friday at 2:00 p.m.?"

"Works for me." As I penciled her into my planner, I wondered why this was so important to Jah.

"Okay, I'll call and schedule the appointment for our girl day. I'll talk to you later, sugar."

"Yolanda, don't call me sugar. Chantal will be fine." What the fuck is she talking about?

Calling me sugar and having a girl day? This bitch don't know me like that! I hope this don't turn into something that I'm gonna regret, but what harm can it do? This bitch got money. Shit, I got money. They say money entertain money, so fuck it. I decided to get out of my feelings and entertain this bitch. See what it looked like. As I looked over my schedule, I realized that I have a laundry list of things that needed my attention this week. Quilla's birthday dinner party is at the top of the list. She wants me to host it. Not sure how that's gonna turn out. I'm not good at that sort of thing. I would prefer to hire the professionals and let them come in and do their thing. And that's exactly what I'm gonna do.

My phone rings again. "Hello. Chantal sp-." Before I could get the rest of my greeting out, a squeaky voice interrupted me.

"Good morning this is Yolanda again. You sound tired. Were you still asleep?"

"I'm good, just had a long night. What's up?"

"Well, I've made all the arrangements for Friday."

"It's too early to think about that shit, Yolanda. Call my assistant and give her the details."

"Okay, excuse me, Chantal. Don't bite my head off. Well, since you're already on the phone, I've placed the reservations under Price for 2:30 at the Beverly Hills Peninsula."

"Yes, I know where the place is. I'll be there at 2:30."

"Great! But no need to drive. I'm sending a car for you. It should arrive at 2:00 and take you to the spa. I have a list of errands to run that morning, so if I'm not there when you arrive, you can get started without me, if that's cool?"

"Sure, that's fine, Yolanda."

"The girls at the spa are wonderful. I've already touched base with them. They're expecting you."

"Okay, see you there, Yolanda." After this bitch disturbed my rest, I got up and started my day. Where the hell was Rosa? One of her job duties was to stop at Starbucks and get two large cups of macchiato. I guess she really don't appreciate that task. I remember one year at Christmastime, she had the bright idea to buy me a latte cappuccino machine with Starbucks ingredients as a gift. I thought she was being funny. That shit is still in the box, and she still stopping every fucking morning for two large cups of that shit. I ran into the mailman coming from Starbucks with my fix. Today was Rosa's day off and I had forgot.

"Good morning, Ms. Laine."

"Hey Harry, how's it going?"

"Oh, it's running like clockwork, ma'am. I love my job."

"That's wonderful, Harry." I could never understand how putting envelopes and packages at a muthafucka's doorstep in the heat of the July sun was gratifying. I glanced through the mail and saw that it was the normal junk mail and invoices. I was as they say, privileged and had a trustee that paid all my bills. Utility bills? I never received anything like that. There was also a letter from Jah and one from Atlanta, Georgia. I did not recognize the name and as far as I was concerned, it was junk just as the rest. Jah's letter:

Hey Chaney, the love of my life,
I miss you something awful. Girl, I need you. I heard you and Qui going to Africa. That should be nice. I wish I was home to go with ya'll. So, business first with the bitch, Yolanda. Just go with the flow. Her peeps up in here got it all taken care of. I just need you to tighten up and stand firm. Moving right along. Chan, I'm tired of this fucking shit in this chain gang. These trick-ass niggas be on some other shit. I know I'm at the door, but it seems this is the longest time right here. You know a nigga don't do nothing but two days, no matter how long their bid is: the day he go in and the day he come out. Everything else is dead time.

So anyway, how you doing? I hope all is well. Shit, it gotta be. You in the free world, getting ready to go to Africa and shit, huh? As for me, I'm doing this shit one fuck-ass minute to the next. It seems I can't get no sleep in this muthafucka. These niggas stay on some fantastic foolishness, baby. Check this, the sissy-ass nigga on the wax with that shit about why the nigga he with don't treat him with respect. Then he say if the nigga don't start respecting him, he leaving. Where they doing that at? Talking bout his nigga, Quincy don't treat him right and Quincy only with him because he rich." So bad-ass say nigga, you the only rich nigga I know that eat state trays. So Norega hollering bout 'it's real disrespectful for y'all niggas to be carrying on like y'all doing in a dorm full of straight niggas. Hoe-ass nigga, you fronting. You ain't made nobody suit up since you been down here, scary-ass muthafuckas. At this point, the whole dorm is off the meter.

It's really off the top today, baby. I can't hear nothing but loudness. These niggas is at it, and that's on the daily. I'm so ready to come home to you and my sister, baby. It's wearing on me. Well just thought I'd share a day in my life with this chain gang shit. Ne way, have fun in Africa and you better get your ass up here before you leave. Chaney, I hope you know, when I come home all that extra business that you got on your plate is a wrap. Well, I'm gonna close this letter. Puttin on my headphones and crank up the chewy. I love you.

From the contents of Jah's letter, I felt his jealousy or maybe it was the fuck shit in disguise. That's one thing that I don't like about Jah. He has always had that jealous shit in him. How the fuck is a dude jealous of his bitch? Where they do that at? But this nigga was. I never understood that, and I'm sure that time in that tank is ever so exhausting, but he'll be home soon. And what the fuck did he mean, that extra shit? I've told him too many times that he can't change me.

Most say that doing time with the one you love in a federal prison is easy time. Shit, I beg to differ! None of it is easy. However, there is a major difference in how you do your time, depending on where you're at. It's known that state facilities offer no benefits for rehabilitation. When you're faced with a long sentence, or even life sentences, you don't get no conjugal visits. No furloughs, no real job training or education. The list of "no's" are endless. Having to sleep in foul-odored, double-tiered bunks in military-style barracks with the same niggas day in and day out. Your mail, phone calls, and every move are scrutinized. My belief is that if you give a real nigga some pussy every now and again, it would control the most problematic ones.

I glanced over the rest of the junk mail, throwing away most of it. I decided to open the anonymous one for the hell of it. It read:

Hello Chantal, my name is Micha. I got your address from our uncle Lance. He encouraged me to reach out to you so that maybe I might get a chance to meet the only sister I have in this world. Our mother, Joyce Oglavee, is incarcerated in the women's correctional facility in California, where she has been for the last seven years for the murder of our father, Jermaine Laine. When she was arrested, she was six weeks pregnant. I was born in that facility on January 24th. I was able to stay with mother for six weeks, then a state representative came and placed me in an environment where they put you when you're not wanted or loved by no one.

For the last fourteen years, my circumstances have given me strength in making the decisions that I have made. Amongst all the obstacles that I've faced, I have been alone. I would like to meet you and maybe be sisters as we should be. I don't want you to misunderstand this. I'm not asking for a hand-out, just a hand up, and maybe get to know you better. We are blood, and from what I understand, our dad would want us to be family. So can I come to California and visit with you? Maybe we can get to know each other and take it from there?

Mama Laine recently lost her battle with diabetes and passed away over a year ago. Mom says hello. She asked if I would include the visitation form that she sent for you to fill out. She says that she would love to see you and that she loves you. My phone # is 404-555-8406. I hope to hear from you soon.

Love you,
Micha

Wow! As I read the letter I thought, '*I got a fucking sister and she's fourteen years old.* This is some crazy shit to find out this late in the game! What's really going on? Could this be a set-up or some shit? One thing I know, foul play will show its ugly face one way or another. My phone rang again. It was Auntie Joyce. I answered, "Hey Auntie." I guess she could hear something in m voice, because she said, "Hey, baby girl. What's going on?"

"Wow, I don't know, Auntie. I got a letter today a letter from who some girl named Micha."

"Oh really? I was wondering how long it would take for her to come out."

"What do you mean, come out?"

"Look, Chan, I knew about Joyce's pregnancy. When she went to prison, they kept me informed of all the details on the girl, and I kept checking on her while she was in the foster home. I never mentioned it to you, as it wasn't important."

"Not important? She's my sister, my dad's daughter."

"Hold up, Chantal. We don't know that she's your sister. You and I both know what kind of life Joyce lived. You know Joyce was a hoe all her life."

I was shocked. "Well, wouldn't that have been settled with DNA?"

"Look, Chantal, I didn't tell you cause I've protected you from the moment you were born like you were my own daughter. When Joyce killed my brother, she killed herself and her whole fucking family wit' it, and everything from that moment on that had anything to do with that bitch died. She died, and as far as I'm concerned, so did her bastard child."

"Damn, Auntie." I couldn't believe what I was hearing. I had a sister!

Auntie said, "Chantal, she's nothing. She's not a Laine. She's not our family. If you ignore her,

I promise you, she will go away. What did her letter say? She want some money, huh?"

"No, she said she just wanna meet me."

"Chan, be careful. She's bad news."

"Why would you say that, Auntie?"

"I can feel it, Chan. Be very selective. Remember, she's an Olgavee, baby girl, and we ain't got no love for the Oglavees. If you're not a Laine, then we don't deal with you."

"Yeah, I know. Auntie. I gotta go."

"Okay. Well, come over to the house around 6:00 p.m. so we can talk. Can I count on it, Chan?"

"No. Sorry, Auntie. I have plans with Quilla, but I will make it up to you, okay? I promise."

"Okay, sweetie. I love you."

"I love you too, Auntie." Wow! What was happening? I feel like I'm in another dimension, stepping out and looking in. I need to process this. I have a baby sister that my Auntie and the entire Laine family kept from me because they don't believe she's my dad's daughter. My thing is, whether she's my sister or not, I should have been told about her and given the choice to choose.

Chapter 12

It's taken two months for the visitor request form to be approved, and the anticipation of seeing Joyce had me stressed out. Ever since I mailed it back, I've had these feelings. Going to visit Joyce after all these years is creating emotional havoc inside me. She has been in prison for the last sixteen years. She caught a free-world charge for sticking a bitch over some shampoo and that added more time to her sentence. I thought the time she received for murdering my dad wasn't enough in my eyes, so with the additional charge, she will sit five more years. I heard it was self-defense, but nevertheless, it resulted in more time which was a plus in my eyes. I guess the decisions that she's made in her life are now consequences that she must face head-on.

It really didn't matter to me if she died in that mafucka. Hell, in my world, she didn't exist anyway. The only reason I agreed to visit her ass was to get clarity as to who this Micha girl is and what the fuck she wanted with me. The butterflies danced in my stomach as I prepared for the visit. I'm skeptical about going to see her, but it would give me some type of closure. That night lingers like a ghost in the night. I haven't spoken a word about it since. Shit, no one could change it, so what was the point in talking about it? Auntie had suggest therapy a few times but what good would that do? It damn sure wouldn't bring my dad back! I guess going to see Joyce would allow me to put it away, hopefully. Secretly, I sometimes wish Joyce could have been part of my life. When I see a mother and daughter on a shopping trip or just having lunch, enjoying each other's company, watching them laugh, I feel like I missed out on something, then I say fuck that. You can't miss something you never had. Besides, my auntie filled a huge void in that area of my life and that was good enough for me.

I've come to understand that life isn't always as it should be. You have to play the hand your dealt. If you stay in regret from the circumstances that have attached themselves to your life, you will surely live and die a slow, meaningless one. However, I have no regrets. I can't live in that place because that is where the pain is. It's rooted so deep inside me that it's made me numb to any type of feelings. I fuck a million niggas with no emotion and I only care about a few. I've learned that Chantal Laine is the only one in this mafucka that matters. I don't need nothing or nobody. All I got is my money, and that's all I need.

I wanted Joyce to know and see that I was more of a woman than she could ever comprehend. I wanted to show her that I am what she always wanted to be, but it just wasn't in her. What I wanted most was to see how she's changed. I wanted to see how the time has whooped her ass and broken her down. I needed to see the pain and the remorse in her eyes. That's what was really driving me to this visit. My heart hates her. Oh my God, this is really getting me in a down spirit! I need a drink to calm my nerves! I drank some wine straight out of the bottle.

Friday was the day of my visit, and I'm feeling all kinds of butterflies. I thought of Teron, one of the best things in my life, the one that I can call and get the comfort that I need. I hope he's home. Ever since our African safari, we have become closer, spending more time and more conversation, bonding in a more substantial way. I decided to make the call. I must be on his caller ID because he answered before the first ring finished.

"Hello, Ms. Chantal. How are you doing?" I loved his African drawl!

"Oh, I guess I'm fine, Teron. How are you?"

"Oh no, you're not Chantal, I can hear it in your voice. How can I help you, Queen?"

"Oh, Teron, don't call me that."

"It's true! You are the most intelligent, beautiful black woman that I know. You are very successful and worthy of such a title. Surely you noticed how they reacted to you when I took you to my homeland. My people adore you and they treated you as the queen you are."

"Teron, I just want us to be less formal and more comfortable with each other."

"Oh, believe me, Ms. Chantal, I am very comfortable with you in my presence. So, how can I help you deal with this stressful situation that you're encountering?" His accent made me feel so vulnerable with him. It was so sexy. It melted me each time he spoke. "Well, I was thinking maybe you could come have a glass of wine with me, keep me company for a while. I just need someone to talk to, you know, listen as you do so well."

"Yes, Chaney. I will be there in twenty-six minutes. Do you need anything else?"

"No, you're enough." When I hung up the phone, I knew I only had twenty minutes before he arrived. Teron was never late. If he said twenty-six minutes, he was there in twenty-three. I needed to get it together so I hurried to my bedroom suite. Twenty four minutes later, the door bells chimed. Shit, there he was, just like clockwork. I opened the door and saw see the appreciation and lust in his eyes. I mean, how could you not enjoy the view? I had managed to get it together, wearing the sexiest and most expensive piece of lingerie that I owned. It was one of my favorites, a little purple silk bodice that fit my body like a glove. The lace that lined the cups of my breasts was very sexy, and the purple diamond teardrop earrings that Teron had given me for my birthday last year were the perfect accessories. I loved them.

Our relationship was very special and very tantalizing. Each time he hugged me, I felt the passion between us. It was a nervous feeling, as if a cocoon had exploded in my stomach. A feeling I never felt with the other tricks. His touch always created a bed of butterflies. He grabbed me with such control, bringing me closer to his body in a very strong, masculine one-arm jerk around the waist, launching me forward, squeezing my body next to his, meshing our flesh. Oh, that shit felt so good! I've never been held like that. I think because we hadn't shared any intimate feelings that made his presence was so stimulating. I wanted him more than anything and even though I tried to play it cool, he knew my attraction to him. The fact that he didn't wanna buy me made it all the more challenging.

Teron said, "I noticed that there's something different about your home. The last time I was here you didn't have this room, right? Wasn't it the library?"

"That's right, Teron. Your eye is observant. I did a little renovation since you were last here. Come. Let me give you a tour." I showed him around the house, almost like a realtor. As we entered each room, I explained the revamping of the space. When we entered the entertainment room, I showed him the new toys and poles that had been installed. "As you can see, I have a pole next to the fireplace now. Keeps things nice and cozy."

"Wow! Chantal, do you used that pole?"

"Of course I do. It's great for upper body strength." From the look on his face he was intrigued. "You want me to show you?"

"Yeah, I would like that sometime."

"What do you mean 'sometime'? I can show you right now."

"Let's just see the rest of your house for now." If I didn't know any better, I would think this mafucka was either gay or allergic to the pussy. He was always turning me down and this pussy right here is the baddest. "So, moving on. I changed all the seating, the floors and the walls. Made it a little more relaxing. This is known as the entertainment room. A little work was done in the kitchen, too. I changed the floors and the granite in there. I just wanted a different look. And now, let me show you the master bedroom which was moved to the lower level. It's a new edition. I love it! Come this way." I led him into what I knew was gonna blow his mind, and he was actually excited. I could tell.

"Damn, Chantal. You got poles all over the house, girl."

"Not all over the house, just in here and the entertainment room cause you never know when the mood is gonna hit you, right?" I have a special build-out with a purple light and glass doors housed all the trinkets and toys. He stood there looking inside that case, examining each one with a curious eye. This space was very exotic, very me, with all the things that I liked. Not many were given the chance to enter this side of the house, but he was special.

We were relaxing in front of the fireplace, feeling the buzz from the third glass of wine and taking a couple of shots of Don Julio. We were feeling very horny. The conversation was nice, the mood was right. I thought this would be the perfect time... "So Teron, can I ask you a question?" I stood up and dropped the robe, exposing my wonderfully sculpted body. "I've never had a man in my presence that didn't seem impressed or excited about getting this pussy. You seem as though you're not interested. What is it?" The tequila was definitely talking right now. I continued my seduction. "You don't want me? Or is there some other reason that you might wanna share?" I looked at him with a curious eyebrow raised.

He caught my meaning and immediately corrected me. "Of course not, Chantal! I don't know why you think I'm not attracted to you. There is nothing in this world that I would rather have. I want you like I've never wanted anything in my life. However, I want more from you than just your body. I love the way we just talk for hours." I stood there, looking in the window to his soul. I saw the dedication, the enduring quest to conquer me. Like Quilla said, his main purpose on this earth was to conquer or die, and the look in his eyes was one of victory. This man was very strong and powerful, showing and giving me what was already in me, passion for life, a passion for love and truth. He knew that I wasn't in a happy place, but who was he to take me from it? Who was he to erase everything I've known all my life? Who was he to love me, to change me? Was I even worthy of such a thing?

I knew one thing, at that moment, I wanted him and I wanted him now. He and I were in this vulnerable space. I was gonna try as I've tried so many times before. I sat on his lap in a straddling position, kissing his neck, his face, his lips, his ears. I kissed him all over. Started grinding on his dick, making the excitement a reality. He held me as if he didn't wanna let me go. He caressed and rubbed my entire body, kissing each little section with so much passion in each touch. I wanted him! As I unbuttoned his shirt, he tried to resist. Upon my persistence, though, he let me continue. One button at a time, revealing his small Olympic-style grandeur. I kissed him all over his body. He was rubbing and squeezing my ass, slipping his finger here and there, but holding back. I knew one thing and two for sure, if I could get to the dick, no man could resist me. I think he knew that, and that's why he never let me get too close. He knew that as much as I wanted him, when I got it, I was gonna own it. I was gonna suck that main vein until it exploded in my mouth. I was going to gobble that muthafucka like Ms. Pacman.

See, once you take a nigga to that place, you gain control. Then it's game over. So I kinda appreciated the way that he was making it somewhat of a challenge. I worked my way down, kissing and licking on his body. I approached the belt. I began to unbuckle it with my teeth. I knew he wanted it. Hell, if he didn't want it, his dick did.

"Chantal, stop, my queen." I looked up at him. I didn't want to stop.

"Why are you stopping me, Teron? What's wrong? Don't you want this?"

"Yes, Chantal, I do. Very much. But not like this, baby. Not like this. I'm gonna leave now." He picked me up by the cheeks of my ass, with the tips of his fingers still in my pussy. He released my G string and it popped back in its place. That did it for me. I was leaking and this nigga was getting ready to go! I tried to control myself. He sat me down and began to get dressed. Shit, just what I needed. This nigga put the tips of his entire hand in my pussy, popped that string on my ass, and would not give me the dick. I was on fire! "I'm leaking and throbbing, and you're leaving? Where the fuck they doing this type of shit at?" I was in absolute awe, wondering how he could fight this. How could he not want me? Okay, I guess this night was over, because anytime Chantal Laine couldn't have her way, then fuck it. Hit the highway. "Okay fine, Teron. You can show yourself out."

"Don't act like that, Chaney. I didn't mean to upset you. I only want all of you, baby, and if you can't understand that, then maybe I should go." I guess he had a point for someone else. But I was Chantal Vivica Laine, and that meant I could have any mafucka on this earth. And what the fuck did 'all of me' mean? "Teron, just leave please."

"Okay, fine. I shall speak with you tomorrow."

"Yeah, Teron. Whatever." I don't know why this is affecting me in this way. Normally, I would just call another trick, bust a nut, and go to bed. But he was different. He wasn't a trick and he was the only person in this world that's shown me a different picture for my life. He was someone that I feel I could actually be with, and be happy. But how can you stop doing something that you've done all your life? It's like eating. If you don't eat you die, right? That's what getting money is to me. If I don't get it, I'm gonna die.

I'm really digging this one though, more than any other and there have been quite a few. I guess the difference in all the rest is that they were trying and he doesn't try. It's just natural for him. I don't know what the feeling is but I'm gonna take my ass to bed and start fresh tomorrow. He was really on some respect shit tonight, and all that did was leave me very horny and agitated. That shit right there was unnecessary. I'm gonna deal with it. That's who he is. When the time is right, it'll happen.

The alarm clock buzzed and I wanted to throw it against the wall. I decided not to, since it was a gift from Quilla. Instead, I reached over to slam the off button. It was time to get up. It was visiting day with Joyce Marie Oglavee Laine. I haven't seen this bitch since I was sixteen years old. Preparing for this day was a challenge within itself. Looking good and smelling better was the plan. I had to wear just the right outfit. The hair had to be on point, makeup needs to be flawless. Proving a point to this bitch was critical.

All kinds of things are running through my mind. What are we gonna talk about? What am I gonna wear? What am I gonna drive? Should I go at all? Hell, I needed a drink and it's only eight in the morning! I'm bugging out. To top it off, I couldn't get no dick last night. I need to get my mind right. Where the fuck is Rosa with my Macchiato? Damn, it's her day off. I guess I should use the machine or drive myself to Starbucks. Now wouldn't that be some wild shit? What the fuck? I pay bitches to do trivial shit like that. Ugh, I feel as if I'm gonna lose my mind! Chan, get it together. It's time to go. Starbucks would be the first stop.

I imagine the hour drive ahead of me was going to be a bittersweet one. The view of the coastal shore is inviting and has that pleasant smell of the ocean. I decided to drop the top on the Bentley and enjoy the shore's ambience. As I approached the facility, all eyes were on me, as if I was a rock star or some other famous personality. It amazed me how a vehicle could arouse so much attention. It was just a car. I was flyy, though. There was no denying it. The attention was the normal for me. I seemed to get that wherever I went.

Once I was inside the prison, the guard assisted me with my belongings and gave me a pass and a locker key. I entered the gated section only to be taken to another gated section for another search. This shit was ridiculous! A guard said, "Visitors, please form a line to the right of the wall. When the inmate's name is called, move forward." It seems that all my life, I've been visiting one prison or another and the procedure is the same in all of them. If someone was to actually analyze my life on a statistical level, the evaluation would be astonishing. It would surely end with a conclusion of a prison term in my future. But I was much better than that, and I would come to this place. Shit, I don't know how they survived in here. It's cold and dirty and had a stench that infused the air. Every prison that I've been to has the same institutionalized smell. This place isn't for me. This place isn't even fit for a dog. But it's just the right environment for someone like old trifling-ass Joyce.

I sat behind the glass in the visiting area and waited for her to be unshackled. There was a little round steel piece of aluminum attached to a 3 ½-foot pole from the concrete floor in which I was expected to place all this ass. I'm sure it was as uncomfortable and unsanitary as it looked. For this visit, my position is standing. It won't take long anyway.

"Hey, Chan."

"'Sup, Joyce."

"Damn, you look good, girl!" She looked me up and down, tip to toe.

"Yeah, thanks."

"How you been?"

"I'm fine, Joyce."

"It's good to see you, Chaney. It's been so long."

"Yeah, it obviously has, because you have forgotten how I feel about you and those calling me Chaney. Chantal will be just fine, Joyce."

"Oh, yeah. I forgot how sensitive you are about your name. I gave you that name, let's not forget. I thought you would have outgrown that shit."

"It's not that I'm sensitive about it, it's just that if you don't know me, how can you be so informal with me?"

"Is that right, Chantal?" The look on her face seemed to challenge me.

"That's right, Joyce."

"Well, I know you. You were my firstborn."

"And what does that mean, Joyce, huh?"

"It means everything. I love you, Chantal."

"You love me? I don't know what that means for you to say that. First off, I don't indulge in that love shit. Because of you, I will never have the opportunity to feel what love is. The only love I know is my money."

"You still grinding, huh?"

"Every day. It's in my DNA, right?"

"I guess I'm responsible for that, too."

"I don't think so. Actually, I don't feel like you're responsible for anything about me, Joyce."

"How can you say that, Chantal? I'm your mother. I'm responsible for bringing you in the world."

"And what, you want a prize for that shit? Cause from the glasses I'm looking out of, me falling from your pussy was the only thing in your sorry-ass life that had any meaning.

"Damn, Chan, do you have to be so disrespectful and bitter?"

"I'm not bitter and disrespectful, Joyce. I hold no regrets about my fucked up-ass life from the hands of you."

"Watch your mouth, Chan."

"Or what, huh? You gonna come through the glass? What you want? Respect? Is that what you want? You deserve to die, bitch, and be put six feet under in a hole. Same thing you did my dad."

"Chantal, I had to do what I did that night."

"What? Kill my dad, Joyce? You was dead-ass wrong for that shit. He wasn't doing anything that I didn't want him to do."

"So you're saying that you wanted to have sex with him?"

"Damn right! I loved him, and he loved me."

"Chan, Jermaine was raping you. You were a minor and I was responsible for you."

"That might be your version, Joyce, but what he did for me was shield me from the bullshit that was awaiting me in this world. He gave me the blueprint on how to apply my worth and take care of myself."

"And how's that, Chan? By becoming a hoe?"

"No. By becoming a hustler, bitch! Look, Joyce, what my dad did was lace me with the same game he taught you. I thought you, of all people understood that. He taught you the same shit, but you never applied yourself, hoe. He taught me how to believe in myself and get money. What did you give me? Not a muthafucking thing but pain! I will never forgive you for that!"

"I'm sorry you feel that way, Chantal."

"Yeah, I know. I know you a sorry muthafucka, Joyce. Always have been. It's just your breed."

"Chan, can we move past this and have a relationship? You know, daughter and mother, forgive and forget?"

"Absolutely not! I will never consider you as my mother. And just for the record, I will never respect or forgive you. You changed my life in a way that you will never understand."

I could tell I hurt her. "You're my daughter! How can you speak to me like that?"

"Yeah, right. And speaking of daughters, who is Micha?"

"That's your sister, Chan."

"Why am I being introduced to her in this way? Why didn't someone tell me about her years ago?"

"There was no way for me to contact you about it. Your aunt returned all my letters."

"Really, Joyce? So that's your excuse?"

"It's not an excuse, Chan. That's how it was. Micha's your sister and she didn't deserve the life she has. Nor did she ask to be here. So I was thinking that maybe you could embrace her with an open heart and not let your feelings toward me hinder that relationship."

"Embrace her with an open heart? That's funny, Joyce. I don't have a heart, thanks to you. So you were pregnant when you shot my dad and you knew that shit. Did he know or anyone else?"

"Yeah, your Godmother."

"Oh, I have a Godmother? And who the fuck would that be?"

"Tiffany."

"Tiffany? That broke bitch is my Godmother? Damn, you're full of the unknown, huh? Maine always said that you was a selfish, secretive-ass bitch. Don't give a fuck about nobody but yourself. You fucked up my life, Micha's life, and took my dad's life. You deserve everything that you get in this muthafucka."

"Okay, Chan. I ain't about to sit here and let you disrespect me no more."

"You feel like I'm disrespecting you, Joyce? See, I told you that you know nothing of me. I call it as I see it, and I see that you ain't shit. Ain't never gonna be shit. That's the way that I feel, and that's me. I will not apologize for being me. I tell you what, Joyce. Since you want some kind of praise or something, check this. This boss bitch that's in your face was raised by a pimp and birthed by a hoe. And that right there makes me who I am."

"Wow, Chan. I'm not even gonna comment on that."

I was dumping out a lot of pain and wanted to make her feel pain, too. I kept going. I said, "You know why? 'Cause you can't. It is what it is."

This hoe said, "I see that you are a full grown woman with a lot of anger. Can we change the subject now? And can you stop calling me out of my name? Cause I promise you, if this glass wasn't between us..."

"What, Joyce? You would kill me like you did my dad? I see this shit ain't going nowhere. I'm ready to go."

"Please stay a little while longer! You know, the other day I was thinking how we used to kick it back in the day." Is this bitch crazy? Or have the fumes in here caused her to lose her fucking mind?

"Well, Joyce, I don't have any memories of us kicking it. Besides, that was so long ago, I don't remember. Hell, I don't remember you! I'm gonna leave now, cause this place is making me nauseas. My Herve' dress is gonna smell like this shit, I'm sure. Matter of fact, I'm gonna have to throw this out just as I've done with our relationship—right into the trash. This was definitely a waste of my fucking time. Deuces! Have a nice life, bitch!"

I could hear her calling me back. "Chan! Chantal! Come back, Chan, please!"

I kept walking, almost in a surreal glide. Something in me wanted to turn around and get the healing process started. Another part of me wanted to shake this spot immediately. See, there's nothing slow about me. I knew that if we could move past it, we could heal from it. I knew that she was the common denominator to the pain and the healing I needed. I didn't want to live with it for the rest of my life, although I was prepared to. I also knew that we shared the pain. I've wanted her to feel the majority of it by losing me and all she had. I wanted to break her. She took everything from me, so I took me from her. I knew it would take both of us to bring us back, but I wasn't willing to bend. So in the blackness of that fateful night, I shall perish. On the ride home, I decided to call my bestie. I needed somebody I could trust to talk things through. "Hey Qui, you got a minute?"

"Yea, sis what's up?"

"Well, first off, I get a letter from Jah. He sends his love. And I got a letter from Micha, my sister."

"I didn't know you had a sister, Chan."

"Hell, I didn't either Qui, but she's my daddy's child, though. Says she wanna come out to Cali and visit."

"You gonna let her?"

"That's the part that I'm not sure of. I know she's family and all, but I don't know this little girl. I'm not sure how old she is. Maybe fourteen or fifteen years old, I'm not sure. She says she grew up in foster care, and had been living with Joyce's brother, Lance for about a year. In her words, her life was totally fucked up."

"So do you think that she has some resentment towards you? You know, for the things that happened to her?"

"No I don't, cause it wasn't my fault. Shit, my life wasn't all that wonderful."

"But it was better than hers, Chan."

I considered this for a moment. "Yeah, you got a point. But anyway, I don't think so. I don't think she would hold something against me for that."

"Well, just be careful." Quilla, the lawyer was always cautious.

"I know what you saying. I still have to make the decision on my own, though. But I will take your advice into consideration. And then, the visit with Joyce was not only a waste of time, but also very draining. She's a trip."

"That's your mama, girl." Quilla laughed sarcastically.

I said, "No Quilla, that's the hoe that birthed me." I changed the subject. "Sis, I need you to do a background on this bitch your brother put me in contact with. I need to know what her life looks like before I get all friendly with her ass."

"Chan, you crazy! What are you and my brother up to now?"

"Girl, you know your brother. She some hoe with business on the table."

"Y'all better be careful! What's her name?"

"Yolanda Price. I guess her brother or relative did a bid down there with Jah."

"What do you wanna know?"

"Everything. Call me when you get something." We said our goodbyes. I was really anticipating this meeting to see what she had to say.

The driver rang my bell at exactly two o'clock. He must have been sitting outside my fucking door to ring the bell at exactly that time.

"Ms. Chantal, I'll be your driver to the Peninsula Spa this afternoon. Are you ready?"

"Yes I am. Let me grab my bag, and I'll be right out." During the ride, I was thinking that I could have driven my own car but this was classy, and I love class. The car phone was ringing, and I didn't know whether to answer or not. I wondered who could possibly know that I'm in this car? I decided to answer. "Hello. Chantal Laine speaking."

"Hey, Chantal, it's Yolanda. I hope you enjoyed the transportation. Was it to your expectations?"

"Yeah, I'm cool." I must say, this bitch was on point. She had a car arrive at my house exactly at 2:00 p.m. She called the car phone right as we were pulling up to the Peninsula parking lot. She even took the liberty of having her recommendations on standby, a chilled bottle of Dom P and the bamboo lemongrass body scrub. She said it was to die for. It was a 90-minute treatment of zesty lemongrass and bamboo, which are blended to make the exfoliating scrub effective and included a moisturizing full-body massage. Oh, how I needed this R&R. I'm grateful to the bitch for this one! With all the drama in my life right now, I need to relate, release and relax.

The ambience was very warm and inviting. I almost forgot how the experience of a spa treatment could be. My way of getting a massage was to call Robert the Rubber over to the house and let him massage shit. He was a pro at that massaging shit, if you know what I mean. Remember, my address book was full of muthafuckas that could get anything you wanted!

I hadn't indulged for five minutes before Yolanda stepped in wearing a white robe with a bottle of Dom P Moet et Chandon Brut 1986, at $1600 a bottle. Shit, she was drinking it like water right out the bottle. She was extremely giddy and excited. Yalonda was tall in stature, which added to the Big Bird persona. It was hard to not elevate the eyebrow muscle in an upward direction when speaking to her. She camouflaged her flaws with high-end custom pieces, but she carried on as if she was the shit. Her arrogance was most amusing to me. Her opinion of herself was based on the shit she put on her back, the house she laid her head in, and the automobiles that she drove.

That was the definition of her worth, her truth, which was bullshit. I could buy this bitch twice. She fucking with a boss bitch that don't play, and I saw straight through her ass, although I was appeased for the moment. This was only a momentary affair. Befriending this bitch was the last thing that I was going to do. She said, "You know, Chaney - I mean, Chantal. Can I call you Chaney? It' so cute."

"Absolutely not, Yolanda! I thought we went through that already." I really don't wanna talk during the massage, but I'm real curious as to the topic of this meeting.

"Well yeah, Chantal, we did. But I thought since we're getting to know each other…"

"Hold up. You know nothing about me. We're just sharing conversation and a girl day at the spa, as you call it. I look at this as strictly business, so I prefer you to call me Chantal, or Ms. Laine, if you like."

"Damn, girl! You sure are outspoken and damn near rude. Every time I say something, you snap!"

I didn't care about her attitude. I told her, "Well, I feel it's the only way to be. You see it's like this, I just don't deal with females. We don't play well together, that's all."

"Could it be the competition that bitches might give?" Was she joking?

"Competition?" I laughed. "Not at all, Yolanda! For one, I don't hang with broke bitches when I do choose to hang with a hoe, so there's no jealousy about money or material things. I got all that shit."

"Well, damn. You got it going on, huh?"

"I just don't need no new friends, that's all. I got one BFF that has been here for me as long as I can remember. That's it. I'm not looking for any other hoes in my life. I deal with the male specimen only, point blank. So we're gonna leave it there, okay?" She was acting high or some shit, but I didn't know this bitch well enough to judge. But one thing I know and two for sho', I will see what I need to see when the time comes. After the masseur wiped our bodies down and escorted us to the changing suites, we dressed and left. Yolanda said, "That was great, don't you think?"

"Oh, yes it was. Thank you."

"You're welcome." While we exited the lobby, Yolanda made a call. It was a mysterious phone call, and it seems as though she did not want me to hear it. Then again, I think she did want me to catch it. I heard her say something about St. Tropez and that she hadn't spoken to me about it yet. The valet pulled around with her car. I was again impressed. Her car of choice was a silver drop-top Bentley, custom made for her. Nice, but not as bad as mine.

While her valet turned over her keys, the other was opening my door. She gave the guy a very generous tip, and we left to make our lunch appointment. I must say that I was curious as to how she got down cause she rolled in style. And I appreciated her fashion game. She was rocking a Gucci dress, Gucci high-heeled, over-the-knee platform boots, Gucci eyewear, Gucci handbag, Gucci perfume. Mr. Francois Pinault would be very proud of her representing him in such a way.

She still didn't have shit on me though. I was that bitch, Chanel form head to toe. White Chanel Carmeuse blouse with a black Chanel leather skirt. Chanel accessories around the waist, black Chanel handbag, and my high-heeled, over-the-knee, platform boots where Chanel. I complemented my ensemble with canary diamonds for that pop of color. Yes, the ears were blinging as well as the arm candy. If you put value to that shit, just my attire was coming in at a hundred thousand. Yolanda was on the low end of ten. I am fierce. I am what the fuck was she talking about when she mentioned competition!

On the ride to the restaurant, I didn't say much. I just listened to her babbling about how she moved to Cali and how she just loved the weather and blah, blah, blah. When we arrived at Mr. Chows, I could see the paparazzi lurking in the cut, meaning that some entertainer or celebrity was inside. As the hostess escorted us to our table, I scanned the restaurant for the entertainer that had the 'razzi's outside. Who do I see? Mr. Teron having a lunch on the terrace with some random, regular bitch and she looked foreign.

My first reaction was to go over and say hi and start some shit, but then I thought about class and decorum. They wouldn't want me to bring ghetto and crazy to the party, so I chilled. After all, he wasn't my nigga so I had no right. Shit, this mafucka didn't even wanna give me the dick, so whatever! We got to our table, and as I sat down, I made damn sure he could see me when he left this mafucka. And he did. He even went as far as kissing my hand, as usual. Yolanda had this curious look on her face and had the nerve to ask me who he was. Using my rudest tone, I let her know that it was none of her business, and that we should move on with the business at hand. Even though Teron had disturbed my appetite, I did my best not to act affected by him being in that restaurant. So by the time the food arrived, I was back in composure and enjoying my lunch, which was my favorite: fresh sole poached in wine with miniature jumbo prawns on shells. I was feeling right and blessed to have such a wonderful life. Everything else didn't matter. The two apple martini's set the entire tone for the day. Now I was ready to do business. I started by saying, "Well Yolanda, I first would like to thank you for this relaxing day. I really needed it. My week has been hectic."

"As has mine, Chantal. Is there anything I can help you with?" What was this bitch talking about, 'can I help'? This hoe is aggressive and really trying! I played it cool. "Oh, nothing that you will be able to help me with. I'm good, just business as usual."

"Yeah, Jah said that you would appreciate this day. He said that you're so busy taking care of him and others that you don't have time for yourself." Shit, if only he knew the truth! I should have told him, but at what cost? Was I willing to tell him everything? I asked, "Did he say that? And when was the last time you talked to him?"

Yolanda said, "Oh no, Chantal. It's not like that at all! Jah and my brother are business partners. They both agreed on me meeting you and spending girl time, as opposed to my brother making contact. I guess your man is a jealous one."

"I don't think jealousy got shit to do with it!" I know a nigga will sic a bitch on you to pull you in. If a bitch can shake you, then he can take you, and that's what's amusing. A mafucka think I'm soft. They really don't know who or what they fuckin' with. They just see a fly-ass bitch on the surface with all the right accessories and what-not. They got a bitch twisted. The only thing that I will ever be loyal to is the game. Truth be told, he should have sent her brother. I would have enjoyed that more than this lame ass bitch. I'll give her credit for a nice day, but now it's time for business. I said, "So what's up, Yolanda?"

She said she preferred to speak on it in the car so she paid the bill and we left. Once we were in the car, she got right down to it. "So here it is, Chantal. We're planning a trip to St. Tropez. It's a business trip with some major players, a weekend excursion, and everything is taken care of. We are providing escort service for two days for some Arab's birthday. They just wanna have fun. The transportation is first class all the way, of course, Global Express XRSG5 will be the carrier there and back. Our clients will join us in St. Tropez. I say we kick it with these fools and get this check. We will be setting up a contact list on that level. You know, go global. What you think, Chantal? You good with that? Jah said that you would be. He said you was a freak."

"Is that what he said?" Fuck it. This was business and I couldn't let my emotions in, so I let that go. "So what the numbers look like, Yolanda?" Her phone started to vibrate in her bag. She excused herself, stepped just outside her car door and took the call. I attempted to listen to her conversation.

"Yea, this Yolanda. Yeah, the uppity bitch is gonna tell me to give her a couple days. I told her we had a small window to make this happen. She's a rude bitch, like she don't need this shit and nothing I'm offering." She nodded her head as she listened to the caller on the other line. "Okay I got you, baby. I'm pushing the bitch but she a trip. I'm gonna get that bitch on that plane one way or another. I love you to, Freeno." Did she say Freeno?

She got back in the car. She seemed agitated, but then she shook it off. She instantly started back on the business discussion, saying, "Chan, if all goes accordingly, our profit would be a half million apiece." Hmm, five hundred thousand wasn't shit. What was the total wap? But to get further into the details, I said, "Okay, Yolanda. That sounds profitable for a weekend fuck. Give me a couple of days to check my schedule. I'll have my assistant get back to you with my answer, and by the way, if for some reason I'm unavailable, can I send in a replacement girl?"

She said with a high tone in her voice, "Is you crazy, Chantal? Hell naw! First of all, it's gotta be you. I need an answer right now. Either you wit' it or you not. We leave Thursday at noon." Now she had me twisted. I was down with trying to be poite with this bitch. I said, "Hold up, Yolanda! First off, watch your fucking tone with me. I ain't one of them bitches that can be easily handled! Second, I'm going to let you know whether I'm wit' it or not. Either you wait or go by your fucking self. Or better yet, how bout this. You tell whoever you gotta tell that Chantal will be getting back with me on her answer after she checks her schedule. Or fuck it. Honestly, I don't give a fuck anyway.

Sounds like you mafuckas need me. Talkin' that shit about how it can only be me! I'll call you in forty-eight hours, and if that's not good enough, fuck it." I exited this bitch's car and didn't even say bye. She had me twisted. Jah wasn't trying to pimp me, was he? I laughed at the thought of that shit.

Chapter 13

Keisha called with the details of our African Safari trip. She said, "I got the information for you on the African safari. Ms. Jones has room available in her schedule for August 5th, which is in two weeks. Your schedule is also open at that time." I told her I would check with the Congo brothers and asked her to email the itinerary to Teron. Another call came in. "Hello, Chantal Laine." The other voice on the phone said, "Hello Ms. Chantal. This is Sheila with Roth, Mayer, and Jones. I have Ms. Jones on the line." Quilla came on the line and said, "Chan, meet me for drinks in an hour. "Got some info for you."

"Great. I was getting ready to call you with the same invite. Africa is happening bitch! I'll talk to you when I see you. Let's meet up at the Ivy in an hour." When I arrived at the Ivy, the valet took my vehicle. My emotions were all over the place. The host actually startled me with his presence. He said, "Good evening. Welcome to the Ivy. How many will be in your party?"

I said, "Thank you. I'm joining someone on the lanai." When I approached Quilla, I said, "What's up, girl?" Then we exchanged air kisses – mwah, mwah! I glanced over her look as if I was the fashion police. Giving her the side eye, I said, "Sis, you're looking awfully casual today." She knew it was a smart ass remark and replied with her middle finger in the air. Quilla reached for an envelope filled with documents and handed them to me.

Getting straight down to business, Quilla said, "Ok, this Yolanda girl that you had me do the background on, well she's a thief. She did a twelve year bid on robbery charges. Dumb bitch got caught in a jewelry store. It's all in there, where she lives, works and reports to parole. You got her whole life in that envelope. She ain't shit, sis. Stay clear of her for sure." She sat back, satisfied with her work and sipped her cocktail.

I said "Is that right? So she scandalous, huh? I thought, Shit, I guess you can't see the snake if they camouflaged themselves with the same colors as you. Yeah, I'm glad I decided not to go with that bitch on her little rendezvous. Jah is so gullible to those chain gang games. They ain't got shit else to do but con a mafucka. Stupid convicts. I said, "Thank you, Quilla. I'm done with that. So, now the news I wanna talk about. It's time for some rest. Keisha got all the details handled for our safari, girl. It's booked and I'm ready to go! It's the first week in August, and I can't wait!

"So it's official?" I wasn't sure, but I think she looked a little scared.

"Hell yeah! We leaving August fifth. She confirmed with Sheila and you are free! Keshia has taken care of the accommodations and transportation, with Teron's assistance, of course. The only thing we need to worry ourselves with is the African wardrobe. As a matter of fact, how about tomorrow we go shopping. Are you free?"

"Absolutely! I always got time to shop. You know Chan, I haven't taken a vacay since we graduated high school when we went to Hawaii."

"All the more reason to go, Qui. You way overdue. Okay, Quilla. I got shit to do. The meal was nice. Thanks for treating. I love you and I'll talk to you tomorrow."

Quilla caught my sly move and said, "Wait, who said I was treating, bitch? Love you too!" As I exited the restaurant, I noticed one of my clients with his wife. I was pressed for time but I wanted to go over. I didn't have anything against his wife, or any of my client's relationships. That was none of my business, so I just kept it moving.

The day finally arrived! Destination Africa. It's gonna be very exciting. From the moment I spoke with Teron regarding the trip, he insisted that he create the itinerary. Between him and Keisha the plans were gonna be spectacular. Quilla and I were ready. We spent over ten thousand dollars on things individually. We really didn't need all those clothes and I'm sure I was gonna shop in Africa, but who doesn't love a shopping spree in Beverly Hills?

Teron and myself, along with Orlon and Quilla embarked on the most wonderful South African adventure to the land of Durban, where the brothers' lineage began. Orlon insisted on being Quilla's personal escort, saying he wanted to show her his land himself. We were flying aboard a

Gulfstream G550, which was custom made for the brothers. The aircraft was a fourteen passenger machine with ostrich-leather seating, wood grain, and marble throughout. Very upscale and luxurious. It offered all the necessities one would need for an eighteen-hour flight. Servants, a personal chef.

From the sky, you get to see the essential part of KwaZulu Natal. When we landed at the Durban International Airport, the first thing I noticed was the difference in the air. I could smell the seawater, which for me, was very familiar and refreshing. I loved the sea. Teron got very excited when explaining to us that in Zulu, old cultural homes are known as emakhaya. When he spoke of the beauty of his country, he did it with pride. The establishment was set in the heart of Umhlanga, Durban, a premier tourist hot spot. We were in a subtropical climate filled with amazing vervet monkeys, which are a constant reminder that you're in Africa. Quilla was scared of the monkeys. That was one of the funniest things to see. Every time she saw them, she would yell at them and they would yell back at her. It became a game for the monkeys and an irritation for Quilla.

The Fig Tree Cottages and Swazi mats on the quarry-rock-tiled floor and comfortable beds with mosquito nets was very nice, very romantic. The private viewing deck and open-plan kitchenettes off the living room were spacious. We opted out for the TV's. We wanted to embrace the quietness of the atmosphere.

Teron had taken extra precautions when finding our accommodations, as he knew Quilla was a city girl. He had to find a location that wouldn't throw her in too much of a culture shock. His choice was one of class and fabulosity, kudos to him. However, I would have been content to live in a bush as long as I was there with him. Our first day on the itinerary was to visit the Mkomazi River. Teron explained to us that within his culture, they referred to it as the Duma Manzi. The Zulu phrase meant Thundering Water. Its majestic sandstone cliffs not only gave the place its name, but also its energy, encouraging its guests to be fully immersed in the ambience. Orlon thought it was the perfect place to show Quilla. I think that's where they started really checkin for each other.

After a small rest, we decided to go to the city known as Kakamega to meet his family and be the guests of honor for a tribal ceremony. Teron's sisters and mother treated him like royalty. They made sure he was fed and comfortable at all times. There was one lady that stood near him the entire time, as if in a servant manner. She made sure that if he coughed, he had water to clear his throat. They weren't as attentive to Orlon, although he got the same care and attention. Just not to the same degree as his brother. Teron was the next in line to be king.

As the ceremonies began, the chief entered, wearing a leopard skin with the bright colored feathers of the bishop bird as a headdress. The warriors' traditional clothing consisted of a loin cloth and skin to cover their ass and dicks. It brightened by hoops and necklaces. All of the married women wore hats, or isichols as they're called. It was made out of a piece of hand-woven cotton or vegetable fiber, then dyed with ochre and placed over a basket. His family gave us some attire to wear for the evening. They made sure that Teron and Orlon were impeccable in style and well-tailored. He described his outfit as senufo-grand, bubu-styled jackets. They were also hand weaved.

The village women gave us beautiful tribal attire and jewelry for the ceremony. Although Quilla thought it was cheap and ugly, she didn't let that ruin the effort with petty complaints. We spent two days in the East African colonial village. The level of respect Teron has for me is flattering, but at times it is nerve-racking. I knew that getting some dick on this trip was out of the question. Hell, it had been three days and nothing had happened. I felt like I was gonna die. I appreciated how he just wanted my presence, not my pussy. Imagine that! But I needed sex just for the fuck of it. Then I needed to get home and back to business.

Chapter 14

It's been three months since that visit with Joyce, and two since my African Safari and I haven't had a good night rest since. I wish that bitch was dead. Here it is two-thirty in the morning, and my mafucking phone ringing. When I answered it, I could hear the excitement in Qui's voice. She said, "Chan, they releasing Jah as we speak! Get your ass up, bitch!"

I jumped out the bed, damn near breaking my toe on the pedestal. "Fuck!" I yelled and held my foot as I hopped around on one leg. Normally, when you're released from a federal facility, you're date stamped, meaning you know the date, and time you go to the door. With Jah's case being one of those under investigation, he was released pending the results. Damn! The day is here! I have waited for this day for fifteen years. It seemed like a lifetime, but not so much with all the extra shit that went on in my life. A lot of time has passed.

The facility could have given more of a heads up, but I was ready. Shit, I had been ready for the last six months. Waiting on that phone call, like a pregnant women waiting to go into labor, and now it was here. I got up, immediately called Keshia to finalize all the details, which was basically telling the team. Rosa was coming with my coffee and eight more cups for the team. Things were very hectic in the house so early in the morning. Everyone was on point with their assignment for the celebration. Every detail was five star.

Quilla put everything Gucci on Jah. Linen suit, loafers and eyewear. She arranged for a stylist to pull some high-end pieces, and meet her at the house. There was nothing but the best on her rack when she arrived. Versace, Gucci, Louis Vuitton, Prada, and Hermes, just to name a few. She spared no expense and arranged for a personal barber and a masseuse for mani/pedi and massage. Jartz, my diamond connection, came through with that bitch, Monica on his arm. She had conformed to her new life from a stripper bitch to blackadish hoe. Shit, I should have charged Jahrtz's ass a finder's fee cause I gave him a bad one! I couldn't be mad at her, though. She was at her money. He brought some of the highest clarity VVS stones from his vault. My platinum chain, paved with black diamonds, four carats for each ear, eight carats on the pinky, and Audemars Piguet black diamond watch came in, also.

8 a.m. The phone call was right on time. I thought it was the driver but it was Jah on the line, very excited. Actually, he seemed like he was under the influence, whispering something about getting out early. He was already in the city and would be here later. I was somewhat confused and disappointed. I had a feeling that all the plans that I had made for him on his release day were gonna go out the window. I got myself together and released most of the team, letting them know that

they could invoice me for their time. Quilla asked the stylist to be on call.

I felt embarrassed and hurt. All kinds of things were running through my mind. All kinds of emotions too, but I pulled it together and tighten the fuck up. Quilla was so hurt by his actions. She said, "It's just like him not to act right." She was so mad that she left without saying bye. I felt her, though. After all the time we had waited for this day, all the preparations, and he just fucked it up. Jartz hung around for as long as he could. I tried calling the number Jah had called from a thousand times, to no avail. Jahrtz was kind enough to leave the jewelry, stating that we would take care of it later. Feeling embarrassed, I apologized to everyone saying, "I'm sure there's some great explanation why this nigga wanted to play games on the day of his release. I apologize." I released everyone for the night and went to bed angry and disappointed.

Well, that minute that Jah talked about turned into three days. Shit, I didn't think he was ever coming, and that was fine with me. Teron stopped by with coffee the day after the fiasco and it was a welcome surprise. When I opened the door, he stood there, looking wonderful. He said, "Good morning, Chan. Wow! You're beautiful even at seven in the morning. Did you wake up like that?" I giggled at that like a school girl and said, "How flattering, Teron. Yes I did. Come on in. Let's go into the kitchen. Please excuse all the boxes.

We were planning a celebration and those are the gifts."

He said, "Wow that's a lot of boxes."

"Yeah, I know." Even I could hear the disappointment in my voice.

Teron noticed, too and said, "Are you okay, Chan? You're not your bubbly self."

"Oh, I'm sorry. I just got a lot on my mind."

"Well, I'm here. Let's talk. I promise I'll listen."

"Thanks Teron. I appreciate that, but even if I talk and scream, it is what it is. I can't change it."

"Yeah, but talking about could make it more clear, give you some kind of relief."

"Maybe you're right and you are a good listener. Let's go sit in the entertainment room. I feel like listening to some music." I must admit, just to have Teron's presence eased some of the tension. For the moment, I forgot about Jah and his foolishness. It only seemed like maybe an hour had past. We talked and shared laughs, fruit, cigars and then eventually upgraded to a bottle of wine. By the time we looked up it was noon. I said, "Teron, would you like another glass of wine?"

"No. I think one is enough. I have to go to the office later."

"Yeah and I have clients this afternoon as well."

Teron was quiet a moment, then he said, "Come here, Chantal."

I immediately felt butterflies in my belly. I said, "Oh, Lord. You're calling me Chantal. Should I be afraid?"

"Never be afraid of me, love. I promise, you'll never have to be afraid me. I would never hurt you." He was looking intently into my eyes with so much compassion and dedication. It kind of shook me for a minute. I didn't know what to think or do. He leaned over and kissed me on the forehead, then on the cheek. Then he reached my lips. He had so much passion in his kiss, sticking his tongue deep in my throat. I felt his heart beat fiercely, we were that close. I could feel his hand rubbing my leg and going in an upward movement. Shit, just the thought of what was getting ready to happen excited me. I've been waiting on this for a long time. Might as well celebrate this victory and what better way than some dick to calm a bitch's nerves.

He whispered, "Is it okay, Chan?" He was such a gentlemen, asking for permission! He asked for permission as he got closer to my pussy! All I could do was open my legs, giving him all the permission he needed. I was speechless and very excited now. He lifted me up on the bar stool, making sure my ass was slightly hanging off the edge, then gently leaned me over the bar, spreading my ass cheeks. When he found the right spot with his finger, he lifted my ass off the chair and stuck his dick so deep and so gently into my pussy.

Everything in me went numb. He held my ass, bouncing it up and down on his dick in a very masculine and forceful stride. His dick was in and out of my pussy at an almost unbearable, rhythmic speed. I could see his expression through the mirror on the wall. He looked at his dick in my pussy, going in and out, in and out. He was a man in heaven, very well satisfied at that moment. And then... The way he turned me over and licked my pussy on that bar let me know that he had been wanting Ms. Chantal for a long time! I must say, he was strong to resist as long as he did, but I knew one day... Well, today was that day. I knew he would give in. After the sexing, we both laughed as if we were kids, like we had did it for the first time. I said, "That was amazing, just what I needed. Thank you."

"Don't say it as if it was a service, Chan."

"Oh no! I'm not. It was all that and more. I'm just very appreciative, that's all. Besides, I don't know why it happened now instead of all those other times you turned me down."

Teron said, "It wasn't our time."

"So now was our time, huh?"

"It just seemed liked the perfect time. Do you feel better?"

I laughed and said, "If you only knew how much."

"You know, Chan, you are a beautiful woman, inside and out. I want you to know that there is a love in my heart for you. All you have to do is come get it. I promise to take care of your heart with everything in me. You would never have to worry about anything." He was talking some real deep shit, but I didn't wanna go there, so I jokingly said, "Teron, you know I take care of myself, and I don't worry. It causes wrinkles." We shared a laugh, but I understood exactly what he was telling me. How could I even entertain the thought of his offer? My life was complicated enough, although the time here with Teron was pleasant, I felt as if I could never have someone of his caliber and gracefulness. Truth was, I felt like I wasn't worthy. I was hoe, albeit a high priced one. I was never exposed to his type of life. It was safer to keep doing me. I was comfortable in my space. To be honest, I couldn't even see myself in any other light.

It was time to get it together and start the day. Just as I was walking to the bedroom, half nude, the doorbell rang. It rang and then rang once more. I thought it was Quilla because she was the only one that laid on my doorbell like that. I glanced back at Teron to make sure he was decent. As for me, I was half naked with a leopard print throw across my body. I wasn't in the least ashamed. I opened the door and what do you know? Mr. Jaheim Jones, three days and many hours later, is standing in front of me. I didn't know whether to slap his ass or shoot him. He actually had the nerve to come in, boss talking a bitch. Little did he know, I had a warrior in the next room that was ready, willing and able to shut his shit down. He fell in the door, looking like he hadn't had any sleep. He smelled like a distillery. He said, "Sup, Chan. Open the door. I been ringing the bell. What you doing? You ain't got no clothes on." Then this mafucka snatched my cover off, exposing everything right there in the foyer with the door wide open. With slurred speech, he managed to say, "Dayum! That's what I'm talking bout! A bad bitch at the door, ready to suck a nigga's dick. Come on, girl. I'm ready."

"Hold up, mafucka! What, you drunk?" I could see Teron approaching the door, as I tried to cover myself. Teron said, "You okay, Chan?" Jah said, "Hold up! Who is this nigga? Look, bruh. I don't know what you got going on with my bitch but you can leave now. Anything you thought you had with her is over with, patna." Jah was flexing like I was his. Teron came completely out of character and went straight into warrior mode. He said, "What, fuck nigga? I'll break your fuckin neck!"

The tone and seriousness that came from Teron scared me. I had never heard his voice leave an octave tone of 3 maybe 4 levels, but he went in. He meant that shit! I tried to get control of this situation and said, "Wait, this is not going to happen. Jah, you need to respect my house and leave." It didn't matter what I said to him because you can't do shit with a drunk mafucka but smash 'em. Jah, with his drunk ass, said, "Bitch, what you mean 'leave'? This my house!"

"I ain't gonna be too many more of them bitches you calling me, Jah, and as of three days ago, you're no longer welcome. You made that choice, so go where you been." Before I knew it, Teron reached around my back and snatched Jah in the throat, telling him to take his bullshit somewhere else. Jah was trying to get the grip of Teron's hand from around his neck as he was starting to lose consciousness. All I could do was scream at Teron to let him go. He pushed his ass out of the doorway and slammed the door. Jah had no choice but to leave. Teron was furious, but at the same time eerily calm. He pulled me into his arms and asked if I was okay. He said, "Chan, I'm sorry you were treated that way."

"It wasn't your fault that Jah came with that bullshit, Teron. You don't have to apologize for his nonsense." Then he asked me, "What was that all about? You kept saying "three days ago." I knew then it was time for me to tell him the history of Jah and our twisted relationship. "Teron, there's not enough time in this day to tell that story."

He said, "Well, were gonna make time and I can't trust what's his name." He made a call to his assistant and asked her to bring his office to my house. The way it was done really impressed me. This man was interested and wanted to protect me! He said, "Now clear your schedule or bring it home, whatever you need to do, cause I'm not leaving until I know your safe." How could I refuse that kind of support and God knows I needed it. It had been a long time.

"Okay. I'm gonna go freshen up and when I return, we'll talk. I asked him if he wanted to join me and to my surprise, he followed me to my bedroom suite. We got into the shower and he stroked my back and my breasts. As the soap lathered, he kissed me gently all over my body. Round two was even better than the first. It reminded me of the way Scooby used to make love to me. He watched the soap trickling down the crack of my ass was instantly aroused. He spread my ass cheeks and entered my pussy walls, thrusting his dick into me like he owned me. In that moment, I felt the same love and passion that I thought was buried in the grave with my daddy. Teron made love to me in that shower. That was something that no one has ever been able to do since Scooby left me.

We were so into it. We lost all kinds of time. Teron's assistant had been ringing the doorbell and calling the phone for thirty minutes. He jumped up and said,

"Oh shit! I forgot about Diana. Can you show her where she can set up? Tell her I'll be down in a minute." I was all smiles. I said, "Sure." Shit, he could ask me for anything right about now! He called her cell phone to let her know that I was on my way down. I grabbed my cell phone and I saw that I had 42 messages and 24 missed calls. The damn thing started ringing in my hand. This is one crazy day. I opened the door and said, "Hello, Diana. Come in. You can set up in the office on the right." She said, "Thank you, Ms...?

"Chantal would be fine. Teron will be down shortly."

"Okay. Thank you, ma'am."

"Diana, please don't call me that. Chantal will be fine". Bitches act as though they can't hear me when I tell them to do something but I will check that ass real quick. Teron came downstairs and went straight into work mode. He gave me a kiss on the forehead and told me it wouldn't take long. That gave me a chance to return all these calls. Hopefully, I would be able to reschedule my appointments, which will be hard. When these niggas want a piece of Chantal, they act like the world is going to end if they don't get it.

But today was totally an off day, and for once I didn't mind calling these niggas to cancel. Shit, I haven't had a day off in years. Of course, all the messages were from Jah. He called from three different numbers. Each time I called back and he answered, I hung up. I was gonna have to show him better than I could tell him. He fucked up. He was disloyal and disrespectful. After all the years I held him down, he couldn't give me the gift of his presence. Because of that, my heart feels nothing for him, good or bad. The rest of my clients weren't at all happy, but they understood. I didn't really care if they didn't. They were loyal. Those mafucking tricks weren't going anywhere.

By the time Teron joined me in the kitchen, I was cooking shrimp and fettuccini and sipping on some Meroni. He seemed very relaxed. He was so handsome, standing there admiring and adoring me on another level. It felt good. I looked over at him and said, "You hungry?" I felt domesticated.

He brought something out of me, showed me that deep down inside, I was good. The things I shared with Teron, I would never give to anyone else. He said, "Yes I'm hungry and it smells good. Whatcha cooking? I thought you would have wanted to go out."

"Nah, I wanna enjoy you. As a matter of fact, I don't want this day to end." "Neither do I, Chan." He bent down and kissed me, then held me so very tightly. I swear I melted in his arms. I know this feeling is temporary, in the here and now. Tomorrow I must face my reality, for Jah will surely be back. After Diana printed and organized the documents for Teron's signature, she was gone. On her way out, she said she would send a messenger in the morning to pick up the papers. How did she know he was gonna spend the night? Well it did sound good, cause I sure didn't wanna be alone or spend the night with a trick, not tonight.

The sun was setting and there was a nice breeze on the lanai. After we ate, I suggested we sit with a bottle of wine and talk. Teron was ready for whatever I wanted. I felt our bond was closer than ever, and I also felt that he deserved the truth. All my truth. So I started at the beginning and kept going to the present. By the time I ended my story, he gently held my hand looked me in my eyes. He said, "We all have our own story, Chan. I appreciate you for sharing yours." I could tell he was still processing everything that I told him. After a long pause, he said, "You've been through a lot, young lady. And you've managed to come out of all that flawlessly. Even your flaws are flawless." I smiled and lowered my head. I'm used to be complimented constantly, but this felt different. He said, "You are remarkable, do you know that?" I want you to know that I'm your gift from God. I'm here to protect and love you." Then he asked, "Will you let me do that, Chantal? Let me be what you need? What you deserve in this life?"

Damn! Now that was some boss shit! I never really needed anything other than money, but what he was saying sounded good. I've been way too familiar with over a thousand niggas from all races and different parts of the country, but this one right here was grand. He stood out in a crowd of niggas, and a bitch like me got everything anyone could ever ask or want for. I could buy anything I wanted, anywhere in the world, but he was special. Maybe he was a gift. I never thought that kind of magic would ever happen to me.

We went into the bedroom and retired for the night. He held me close all night long. The next morning, Teron was extra appreciative from the night of ecstasy that was given to him. I sucked that nigga's dick as if it was the first time he had ever experienced it. I put all my skills into it. Yeah, I blessed him for no reason other than he deserved it. He didn't wanna leave, but we both had business to take care of. He promised he would be back after work and for some reason, I wanted that. A lot.

Thirty minutes after he left, here comes Jah. It was as if he was waiting outside for my nigga to leave. Scary ass nigga. What I want with that? I couldn't get into the kitchen good before the phone started ringing and the doorbells chiming. Now that pissed me off and I started talking to myself. "This shit is ridiculous. I promise you, I'm gonna start turning the fucking ringer off that phone, cause mafuckas don't know how to respect my time. It's too damn early for all this shit.

I answered the phone with attitude. "Yes, hello? Chantal speaking." I'm sure the caller could hear the frustration in my voice.

"Hi, Chantal. This is Micha."

"Just a minute, Micha." Jah was on that damn bell like he was a nut fresh out the crazy ward. I screamed, "Hold the fuck on! I'm coming!" I opened the door and said, "Get off that damn bell like that, nigga."

Jah stood there, looking dumb. "Good morning, Chan. Can I come in now?"

"Yeah. Hold on. I got a call." I led this nigga to the kitchen, and went back to my call. "Ok, Micha. What's up?"

"I was calling to see when I could come out there. I've been waiting for you to call me or write me or whateva."

"Micha, I've been really busy. I have a lot on my plate. Let's try and do it in the summer. I'll try to make some time then.

"Well Chantal, I didn't think my visit was an appointment." Well, I'll give it to her. She had some balls. I liked that.

"It's not, trust me."

"I won't get in the way of you handling your business, Chantal, I promise. Please let me come. Uncle Lance said that I can't stay here after I graduate."

"Why would he say that?"

"Not sure. He just said that he had to move and I had to find some place to go." One thing I know about living in someone else's space is that there's rules and boundaries that you have to adhere to. You must respect that person, or you will definitely wear out your welcome. I said, "There must be a track record on your part of being irresponsible, Micha."

She said, "No, he just said that he has to downgrade and won't have room for me." I still didn't believe her. "Really?"

"Really. So can I come?" Now I know that whatever shit she has done for him to ask her to leave, I don't want coming this way. But to appease her, I said, "Okay, Micha. Let me think about it. I'll let you know." In reality, I didn't have to think on it at all. It just sounded good to tell her that. She said, "Okay, Chan. You got my number. Just call me, but please let me know soon." Whatever. I said, "Yeah, okay. I'll call you. I got to go. Bye." I hung the phone up before she could say bye.

Now it's time to deal with this mafucka who has already made himself at home, eating a big ass sandwich and shit. Drinking my juice out the container. How am I going deal with this institutionalized ghetto ass nigga in my crib, disrespecting my shit. Lord, give me strength! I'm definitely not in the business of keeping no nigga, no way. He should feel privileged and enjoy the fruits of my fucking labor quietly and respectably. He needs to understand that hard work bought and paid for this shit.

With a mouth full of food, he said, "How you doing, Chan?" I said, "I'll be doing better if you clean up your mess. Don't come in this mafucka disrespecting, Jah." He said, "Damn, you going in on a nigga already! You ain't gave me no kiss or nothing. Come here, baby. I missed you." He really got the nerve to come here like he didn't fuck everything up, and now he in here like it's all good. Asking me if I'm okay. The nerve of this nigga! I said, "Jah, don't come in here with all that. You made a choice and so live with it."

"I didn't make no choice. My friend asked if she could pick me up, and I let her. What's the problem?"

"Whats the problem?" Was this nigga for real? He said, "Don't worry about that. Come here. Ain't you happy to see me? Give me some love baby." I thought for sure this nigga crazy.

"Give you some love? Jah, listen. I'm very disappointed in your actions. You disrespected me and you weren't honest with me. I'm not that little girl you left in the projects."

He considered me for a moment, then said, "Naw, you not and you been hustling like a mafucka, I see."

"Call it what you want. Tell me this. What are your plans? He looked around him and said, with a smirk on his face, "My plan is to be with you." I said, "I can't tell! Look, there's all kinds of shit in the living room that was bought out of love for you. Take all that shit with you." He looked at me dumbfounded and said, "What you mean, 'take that shit with me'? I ain't going nowhere. This my house. You better stop playin' and let that fuck nigga know not to come back here." Now that was funny! I thought to myself, "Why? Cause you don't want your ass beat? Instead, I said, "All that changed when you made a decision to go left."

"Girl, I didn't make no decision to go nowhere. Now I'm tired of all this talking. I want some pussy and I want you to come over here and suck on this dick."

"Well, that you ain't getting. So what else?"

That cocky mafucka said, "Oh, I'm gonna get some of that pussy! You crazy." Jah started walking round this mafucka, talking about what he gonna change and what he gonna do. I guess he really believed that everything was okay. He don't even know me! It's either left or right with me, and I always choose right and what he did was wrong. Dead to the left! I said, "Look, I really don't have time to play with you. I have appointments this morning, so time is ticking. What's up?"

Not catching the hint, he said, "Well, go on to your appointments and I'll see you when you get back." Oh no this nigga didn't! As if! I said, "Nope, that's not happening. Call your sister and I'll slide you over there." This nigga actually thought he was gonna stay in my house all day, rambling and rummaging and shit. He really got me fucked up! "Quilla's number is on speed dial. I'm going to get in the shower."

He looked surprised. He said, "Damn, you serious, huh? We can't talk about this, Chan?" I wasn't playin.I said, "Dead ass serious. What is there to talk about?" I could tell I threw him off with that. He said, "There's a lot to talk about. What, you tryin to leave a nigga?"

"Leave? You still don't get it, do you?"

"Get what? All these years we got invested and you gonna just try to leave like that? Chan, I'll..."

"You'll what?" When that nigga said 'try and leave', he had a look on his face that spoke volumes. It kin a shook me, but a nigga ain't never been able to intimidate a bitch like me. I said, "Listen, I got shit to do. Go spend some time with your family and I'll see you later."

"Yeah, later. Okay, Chantal."

I could tell he was heated but I dismissed him by saying, "Now go sort out some of that shit in my living room and call Quilla. I'm going to get in the shower." I left the room before he could respond. I somehow managed to get dressed in peace and get Jah out of my house. On the way to Quilla's, he kept guessing how I got all this money that he saw. Shit, when we got to the garage, he was like a kid in a candy shop, jumping around the collection, talking 'bout, "Let's roll in the Bentley. Give me the keys and I'll drop you off."

Those words gave me all the confirmation I needed. This nigga ain't shit. He was one of those niggas for sale, looking for a bitch to keep him. Oops, wrong bitch! As we pulled up to Quilla's driveway, he was again in awe. Quilla had moved a couple of months ago into 20,000 square foot traditional out in Malibu. Great place she could call home. She even let me help with the purchase and I gave the final thumbs up. She was not too far from me, so we're almost neighbors.

Jah was talking shit. "Damn! My bitch bad. My sis bad. I'm rolling in the range, all white everything. Yeah, this it! I'm straight!" I got my cell phone and called Quilla to come out cause I couldn't come in. Time is money. She came out, screaming and running and carrying on. "Hey baby! Get out that car and give me some love, nigga! Where you been?"

Jah said, "Ah, nowhere. Just tryin' to be where I'm supposed to be." He looked me, as if waiting for a reply.

I said, "Well, ya'll have your little reunion. I gotta go." Jah was the first to speak. He said, "A'ight. Call me when you finished. Give me a kiss." At first, I didn't wanna kiss this nigga, but I didn't want Quilla to feel some type of way, even though he was gonna tell her everything. So I gave a fake kiss, a little a peck on the lips.

He got out of my car and I was gone. I haven't spoken to my aunt Jackie in a while. with all that has being going on. I'm sure if no one else understood how crazy my life was, it would be her. She deserved a phone call, so on the way to my first appointment, I called her. "Hey, Auntie."

"Hey, baby girl! What's going on? I haven't heard from you. Is everything ok?"

"I'm okay. How you doing?"

"I'm okay, baby. You don't sound right. What's wrong?"

"Wow, I don't know, auntie. I just got a lot going on. Jah got out with all kinds of nonsense and Micha's calling me."

She said, "Well I didn't know Jah was home but more importantly, what you gonna do about that Micha situation, baby girl? And what do you mean Jah is acting crazy?"

"He came to the house three days after he was released and to top it off, he was drunk as hell."

"Are you serious? So you didn't pick him up?"

"No. He said some girl came and got him."

"Some girl, huh? So where is he now?"

"I dropped him off over Quilla's." I guess she could hear the hurt in my voice. She said, "All that planning you did and he didn't even show up. You need a drink and a massage. Meet me at the

Beverly Hilton, my treat. I wanna hear the rest of this crazy mess you got going on. I'm gonna help you work it out, okay Chan? I'm not taking no for an answer."

"Okay auntie, but I have to get to an appointment. But I promise, immediately after, I'm there. Is 3 o'clock ok?"

"Yes, I'll call you then. Smooches. I love you."

I wanted to get off the phone before she could ask what kind of appointment I had. Auntie and Grandmother Laine have always been overly protective of me. Being cautious where Micha was concerned was no surprise. But at the end of the day, whether she's Maine's daughter or not, we came from the same bitch. This shit is too much. I knew I had to get it together cause it was time to go to work. The moment I walked into the room, this nigga was already jacking his dick. Good, less work I gotta do. I gave him what he paid for and got the fuck on with my paper. One hour, that's all you get. My time is money. I don't play that overtime shit, unless you pay for it.

While the valet was getting my vehicle, I thought it would be a good time to reach out to Lance and see what's really going on with Micha. He had a mouthful to tell me. Just so happens, she's wild as hell. He can't do anything with her and don't want to handle her any longer. He said, "She been under my roof for the last three years and she will not follow the rules. She staying out late. Partying with grown folks twice her age. I

done all I could do. It's someone else's turn."
Turns out, he has a new wife and they wanted to
do a little traveling and Micha wasn't a part of that
picture. He was going on and on about his new
bitch and blah, blah, blah.

After speaking with him, I got the feeling
that he just didn't wanna be bothered anymore.
Letting Micha come here could be a bad thing, but
then again, she might actually adapt to this
lifestyle and make something of herself. At any
rate, I knew I had to let her come. My dad would
have wanted me to do that. But she would have to
understand that there would be rules to this shit.

Quilla and Jah had been blowing my phone
up ever since I left, wanting to know what time I
was coming back to get him. Like she was
babysitting a child of mine or some shit! After
talking with my auntie and realizing I don't want
anything bad to happen to Jah or Micha, I decided
that would let him come, too. The both would have
to get their shit together or move on.

I decided to call Micha and let her know that
I had made up my mind and she could come. I also
let her know that I wasn't for no bullshit. She said,
"Trust me, sis. I'm gonna show you." I don't know
what she meant by that. "I graduate next month
and I was thinking, maybe I can come after that.

"Okay, as long as we have an
understanding. This is a temporary situation,
depending on how we mesh...cool?"

"Yeah, that's cool. I need a ticket though.
Uncle Lance said he wasn't paying for shit. He said

that with the kind of money my daddy left you, I should be traveling first class and living the same life you're living."

"Is that what he said? Well, whatever, Micha. Folks been talking about me all my life. I don't listen to that shit. I'll have Keshia make all the arrangements. She will call you and let you know when and where. I'll talk to you later. Bye."

I hung up with Micha and called Keisha to make the arrangements, with specific instructions to book an open coach seat ticket. My auntie was on time with that massage she gave me during our talk. I feel very relaxed in spite of the situations I'm dealing with. I always enjoy the time I spend with my aunt.

On to the next appointment, which is gonna take some time. This particular trick likes me to sit on his face for thirty minutes. He always wants more and he pays for it. I was entering the hotel and there was Teron, standing at the concierge. I tried to go unnoticed, if that was possible, but he saw me at the front desk. He came behind me with a big hug and kiss saying, "What a surprise. What are you doing here? Oh shit.

I said, "Oh, hey! This is a surprise! What are you doing here?"

"I had some business to take care of." I glanced over his shoulder and his assistant, Diana, waved at me and nodded hello. Next to her was a slender lady with dreadlocks, standing gracefully. She was very well put together. I turned back to

Teron and said. "I see. Well don't let me keep you."

"Oh, no. Chan I want to introduce you to someone." I said, "Teron, I have an appointment. Maybe some other time." I didn't wanna meet anyone right now. I was booked today and time was money. But he insisted, "Oh come on. It won't take but a minute."

As we walked over, the expression on the women's face was confusion. It was obvious that she wanted to know who I was. I admit, I was also curious as to who she was, although it ain't in me to trip. Even if I've been with a nigga sexually and I see him with a bitch, it don't move me. I own no nigga and no nigga owns me. Teron immediately introduced us with excitement. "Chan, I would like to introduce you to Mrs. Melissa Mateow. Melissa, this is the lovely Chantal Laine."

She spoke with a European accent. "It's my pleasure to meet you, the very lovely Chantal." We all gave out a little chuckle and I said, "Likewise." Teron put his arm around me and said, "Chantal, this is my sister. She lives in Europe with her husband and three children."

Yeah, that's nice, but my money is waiting. I said, "Oh, that's wonderful. Look, it was nice meeting you, but I'm running late for an appointment. I have to go, Teron. I'll call you later." He gave me a peck on the cheek and I left. I got on the elevator. I couldn't help but think, why hadn't I met his sister on our African retreat? But anyway, I needed to regroup. It was time to go to work.

Later that evening, Teron was ringing my phone. When I answered, he said,

"Hey gorgeous, did I tell you that you were most exquisite today? Are you busy?"

"Not really. What's going on? And thank you for the compliment."

"You're most welcome. Well, the reason I'm calling was to invite you on a little vacation. I know you could use one, help get your mind off all the madness." Now this was unexpected. "Really? And where will this little vacay be?"

"Just a short trip to Antigua. I got about 2 hours of business there and then I would be all yours."

"All mine? You promise?"

He said, "I promise, baby." Lord, the way he said that made me say yes to the invite. I could feel my clit throb with the excitement. I said, "Yes, Antigua. That sounds delicious. When are we leaving?"

"Next Thursday, my love. I'll have Diana call Keisha with the itinerary." He was super excited. We said our goodbyes and hung up. Oh what a day! All I wanted to do was take a hot bath and lay it down. But that only sounded good cause just as I was stepping into the tub, Quilla called to let me know her and Jah were on the way. Damn! I wanted my house to myself tonight. Before I knew it, the doorbell was ringing like crazy. Imagine two loud mafuckas on your bell like they stupid. I poured me a glass of wine and let them have fun ringing that bitch until they got tired. Then they started banging on the door. When I opened the door, I could see they were both faded.

"The hell you ringing my damn bell like you ain't got no sense?"

"Ah baby, stop being so mean."

"Fuck you, Jah." I was not in the mood.

"I see you still mad at me, huh? Chan, I'm sorry."

"Ya'll really need to stop tripping."

"What is it that you want me to do, Chan? You want me to leave?"

"No, I want you to be right."

"I am right."

Quilla walked in and said, "Chan where the wine? Ya'll tripping."

I needed to nip this right in the bud now, so I told Quilla to go to the cellar and get another bottle. Then I looked at Jah and said, "Listen we'll talk, okay? Privately." Jah and I had a long talk that finally ended after he kept asking a thousand questions that never got answered. Chantal Laine don't answer to no nigga. I learned that at a very early age. My dad's spirit lives on in my heart and his teachings have lived on in my life from day one. He would say all the time, "Never push a loyal person to the point where they no longer give a fuck. Loyalty is not bought, it's earned. Through one's actions, you can see all you need to see. Pay attention. Perpetrators come in all sizes and shapes. Never let anyone in your heart cause they will surely crush it. Get your money and fuck the world! With Jah and Micha coming into my life, I know things are going to be different, but I run Chan, my house and my business the way I want to. Nothing and nobody is gonna change that, and if these two mafucks got any kind of agenda of malice intent, I will cut they ass off real quick.

Chapter 15

I was born Jermicha Junice Laine. People call me Micha. I am Chantal's baby sister. I didn't know what came with that, or who she was, but I would soon find out. It's been over six months since I heard from my sister. Living here in Atlanta has been a nonstop party. There's always a party, bar-b-que or fish fry, or something. Down here in the south, they know how to eat and how to party. And don't let the Falcons be on that football field. Atlanta turns up! The shawties ain't nothing like them San Diego niggas.

The lessons I learned living in San Diego taught me how to manipulate a mafucka, but here in the A, those skills weren't necessary. Georgia got some cool mafuckas. California niggas are too uptight and the hoes ain't shit. I've never gotten along with bitches, no matter what state I'm in. Can't trust them. Growing up, I had to learn to take care of myself. Living in one foster home to the next, I've seen a lot of different faces and most mafuckas got two of 'em. So I choose my circle very carefully, but never really having a *friend.* When I was eleven years old, my uncle decided to take me in. Said he wish he had done it earlier and asked for my forgiveness. Hell, why not forgive him? Mafuckas been sorry for the way they turned they backs on me all my life. He wasn't any different. At least he had the nerve to say sorry, even though it didn't mean shit, I accepted his apology, and he kept his word. After all the paperwork was completed and several home visits from the Department of Child Services, and a year, it was finalized. The fact that I had ran away seven times didn't help, but they agreed that he had a stable environment. Hell, the state was glad to let me go!

My mom was the only person that ever gave a fuck about me. She just wasn't in a position to take care of me. I miss her, and need her in my life. Well, it was time for my theray session. I walked in and said, "Hello, my name is Micha Laine and I'm here for my session." The old lady behind the desk told me to have a seat. I thought this is a waste of time. These classes are suppose to teach you how to adjust if you're the product of the foster care system. If there were disciplinary sanctions in your file, counseling was mandatory in order for you to be able to transmission into normalcy. I was suppose to learn how to deal with your feelings and control your behavior in a more productive way with positive actions instead of taking out the anger in a violent manner. If you ask me, I say their trying to erase the effects from growing up in the system or being abused, which is the same thing in my book. In my opinion, they could never be erased or forgiven.

I hated these group sessions. They were ordered by the court and I had to attend classes every Wednesday until they felt I was rehabilitated. This was the most ridiculous thing that I've ever had to do. You sit there and share all your problems and personal business with strangers and then they judge you on that shit. They must have thought I was a mute, cause I never said nothing. Officially, I have only four more sessions left and then I would have a piece of paper that said I was rehabilitated. Yea, right! I'm smart and from the moment I realized my potential everything that I've did up to this point in my life has been planned. My love for books has enabled me to excel in just about everything I do. Let's just say, I ain't no dumb bitch, and my manipulation skills is on point!

There was this girl that lived across the street from my Uncle's house named Leslie. She was also in group session. She was the only female that I've talked to in a long time. She was also given to the state at a very young age and finally being adopted at the age of ten. Leslie liked being around me. She said I taught her how to play people and get what they got. She got on my nerves though, always complaining and asking questions. I liked the fact that she wasn't messy. You know, the hoe that's always in somebody's business, running her mouth. It seems like Leslie and I have been on the same road, just at different rest stops all our life. We had to grow up fast.

Although I loved living in Georgia, I got big plans. I'm going back to California. Beverly Hills, not no damn San Diego. My punk-ass sister live out there. Yeah, she's some rich bitch. I'm gonna just go and manipulate her ass and get what the fuck I want outta of her, like I've done with everybody else. You see, it's simple: Put real thought into whatever it is you desire, evaluate the cost of achieving it, and get it. One must be in the habit of wanting something, and I want a lot.

My girl, Leslie was outside, blowing the horn. One of her friends was driving us to the club tonight. The bitch was outside, screaming and hollering. "Come on, Micha!"

"I'm coming. Hold on," I yelled out of the window. If this bitch blows the horn again, I'm gonna tell her the fuck off. I definitely ain't trying to befriend theses hoes. They are rude and impatient. I just needed a ride, and that's what this hoe is being used for tonight. We pulled up in the parking lot and it was full of cars and niggas. Yeah, it was turnt! I pulled the lipstick and a blount out of my bag. I said, "So ya'll wanna smoke this blunt before we go in?" Everybody in the car answered at once. It didn't make me none cause I was doing my shit with or without these bitches.

A girl in the back seat said, "Hell yea! I got a lighter." I gave it to her to spark. While the blunt was in rotation, the compacts and mirrors were put to use. We started lip glossing, touching up makeup, and fixing weaves, trying our best to look our best. See, a bitch put her best shit on for two reasons. One, it's her thing, which is natural, or two, she stunting on another bitch. Most times, both are the case. The fellas could care less. They just want the pussy, and the more clothes you got on the less their interested.

Club Lime Cay was crunk tonight. It was a hole in the wall that mainly played Jamaican music, but every now and again the D.J. would mix in some rap. The niggas were grimey, with that sexy Caribbean drawl, just how I liked them. Tonight is ladies night. The good thing about this club is that they never carded anyone. I'm only sixteen, but didn't nobody know that shit but me. If you looked the part, then cool. The dude at the door said, "Cum nah, give me your ten dollas, girl and enjoy yourself." He said that to everyone that came in. I paid my ten dollars and knew I was looking good by the look on his face. Let me know I was looking extra delicious.

I got my sexiest black sheer dress on. It showed the florescent pink bra and G-string panty set perfectly. All the niggas was gonna holla tonight! My shit might come from the thrift store, but I know how to wear it and make it look like some designer shit. I'm used to things not being new and fresh, so I make it work. Had to learn that when I was real young. We found the perfect table, right next to the dance floor. I wanted to sit at the bar, but these girls wanted a table. I played kosher with these hoes cause I needed the ride home.

Just as we were sitting down and ordering our drinks, this tall, dreadlocked, chocolate brother named Kenzo appeared out of nowhere. I think the dress caught his attention. He was hot! He said, "Irie Irie, weh yuh up to? Can I have a dance?" The way he said that shit turned me on! His accent was very rural and deep. He called it Jamaican patois. I called it sexy! He said he didn't speak it that much around Americans, but I wanted to hear it all the time. He said, "Cum nah, let's go and partay on the dance floor."

I was so happy that he asked me to dance. The closer he got, the more I wanted to smell his hair. That shit smelled so good! Once, I'd asked him why it smelled like that and he told me, "Dem juice and berry, mon, with the coconut." That scent lasted in my memory for four days. It was like voodoo. I was liking him for real. While we danced and danced, the other girls were my purse watchers. Although Lez was doing her thing, the others were just in the cut, hating. Kenzo said, "I-yah gwaan outside and have some fun. Let me lick on the pum pum, yuh think?" When he asked me to come outside with him, saying he wanted to have some fun. I knew what he was doing. He must have thought that I was a naïve little girl. But I know how this shit work. I wasn't a virgin. Shit, I lost that at one of them foster homes from the hands of the very mafuckas that was suppose to be taking care of me a long time ago.

He opened the door to his car and I slid in, booty first. Hell, I didn't know if this muthafucka had HIV or what. All I knew was that his dick was big and I wanted it. When I sat on his dick and rode that shit the way that I did, he knew wasn't nothing naïve about me. We saw each other every other day after that. Skin to skin and nut to nut. He would always say, "The pum pum is turn up!" meaning my pussy was the shit and it fit his dick perfectly. I would ride the bus over to his condo and we would fuck all day.

He was really into that Kama Sutra shit. Sex toys were his thing. He had a fetish for the pussy. He had this sex harness, a swing that extended from the ceiling, which makes having sex in many unusual positions possible. I was nervous as hell the first time I saw it, wondering if it was anchored tightly enough to hold me. I wasn't a big girl, but I was thick with a lot of ass. I didn't wanna fall. Kenzo would put me in different positions. He would hoist me up in the center of that shit, positioning my legs by separating them as far apart as they would go. Then he pulled the straps to stretch them open until they literally wouldn't go anymore. He would then lock them into position and grab a chair, sitting in examination form, as if he was the doctor and I was the patient. He would stroke the pussy, lick the pussy, suck the pussy. I think at one point, he counted the hairs on the pussy.

That shit drove me crazy! Imagine a muthafucka sittin there in front of your pussy for what seemed like an hour. This nigga put a cup just below my pussy so it could collect the cum that dripped as he played with it. He would tell me, "I'm gonna make you fill that shit up tonight." And a few times, he almost came close. He would eat the shit outta my pussy, like he was dining at a buffet. No amount of resistance could be made. When you're tied up in an east-west position, all you can do is squirm and enjoy it. After your body is totally numb and accepting all that this fucking journey is offering, then he would thrust his big, black dick into my swollen pussy and hit it until I cried, good tears of course. I wanted him to stop, but I couldn't speak to tell him.

He made me feel like, I meant something to him. No one has made me ever feel that way. But I knew it was just a fuck, and a good fuck it was, so I would just play along with his ass as long as he wanted to play. When I found out about his wife, I was hurt, 'cause I enjoyed the dick so much I wanted to keep it. But it didn't matter to me one way or the other. Fuck him too. Kenzo had issues that I wasn't ready to deal with, anyway. His shit was extra. One day, we were kicking it, and who pops up but wifey with all her drama. She was screaming at this nigga 'bout his daughter and the time that he wasn't spending with her.

Listening to this bitch rant really fucked me up, but it's not my place to interfere with this nigga and his bitch. She went on until she threw her beer at his ass and tried to walk away. What she didn't know is that shit got on me. I jumped off the ledge where I was sitting and hit that bitch so hard, I don't think she knew what happened. When her teeth went flying by, she realized it, though. I whooped that hoe like she stole my man. See, it was cool with her cussing him out; that was their problem. But never will I let her or any trick-ass hoe disrespect me for any reason. I lit into her ass like lightning. Kenzo was in the background laughing and enjoying the show, just as niggas do. I knocked all that bitch's front teeth out.

She tried to put charges on me for that stupid shit. She said I assaulted her. Shit, that bitch assaulted me with the disrespect! She threw the beer first and I was a minor - case closed. One thing I know, I was the last person in real life that hoe bitch ran up on talking about a nigga. I let that bitch have it, and I'll give it to any other hoe that think she can just run the fuck up on me! Kenzo had gotten into his vehicle right after I beat her ass and went after her. I never saw him again, although he called many times. I guess he wanted to apologize for his actions and get some more of this pussy. But it didn't matter. I was through fuckin' with him, so I never accepted any of the calls. He lied so much to me. Come to find out, the condo that we have been in all this time that I thought was his house, wasn't. It was a fuck nest for the homies. They all had stake in this muthafuckas equally, sharing the expenses. It was a spot where they could play and cheat on their wives. I had to give it to them, it was a fly-ass concept. It had all the necessary amenities for fucking and not much of anything else.

Tonight was the rapper, Mutiny's album release party at Lime Cay. Leslie asked me if I wanted to go with her and her sister. At first, I didn't, cause I was sure to run into Kenzo. It had been six months since the last time I had seen him. After we had our Jerry Springer ordeal. But fuck it, I'll go and show him what he was missing.

As we approached the club, we saw that the line was wrapped around the corner. I'm not one to stand in lines, and the $25 VIP charge was ridiculous, so I began to ease my way towards the security guard. I whispered some shit in his ear that wasn't never gonna happen, but he bought it and we were in, just like that. It was just Manipulation 101.

When the trick-ass bitches that were still standing in the line saw my strategy, they started their hateration, yelling and shit, trying to throw salt on the situation. But them hoes didn't matter. I had game, and all my life I had to deal with that type of shit 'cause my booty was big and my hair was long. That wasn't my fault. Blame it on my fine-ass momma, Joyce Laine. She gave me what I needed, this body and some of her game. I headed towards the bar, which was always my first stop in a club besides the bathroom. Who did I see standing in the corner watching me? Kenzo, with his fine ass. That man knew he had it going on. I tried to act as if I didn't see him. I got the bartender's attention and ordered my usual French Connection, Grand Mariner Hennessy and Martel, straight up. I was on my grown woman shit tonight. Kenzo paid for his drink and tried to pay for mine too, but I refused his offer and paid for my own drink. Then I walked my fine ass away.

Although I wanted and needed him, I ignored his ass. I had all eyes in the place on me, and I loved the attention. I danced my ass off. After the third French Connection, Kenzo was all over me. I wasn't complaining either. We partied until daybreak, ending the night at the fuck nest, buck wild and dead-ass drunk. We fucked until we passed out. The next day, the only thing that I regretted was them damn French Connections. Hell, I look at it like this, I'm leaving next month, and this was a most delightful going away present.

Chapter 16

Well, it's been two months since I talked to Micha. She could have at least called and confirmed that she had gotten the tickets and arrangements. I don't even know her. I'm just gonna chalk it up to the game. I've already done the right thing. I don't even know why I decided to let her come out to California. It could be good or bad. She might actually adapt to this lifestyle and make something of herself. At any rate, I had to take her in. My dad would have wanted me to. She must understand the way I live and the shit I will not tolerate. She must have respect for me, my home, and herself. She assured me that she was gonna do the best she could. We'll see.

Going to LAX Airport always depressed me. The traffic is a nightmare, just too many damn people in California, period. Whenever I fly, it's always private, straight to the airstrip to board the plane and none of this domestic shit. Some say first class is cool, but my thing is, you still gotta stand in the fucked-up lines and walk in that bitch barefoot, exposing your panties in front of the entire airport. It's just not for me. I could have sent a car service to get her, but the anticipation was too much.

As Jah and I approached the airport, we began looking for her among all the other travelers. That's a different kind of experience, especially when you don't know who you're looking for. Not knowing what to expect, who Micha was and more importantly, who she looked like. I said, "Okay, baby, she says she's wearing a red blouse and black boots. Just look for a little girl wearing those colors. I don't know if I'm excited or nervous."

"Everything is gonna work out, Chaney. This is your sister. She family, right?"

"I know, right? But what if she looks like that bitch, Joyce?"

"Baby, don't talk like that. That's your moms."

"Don't go there, Jah! You know how I feel about that bitch."

"Alright. Alright. Micha's just a kid, right?"

"Yeah, she's sixteen years old. Same age I was when I lost my daddy."

"Baby, I'm sure she's been through more shit than you can imagine. Living in them foster homes was probably like living in chain gang."

"I hope she comes here with a different look on life, cause I ain't got time for the bullshit. Oh look! Is that her? Oh my God! She looks exactly like my dad!"

Jah said, "And she damn sure ain't no little girl!" He looked impressed. He looked... I said, "What the fuck that mean, Jah?"

"Nothing, baby. I'm just saying." I looked at the girl again and said, "Damn, she do got a shape." We pulled over to the loading zone, and she was very excited. She looked exactly like my dad and auntie Jackie. She was an attractive young lady.

Jah stepped out to help her with her bags. She got into the vehicle with what seemed like an attitude. But maybe I was tripping. It could be that she's just not comfortable yet. I broke the ice. "Hey, Micha. Welcome to California."

"Thank you, but this isn't my first time here."

"Well, I'm glad you're here now. Are those all your bags?"

"Yep. That's all I got."

"That's cool. I'm gonna take you on a shopping spree. Anyway, we're gonna have fun. Can I have a hug?" I reached towards the back seat. She seemed shy. She said, "Yeah, sure. Why not?"

"Micha, this is my husband, Jah."

"Hello, Jah. What's that short for?"

"Jaheim."

"Oh, Jaheim, that's a nice name." Did I detect a little flirtation in her voice? I was probably overacting, so I brushed it off and said, "Um, anyway. Micha, are you hungry? What's the A like? I haven't been there in a while."

"Well, I don't know how it was when you were there, but it's still the south, if that's an answer."

"Yeah, that good ole southern hospitality, huh?"

"Yep. Chantal, this a nice truck. What's this? One of them Range Rover? All white everything. I heard that, Sis! They said you had money. Said you was one of them boojie bitches."

I looked in the rear view mirror and asked, "Who said that?" She never looked up, just rubbed my leather seats and said, "Mama and them."

"It's just a car, Micha. I work very hard for my money and my things."

"Yeah, I'm sure you do. If it's just a car, can I have it?" This little bitch ain't been here six minutes and she already at it. It's a good thing Jah interrupted that one. He said, "Let's get something to eat, ladies. What y'all got a taste for?"

Micha said, "Jah, you treating?" Again with that voice. Micha suggested that we go to the world-famous Louisiana Chicken, dead smack in the middle of the 'hood on Normandie and Manchester. Jah said, "Oh, yeah. I haven't had that shit in a minute. Let's go!"

I said, "Um, I don't think so. I don't go to that neighborhood or any other in the LA basin."

"Come on, baby. I want some chicken, too. I haven't had any of that shit in years!" I gave in. "Fine, but I'm not getting out of the car." Micha said, "All right, that's cool. Me and my brother-in-law can handle it. Come on, Jah." She grabbed my husband by the hand as if they were a couple. She had barely known him for fifteen minutes! When they closed the doors, I immediately locked them. I spent time in the hood, so I know how that shit go. I'm out here shining like I am and a nigga will get my ass. The parking lot was always filled with common bootleg hustlers, selling everything you needed. I didn't knock their hustle as long as they was on some getting money shit.

When we got home, I just wanted a hot shower and a glass of wine. They can have that chicken. We pulled into the driveway. Micha was in the back seat, taking it all in. I said, "Welcome, Micha. We're home." I don't know if it was jealousy or excitement that Micha felt when she walked into my house. She said, "Chan, is all this one house?" I thought that was cute. She asked me where her room was. I told her, "Upstairs, third door on the left."

Then she asked, "And where is your room?"

What the hell? "Why?"

"I just asked."

"Okay, well go unpack your things. We're gonna have a family meeting after you get settled. There are some things that we need to address." I went upstairs and got comfortable. Micha and Jah went into the kitchen to eat what looked like a bag of grease. Micha was skipping all around the house with a smile on her face. She definitely loved my home. Ms. Micha and I are gonna have to have a long talk about the rules of my shit. I might have to include Jah in that conversation. Since he's been home, his living skills are not what I would like them to be. I should have had a clue that this li'l heifer was gonna be a problem right away, but I was gonna nip that shit in the bud ASAP. I will not let these two come into my world and fuck it up.

Micha said, "Okay, Chantal. I'm ready for the talk." No this heifer didn't! She had the nerve to come downstairs with a wife beater on. Her nipples was busting through that shit and she had some boy shorts on, showing all her ass. Don't nobody walk around this muthafucka like that but me! I went off. "Hell naw! Hold up, Micha! I was gonna hold off on this little meeting until tomorrow cause we all tired and it's been a long day, but check this, little girl. You will not walk around my house exposing your ass and titties in front of my husband, period! Now I suggest you get back the fuck upstairs and put on some clothes. And if you're not gonna be able to deal with that, then I can a call car service and have your ass back on a plane in forty-five minutes to anywhere you wanna go. Let this be the last time I say that."

"Chan, you tripping! I ain't got nothing Jah ain't never seen before. I mean, excuse me, but if he seen one, he seen them all."

"Just go upstairs and change, Micha, and make this the last time we have that conversation." The nerve of this little heifer! She got the right idea, just the wrong bitch. Jah was sitting on the lanai, smoking a blunt and having a beer, which was a normal routine for him. He didn't come to bed until 3:00 that morning. He was on that damn lanai drinking and smoking, playing that damn game all night. He spends more time on that damn game than in the bed with me. When he was in prison, he couldn't get enough of the pussy. Now that the nigga home, he barely touch a bitch. The statistic is right: when a nigga locked down, the dick is faithful and the heart is humble, but once a nigga get out, he realize all that he been missing. He goes after that shit. Good or bad, it don't matter. All that I sacrificed and put myself through, doing the time with him, and all that comes with that shit is worth nothing. A nigga will praise her to the door, but once them chains drop, that nigga will spit in her face at the gate. Or he will slide up under her ass and take and take. Drag a bitch 'til she ain't no good for no other nigga. It's been a long night. Time to get some sleep.

"Good morning, Chaney."

"Hey, Jah. What's up, baby?" I rolled over to give him a morning kiss. "Baby, you stayed on that damn game all night."

"Yeah, I'm fucked up, Chan. Give me some pussy."

"Damn, you must be high."

Jah grabbed my shoulders and said, "Come on, bitch."

"What's the fuck wrong with you? Who you calling a bitch? You ain't that high!"

"Man, come on. Give me some pussy!" His dick was ready, too. Poking me in my ass, trying to get to the spot. He started by sliding his finger in my pussy, making me very wet, one finger at a time. I relaxed and arched my back into a position of comfort so that I could enjoy the finger fuck, even though I was a little irritated by the way this nigga was acting. But shit, this muthafucka finally getting ready to fuck the shit outta me. I ain't gonna fuck that up with no bullshit about being called a bitch! Shit, I'ma be that bitch if I can get a good fuck out this nigga!

So I got into a 69 position and let it happen, blessing his dick. It was what I wanted, what I needed. I kept licking and spitting saliva on the head of his dick. It drove him crazy! I couldn't understand why he didn't want that shit every day. I'd suck the tip, you know, how a baby would suck their pacifier. Maggie Simpson ain't got shit on me! I just kept popping the head in and out of my mouth and grinding the dick as if I was grinding pepper. All the while, I was shaking my ass in his face as he sucked on my pussy. He seemed to always get me wetter than an umbrella. I'm talking soaking wet. Then he would suck all the cum right back out of my ass.

I loved the way I could tell when his dick was getting ready to cum. His main vein would start swelling and throbbing. Sometimes I would stop just at the middle of the erection and jack it in my face. It's the best moisturizer I know. That shit on the market is weak. Blemishes, acne, cum will clear right the fuck up. Let your dude skeet that shit in your face. Then let it sit maybe twelve minutes and rinse with warm water...that shit works!

Anyway, during our lovemaking escapades, I would back that ass up in his face and suck his dick until he skeeted all over the fucking room. There's this game we play sometimes. I installed a cum bull's eye. Basically, it's a round disc that gave off a luminous light. When moistened, it would blink neon purple. It was just one of my bad-ass tricks. I love playing with toys. I placed it on the canopy above the bed. Whenever I sucked Jah's dick and it was time to skeet, I would aim it at the bull's eye. He has yet to hit that muthafucka. One day I'ma make him hit that shit, though.

We were at it full steam. I was definitely cumming in his mouth and he was getting ready to bust in mine. I turned and looked in my mirror and saw Micha standing in the cut, watching us with her finger in her mouth. Seems I wasn't the only one getting pleasure. What does she think she doing? I see we are cut from the same cloth. I'm a freak as well, and sometimes I would invite another freaky bitch in to join, but this shit came with rules. Micha had already begun to break them. I wanted to stop and let her have it, let her know that she needed to respect my privacy, but this shit was feeling too good to stop. So for the moment, she could enjoy the show. I tried to continue sucking Jah's dick. I couldn't get the tip out my mouth fast enough. He was cumming all over the place. I didn't get the chance at that bull's eye. Now I see a bitch gotta start closing her door real tight.

Jah said, "Damn, Chan! You got shit everywhere!"

"I know, right? Get me a warm towel, please. I don't wanna get up just yet."

"If you let that cum lay there and nest, you gonna fuck around and get pregnant. Wouldn't a baby fuck up your business? I mean, that's what you said, right?" I knew where he was going with that shit. He had talked to me on many occasions about starting a family, and I would shine that shit on. Honestly, I don't think I'm ready for a child, not now. Hell, I don't think a child was ready for me! I really needed to get my ass up though and start preparing for my trip and take Micha shopping before I left.

The next morning seemed different, being that I had a little sister in the house. I said, "Good morning, Micha. How was your rest?"

She said, "It felt good to be in a clean, nice comfortable house."

"Well, I'm glad you enjoyed it. I was thinking we could go shopping. I'll be leaving in a couple of days and I wanna make sure you and Jah will be okay while I'm gone."

"Where are you going?"

"Just on a trip for some business." My trip was more pleasure than business, but she didn't have to know that. She asked, "How long will you be gone?"

"Just the weekend."

Micha thought, "I hate this bitch. I don't even know why I'm standing here conversating with her, but it is her house, so whateva. I haven't been here twenty four hours and this hoe already leaving for two days. She said, "That's cool, Chan have fun. I'm gonna go to my room and use the phone."

The shopping experience with Micha was one to definitely remember. She was out of her element. A shopping trip with Chantal Laine is an epic experience. I only shop at the best stores, drink the finest champagne while doing it, and I don't look at price tags. I don't try shit on. A staff of people attend to my every need and want in every store. Along Rodeo Drive, I'm well known in the retail industry. Micha couldn't believe we had spent ten thousand dollars and only had four bags. She kept saying, "Chan, that cost too much. You gonna buy that? She was cute, but at the same time jealous. I spare no expense when it comes to what I want. I thought that H&M would be a perfect place for her to shop. She thought it was boojie. She thanked me, saying, "Chan, I never bought a pair of shoes for fifteen hundred dollars. Hell, I never even had fifteen hundred dollars."

When we returned home, she ran to her bedroom in excitement. She even thanked me several times. I knew that she wasn't used to having shit and her appreciation was thanks enough. Jah passed her in the hallway and he could see the excitement on her face, too. He was on his way out, as usual. Micha ran to call her friend Kenzo, whoever that was. She said, "How are you?"

"I'm good, and you?"

"Shit, bored! It's been three months since I been here in Cali, and this shit is boring! All these crackers and shit...I'm outta my element! Boujie-ass muthafuckas! I would really like for you to come see me, if you can."

"Hell, yeah! I'm down for Cali! Shit, I always wanted to go to California. I need a vacation, mon! Stupid-ass bitch is getting on my nerves and this job tripping!"

"Oh, you still going through that foolishness with your wife?"

"That bitch ain't my wife. Don't start that shit, Micha!"

"Yeah, whatever. I'll make all the arrangements. Leave it to me."

Kenzo said, "Is that right? You mean to tell me you're gonna buy me a ticket to California and put me in a mansion while I'm there?"

"Nope, my sister is."

"Damn, that's what's up! Let me know when to go to the airport."

Micha said, "I'll call you in two days with your itinerary. How long did you say you could stay?"

"Shit, baby, get me some one-way shit and we'll take it from there! If you got it like that, I can stay as long as you want me to!"

"Bye, Kenzo."

"Yeah, mon, bomclaud rasta fucking right! I'm going to California!"

Chapter 17

My flight was leaving in the morning and it couldn't be soon enough. Jah stayed out all night in my damn car again. As I was walking out the door, here he comes, pulling up in the driveway. I snatched my keys out his hand and didn't say shit to him. Teron sent a car service for me and the timing was perfect. I was very excited and ready to go, Micha was so devious and transparent. I could see the hate that she had for me when I left. I wondered what I would return to, but for now, I'm not thinking of any of that. Just Teron and his big black dick and this wonderful time that awaited me. The car pulled onto the landing strip and there he was, holding a million pink roses in his hands. He had the biggest smile on his face.

He said, "Chan! My God, you look exquisite." He always complimented me, even if I had on jeans. My intention was to fuck all over that plane, so I wore a really short mini with easy access. He was in for all kinds of surprises this weekend, he just didn't know it. The private jet was fully stocked with champagne, food, and Chantal in red stilettos. I couldn't wait to fuck this nigga! When we were in the air, I was ready. I'm a nympho. I needed sex like a vampire needed blood. I didn't give a fuck about nobody but what I needed and wanted, literally! Teron kept saying that he wanted to love all of me- mind, body, and soul. Said that sex didn't have to play a major part in that. He said, "Besides, I don't want the white boy to see us. Just wait till we get to the island, Chan."

"What white boy? Who? The fucking pilot?" My God, if only this nigga knew. The pilot can join in! Watching ain't shit. Besides, he was paid to fly the fucking jet. Do that! But Teron was such a gentleman. I knew I would have to wait. The itinerary was for three days in paradise. Teron suggested we take a nap, saying how tired he was and when we wake up we would go out to dinner. This is not what I had hoped for upon arrival. I wanted to fuck and he talking about he tired. What is the problem with these niggas turning this pussy down? To make it worse, these the mafuckas that I'm willing to fuck for free! Just goes to show you can't just give to a nigga. He gotta earn it in order to appreciate it. Him not wanting to fuck irritated the hell out of me. He made up for it, though. Our little vacay was more than anything that I ever knew or been exposed to. He treated me like a queen the entire weekend, loving on me, caressing me and holding me in his arms. We did very little fucking.

Instead, he showed me how to be with someone intimately. He made love to my soul, just as he said he would do. We didn't talk about business, home, or any other irrelevant subjects. We just held each other close and whispered softly in conversations, and to be honest, I liked it. For the first time, I enjoyed the company of a man. Granted, I could never, and I mean never, imagine someone like me with someone like Teron. We had a memorable time in Antigua, but all good things must come to an end. This escapade was only for the moment. It was time to get back to my madness.

Meanwhile, Micha was back at my house causing all kinds of drama. Micha said, "Hey, Jah."

"What's up, Micha?"

Micha shook her head. Look at this muthafuckas. He just as lame as his bitch. She said, "I see you like football. Who's your team?"

"The Sea Hawks, no doubt."

"Is that right? Who is this playing now?"

"The Saints and the Falcons."

"Oh. Do you mind if I get one of your Heinekens?"

"Naw, go ahead, Micha."

Micha grabbed a beer and made herself comfortable. "So who's winning?"

Jah finally turned his attention to Micha. He asked, "Do you know anything about football, Micha?"

"Naw, I just like to see niggas watch the game. The passion they have for the sport is kinda sexy."

She definitely had his attention now. He said, "Really?"

"Yeah, really. So, Chan's on a trip, huh? Shit, she got more business than Wall Street. What does Chantal do for a living?"

Jah answered, "She's a consultant. Why didn't you ask her, Micha?"

"A consultant? Is that what she calls it?"

"You know what, Micha? If you sit down and talk to your sister and establish a relationship, which is what she wants to have with you, I'm sure she would tell you all you need to know."

"Is that right, Jah? Has she told you everything you need to know? I see she got you fooled like the rest of these mafuckas round here."

"What you talking about?" She had his undivided attention now. She was gonna play him, just as planned. Micha asked, "Do you know the truth, Jah?"

He said, "Look, Micha. I love Chantal for who she is, period."

"Is it because you don't care, or because you're too afraid to know the truth."

"What truth? What you talking about?"

"Jah, Chantal sells her pussy for money. It's about time you knew, bruh."

Jah sat up in his chair. "What the fuck you say, Micha?"

"She a hoe, Jah."

"Get the fuck outta here! Don't be saying no shit like that!"

"Don't sit here and tell me you didn't know that this bitch is selling her ass all over the hills of Beverly. It's a whole lot to her story, Jah. Do you even know the story?" At this point, Jah was completely silent. The pain in his eyes reflected the hurt. At that moment, Micha knew this shit was gonna be easy. She said, "Jah, you straight?"

"Yeah, Micha. I'm good. Let's freeze up on this conversation. I'ma holla at you later, aight?"

"That's what's up. I'm gonna go take a shower. You wanna join me?" Jah seemed to have gone into another space and time. He looked at her with a blank stare, probably from the shock of what he had just heard. Micha tried to conceal the fact that his lame ass was hurt, but really, she was pleased by it. She asked again, "I asked if you wanna join me in the shower."

He just looked at her with a smirk on his face and a lump in his throat. She laughed and went upstairs. Jah was mad as hell. He cranked the TV up loud and started drinking the hard shit, even sparked a blunt right there in the family room. He never smoked in the house. Micha realized that the shit was gonna hit the fan tonight. She couldn't wait for Chantal to get home. She thought, "Ha, ha. Moms is gonna be proud!"

Upon returning home, I could see all that had been going on from right where I was standing. The foyer was dingy and the house smelled horrible. The scent of weed was in the air and it was very strong. I put my bag down and glanced over at the mail. A letter from Joyce...here we go! It was addressed to both me and Micha. I thought that was strange. I guess the hoe gotta save stamps so she put two letters in one envelope. I'll read this shit later. I'm sure it didn't say much anyway. My mini vacay was super awesome, but return to this bullshit, I must. I shouted, "Hey, I'm home. Who's here?" The TV was at maximum volume. "Micha, you here? Jah? Where are you guys?"

I stepped down into the family room and there was Jah, laid out on the couch drunk, high or whatever. I was heated. "Jah, wake up! Wake up!" I tried to shake him back to reality, but he just shrugged in a leave-me-alone kind of way. I wanted to let him have it about smoking weed in my house and all these empty bottles everywhere. We already had an understanding about this shit, but this muthafucka was doing what he wanna do. I shook him again. "Jah, wake up!"

"Oh, hey Chantal."

I turned around at the sound of my sister's voice. "What's up, Micha?"

"Nothing. He been like that for about two hours now. "He was watching the game, drinking tequila out the bottle, and smoking weed until he passed out. He straight, I guess. Just drunk."

"What else has been going on?"

"Nothing. I just lounged around and Jah watched the games all weekend. Rosa came. I told her that I would clean the house and she didn't have to work today."

"So why the hell didn't you clean up, Micha?"

"I fell asleep."

"Micha, since you been here, you have been basically doing you, and that's not cool. Don't get me wrong, for a grown muthafucka, it's cool. I wouldn't have a problem with it, 'cause you would be taking care of yourself. But since I'm your guardian and sole provider, you gonna have to offer respect and gratitude. Disrespecting me and mine is a problem. You can't come into my house and tell my maid that I don't need her. You cannot come in my house and walk around as if it's yours, half-naked. I need you to respect my space, and all that come with that. Do you understand me?"

"Huh?"

"You heard me, Micha! I'ma tell you like this, we're starting off in a real negative way, little sister. I want us to bond and be BFF's. There's so much that I can teach you. Dad gave me so much, and I would love to share all those things with you. I'm glad you're here. I know it's different for both of us, but I think if we just respect one another's space, we can do this. Scooby would have wanted it that way.

"Who"

"Dad"

"No, what did you call him?"

"I called him Scooby. It's just a nickname I gave him."

"Why? You didn't call him daddy?"

"Of course I did. I called him all things because he was all things. He was a great guy, Micha. A remarkable man. You would have loved him."

"Really, Chan? Would I have loved him the same way that you did?"

"I'm sure you would have, Micha. It was impossible not to."

"Do you think he would have had sex with me, too?"

I stepped closer to her. "What did you say?" Although I knew what she said and where it came from, the words cut like a knife. Cut right through all the pain, all the hate, in a matter of seconds. The secret had surfaced. Someone else knew, and that someone only knew one side of the truth. The night Joyce killed Scooby, in the eyes of the law, it was for him putting his hands on her, not for having sex with me. That was our truth. Only three people knew. One was dead and the other locked up and dead to me. I tried to shine it on, but she came full throttle with the question again. "Huh, Chantal? Do you think dad would have fucked me the way that he fucked you? To the point of falling in love with him?"

I actually didn't know how to respond. "Micha, first of all, watch your mouth. Now I don't know where you got your information, but dad didn't fuck me, as you put it."

"Really? What do you call it, sis? Sex?"

"No, Micha, and I'm tired of this conversation, okay? One day I hope to be able to tell you exactly what Dad did for me and to me."

"Why not now?"

"It's just not the right time, Micha." I knew then that our secret wasn't a secret anymore.

"Chantal, can I ask you question?" Butterflies fluttered in my belly, but I answered, "What is it, Micha?" I stood there in complete shock, trying to ignore her. She said, "You know that disrespect that you're stressing about your house and your business and all your things? How you want me to respect that and respect this? Did you give Mama that kind of respect while you was fucking her man? Is that the same or was it different?"

I was speechless. And that was definitely a first for me. But she didn't know the whole story. Or maybe she did. One thing I knew, this little bitch had motives. She hit me where it hurt. No one can touch me there, but somehow she had managed to get to that place. I've never looked at it the way she just put it. For once, I stepped out of my own shell and looked in the mirror and didn't like it. She continued on and said, "I'm listening, Chantal. Enlighten me."

"Micha, you don't know what the fuck you talking about, little girl! Wherever you got your information from, I suggest you go back and tell that muthafucka to mind they business."

"Shit, it was they business, Chantal!" I knew then that it was Joyce that fed it to her. Jah came into the kitchen right on time. I didn't wanna entertain this shit no way. I said, "Hey baby. You want a juice?" Micha didn't let up. She said, "Oh, okay. You wanna change the subject, Chantal? That's what's up. I thought you would."

"Micha, we will return to that conversation at another time, I promise you." This little girl really got me fucked up sideways. She don't know who the fuck she dealing with! I've tried to be open to this shit, but I see I'ma have to check this li'l bitch the way she should've been checked at the door. In an effort to close this conversation I suggested we get dinner. I turned to Jah and asked, "Hey baby, you hungry?" The look Jah had given me was one that I had never seen before.

"Naw, I ain't hungry."

"You not hungry?"

"No, I'm not. Is that a problem?"

"Damn, what's wrong with you, Jah?"

"Nothing. Come upstairs. Let me holla at you for a minute." I went to Micha and said, "Here's my credit card. Get some Kung Pao chicken, eggrolls, fried rice, and whatever else, okay?"

"Okay." Micha thought to herself, "I hope Jah gives it to that bitch straight with no chaser. She talking about respect and gratitude, wanting to be my BFF. Fuck that hoe, fucking my daddy and hurting my mama!

I couldn't understand why Jah was so angry and wanting to talk to me. When I entered the bedroom, he had already gotten into the shower. Talking over the running water, I told him I had gifts for him from my trip. When I asked him what was wrong, he screamed, "Chantal, I don't care 'bout no fucking Gucci and gifts and shit! What you been doing all weekend and where did you go?" Oh shit! I tried to play it off and said, "Jah, I work." He got out the shower and came over to the bed with a towel wrapped around his waist. He said, "Man, you still out there fucking with them tricks?"

"What are you talking about?"

"Chantal, don't play me. You heard what the fuck I said!"

"I heard you, it's just the tone you giving it in." I was stalling and he knew it.

"I don't give a fuck how I said it. Just answer the question, bitch!"

"Jah, you tripping like you don't know what it is. You know who I am and what I do!"

"Bitch, I'll slap the shit outta your ass with that bullshit! I thought we had an understanding about that shit! I'm home now. The hoeing stops. I want a family, point blank." I sat there listening to this rest-haven-ass nigga talking 'bout the hoeing stops. I said, "Nigga, don't you know that's how you living and eating in this mafucka? It's my job, my life, all I know. And Jah, I ain't gonna be too many of them bitches."

"Fuck you, Chantal. You got your li'l sister hollering at me, sayin' you a hoe. Selling pussy all over Beverly Hills and shit."

"Is that right? That's what she said? Hold up." I yelled for Micha two, maybe three times before she came. Meanwhile, Jah was still going in. He said, "No, you hold up. I ain't finished, Chantal." He went into the closet to get dressed. I wasn't tryna hear that. I wanted Micha's ass. I said, "No, fuck that! Wait a minute, Jah." I yelled, "Micha, bring your ass in here! You probably listening at the door anyway!"

Micha popped her head in the door. "Yeah, Chantal? Damn, what's wrong?"

"What's wrong? You sitting up here, telling Jah that I'm a hoe and selling my pussy?"

"Chan, I didn't say it like that. She looked over at Jah as if the words were a weapon. She said in a loud tone, "And Jah know it. He said you were out handling business, and I said something like you had business all over the hills of Beverly."

Jah moved towards Micha and said, "You a damn liar! You said she was a high-priced hoe. Don't be lying, little bitch! I will slap the fuck outta you!"

"Yeah, put your hands on me mafucka, and that ass will be on a one-way ticket back to that prison from which you came! Fuck with me if you want to, Jah!" Micha turned on his ass in a second and screamed, "Chantal, you better get your man, as you call him."

"Okay, okay, both of y'all stop! Micha, I will talk with you later. Close the door behind you." She looked at Jah and said, "That's what I thought, lame-ass muthafuckas. I don't see you jumpin!" I guess Jah wasn't about to take that shit off her. He lunged towards her, breaking my Tiffany lamp on the nightstand, trying to reach her. She turned around with vengeance and hate in her eyes and dared him to touch her.

"Okay, you two need to stop!" I pulled Jah back and yelled at Micha to leave the room. "Damn! You muthafuckas breaking up my shit, acting like kids." Jah said, "Chan, this shit is your fault, with your lies and shit! I'm outta here before I hurt one of you bitches." He grabbed the keys and ran down the stairs. The only problem is that he grabbed the wrong keys. I think that was on purpose. I said, "Hold up, them the wrong keys!"

"I don't give a fuck, Chantal. Get out of my way!"

"Don't take my car, Jah!"

"Fuck you, Chantal. One thing I do know, you better have a decision when I come back." He walked out and slammed the door. I don't believe this shit! This nigga tried to threaten me. I don't play that shit! That's where the fuck this nigga lost me. He left and pulled out of the driveway in a mad fury. I tried to run to the garage to let this nigga know that's a Bentley, bitch, and you don't treat my shit like that, but he was already gone. That's a nigga for you. Instead of him driving his BMW that I bought, he chose to fuck up my shit. I looked up the driveway and saw the food delivery guy. Amid all this bullshit, I couldn't even look at him. I've always held order around my house, and this shit was spiraling out of control. My appetite was gone at this point.

Micha paid for the food and came into the kitchen. I had a few words for her. "Look, Micha. First off, I don't appreciate your attitude. That's the one thing that will get you fucked up. Play with me and I'ma show you something."

"What's that, huh? You threatening me, Chantal?" She looked at me without fear.

"No, that's a promise, Micha. I don't know what's wrong with you. Maybe it's those damn homes you been in all your life. But in this home, there is structure. You know, rules you must follow.

"Oh Chantal, I'm so sick of your rules. Rule this, rule that."

"Well you can always go back where the fuck you came from, Micha. I think you seriously got a problem. If it's help that you need, we can get the best in the business. But if you think you're gonna play with it, you can go upstairs and pack your shit ASAP. You understand?"

"Yeah, I do. Can you hand me a plate?"

"Damn, did you hear anything I said, little girl?"

"Yeah, I heard you."

"Well tighten the fuck up."

"Chantal, I did hear you. No more, what you call it? Fantastic foolishness? And that thing with Jah? I will apologize when he come back. Now let's eat. I'm starving!" I knew she was trying to change the subject. Cooking? I don't cook for nobody. She said, "Really? You never cooked a meal in this nice kitchen? You're kidding!"

"Hell naw! I go out or call this chef named Tony. He will come over and make me anything that my little heart desires." Micha was obviously impressed. She said, "Shit, let's call him now!"

"See, that's what I'm talking bout, bitch! Don't let me find out that you done called this muthafucka to come cook up some shit, you feel me?"

"I know, Chan. That's fantastic foolishness, right?"

"Hell yeah, Micha! We shared a laugh, and I couldn't be mad at her. We was cut from the same damn cloth. Wasn't no raising her. That was done. She is who she is now, and it was my obligation to lace her with the game. But that's only if she wanted it. She had the body and the potential. Scooby taught me well enough to pass it on to her. After all, it's in her DNA, but she gotta want it. I said, "Micha, you crazy, girl!"

"You too, Chan. I guess we get it from Mama." Hell naw! I didn't get shit from her ass! But I didn't wanna ruin the moment so I kept my thoughts to myself. We just sealed it with laughter, which was the first time that I saw Micha smile. Hell, that was the first time I had laughed since I can remember.

Jah went over to his sister's house and took all his anger with him. He called Quilla on the way. "Qulla, I'm pulling up on you. Open the door." When he reached the door, Qilla said, "What's going on, baby?" Jah closed the door behind him. His sister could see the hurt in his eyes. He said, "Shit, I'm just irritated with Chantal. She act as if a nigga not there. That's why I stay gone. I try to talk to her, and she just dismisses my conversation with 'I don't wanna hear it'. Man, Qui, I'm ready to go. It's time for a nigga to change the channel. I should be home enjoying my life and happy, not all fucked up about this bitch. She a good bitch, don't get it fucked up. She just got her priorities fucked up. His phone rang. He smiled when he saw who it was. He answered, saying, "Hey baby, what's up? Sitting here talking to my sister."

The caller said, "That's cool. Are you gonna come see me tonight?"

"Of course I am!"

"Okay, I'll be waiting for you."

"That's what's up!" Jah hung the phone up and looked at Quilla with a huge smile on his face.

"Was that Chan?" Quilla asked.

"No, it was Tanya."

"Oh, so you cheating on Chantal?" Quilla's emotions were mixed.

"Sis, that's what I been trying to tell you. I'm tired of her shit. She don't listen to me, she don't fuck me, and she don't love me."

Quilla said, "It's not cool to cheat. Don't you know if she finds out how hurt she gonna be?"

Jah said, "Shit, she don't give a fuck! I'ma holla at you later. I gotta go. Love you." He got up to leave, but Quilla stopped him. "Wait a minute." But Jah wasn't having it. He said, "Naw, I'm going were I'm wanted. I love you. I'll call you, okay?" Then he was gone. Quilla immediately made a phone call.

"Hello, Chantal speaking."

Quilla decided to tread lightly. She said, "Hey girl, hey how you doing?"

"Good, I guess."

"Jah just left here. What's wrong with y'all now?"

"Shit, Quilla, these mafuckas in my house trying to run it. You know I love your brother but this shit is out of control."

Quilla said, "Well he was saying something about you don't love him."

"Quilla, you know I do. He just tripping. Ever since Micha moved in, shit just been off."

"Like what?"

"Well, you know I keep like $6000 on the dresser under my jewelry box, right? Just loose change in the house. Well, when I returned home it was gone. At first I thought maybe Jah took it, but when I mentioned it to him, he didn't know what I was talking about. I know I'm not losing my mind. I know that li'l bitch done stole my money. I'm so done, and very drained. Can we finish this conversation tomorrow? "Good night, sis."

Micha was down stairs eating. These two mafuckas need to realize this is my money and my house and if they wanna continue to be here, they need to shut the fuck up and have several seats. I called Auntie Jackie. "Hey, Auntie, can you meet me for lunch at your favorite spot tomorrow, my treat? I need to talk."

She said, "Okay, sweetie. Is everything okay?"

"Yeah, I just wanna be with you." "

"Ok, Chan. I'll grab a table around noon." 208 Rodeo was a fabulous secluded spot with outside seating, perfect on a nice evening such as this. Meeting with Auntie Jackie was just the relief

I needed. "Hello, sweetheart," she greeted me when she arrived. "How you been?"

"I'm good, and you auntie?"

"Fabulous, darling. You look absolutely drained, my love. What's wrong?"

I immediately unloaded on her. "Oh, Auntie, I am! Micha has come into my space and caused nothing but havoc. She stealing, lying. I can't take all this drama that she has brought to my life. She's evil, Auntie, with malicious intentions.

Aunt Jackie said, "Chaney, I want you to watch her with every eye and ear that you have from this point on. She is wicked and out to harm you. If you summon the third eye on her, not only will you be on point for whatever she has for you, but she will know that you're not to be played with. You must remember, she's Joyce's child."

I said, "Shit, Auntie, I'm Joyce's child, too."

"Yeah, but you're a true Laine, and that carries a lot with this family. Just remember, my sweet one, don't let her run your house. She is a child, and that is your home. Take control of it. Hell, send her ass back where she came from. Not only does she have you looking bad, but I can imagine the state of your home. Rosa told me that she didn't know what was wrong with you. She said you didn't want her to clean anymore."

I said, "Oh, that's another thing. Micha has been telling her that she's not needed and sending her away. Can you please call her and apologize to her for me?"

"It's done. She will be there Thursday with a special crew to sanitize the entire house." I laughed and said, "Auntie, it ain't that bad. Okay, where is that waiter? I'm starving!" We sat there sharing laughter and food. She was my favorite girl. Whenever were together, we enjoyed each other's conversation. I thought about what auntie had said. How could I let this child come into my space and disrupt it? But that shit stops, and it stops today. I'll send her ass back to Atlanta or wherever she wanna go, but this shit is over! I've tried with this one, and that's something I don't usually do.

Chapter 18

Micha was at home and decided to take a walk around the neighborhood. I guess she was looking to get into some more fuck shit. I don't know what she was looking for. There were only upper class, rich white folks in this sector and fitting in... Well, she wouldn't now or ever. She's damaged goods. When she met Freeno that day, I don't think she knew exactly what was to come from that grimey ass nigga. There he was, standing in the driveway on his phone. She approached him with a sashay and said, "Damn, boo. Who are you?"

"I'm Freeno, baby. Who are you?"

"My name is Micha."

"Well, pleased to meet you Micha. You live around here?"

"Yeah, third house on the right."

Freeno was surprised. He said, "Hold up. You live in that house right there?" Michashould have known this nigga had motives by his sudden change in interest. She said, "Yeah, why?"

"You know Chantal?"

"She my sister. Why? You know her?" Freeno decided to play this out and see where it led. He said, "Naw not really."

"What you mean, not really? It's either you know her or you don't."

"Well I don't know the bitch personally, but I know of her ass. I ran into her a couple of years ago. I mean, not to talk about your sister, but that bitch ain't shit!"

Instead of defending Chantal, Micha said, "You good. I agree, she is a bitch." They thought that was super funny. She asked him, "You live here?" Freeno said "Naw, my uncle live here."

"Damn! I didn't know black people lived around here other than the bitch in the third house on the right." She laughed so hard, but he didn't crack a smile. He said, "I never seen no black people, other than your boojie ass sister. My Uncle Black been living here for a while. He just ain't never home. Micha thought it was refreshing to meet someone that wasn't stuck up. Freeno was a little older than her, but he was a real one in her eyes. Freeno looked at her closely and asked, "So Micha, how old are you, if you don't mind me asking?"

"No, I don't, as long as you won't mind when I ask you the same question. I'm twenty, Freeno." He knew better than that. He said, "Really? You look much younger than that."

"Yeah, well I take care of myself. How old are you?"

"I'm an old man. Turning thirty-five in two weeks."

"How will you celebrate, Freeno?" She gave him a flirty smile.

"I don't know. Maybe with a new friend that I just met."

Micha turned coy and said, "Who, me? Um, I don't know 'bout that."

"Why not Micha? Can I have your number and call you so you can let me know? Come on, you know you want to right now. Ain't nothing to think about. I mean, look at me, shit!"

"Look at you, and what? You ain't all that, sir."

Freeno laughed and said, "We look good together, though. Holla at me. I'm gonna give you my number."

Still playing innocent, Micha said, "But I don't even know you."

"Okay, that's fair. Just take the number and call me to let me know if I can have your number. How about that? Cause I like what I see."

"Umph, that's cute. I gotta go, Mr. Freeno."

"Goodbye, beautiful." Freeno was super excited. He told his uncle that he had just ran into a li'l bitch named Micha. Said she was Chantal's sister. He asked if he knew her.

"Naw, can't say I do. Maine only had one daughter, Chantal. Bout how old is she?"

"Sixteen, seventeen at the most. She tried to tell me she was twenty."

Black thought for a moment, then said, "If she sixteen or seventeen, that would mean she must be from a trick, cause Maine been gone damn near eighteen years now."

"Yeah, that's probably good he gone, cause if that muthafucka was alive today, I'd make sure I took care of his ass instead of his bitch doing it."

"Come on now, AJ. That was a long time ago."

"Black, you the only muthafucka that calls me AJ!"

"Shit, that's 'cause you every bit of that nigga Tonio."

"Yeah? Well, I never got a chance to meet him cause of that Maine nigga."

"He was a cool dude, Freeno. He took care of you and your momma. He loved y'all. He was real educated and shit, you know? Just addicted to the pussy.

"Getting killed over a trick bitch... I guess that is an addiction. It's the main reason I gives no love to a bitch. This fucking Maine nigga fucked up me and my mom's lives. Now his little princess-bitch daughter living on top of a hill looking down at a muthafucka like she own this fucking universe and everybody in it! I been hating this bitch forever!"

***

Teron and I hadn't spoken since returning from Antigua. He had dropped over some blueprints several days ago that I still hadn't looked over. When I decided to take a look at them, he called. What a coincidence. He wanted to meet for lunch to talk. I accepted his request. Micha and I really hadn't said two words to one another since she had the nerve to disrespect me, however I did feel better after our conversation. She said she would try to do better and apologized for being disrespectful. With all of her boo hoo tears, I decided to give her another chance. I see what Lance meant. When I arrived at the restaurant, Teron was very reserved and spoke in a hushed tone. "Hello, Chantal." He pulled the chair out for me. I said "Hello, Teron."

"Thank you for meeting me today."

"It's my pleasure, Teron."

"So how you been?"

"I can't complain. Just a lot going on. It's taking my time to the maximum. I miss your company, though."

"I miss you, too. The last couple days has been crazy for me as well. Shall we order first?"

Something didn't feel right. I said, "Naw, I need a drink. A strong one." The waiter came over and took our drink orders. I noticed that Teron came bearing gifts, as always. After three martinis, our table was ready. We sat down for lunch. I asked, "So what's going on with you?"

"Just business, and that's something that I wish not to speak about. I'd much rather enjoy you for a moment, Ms. Chantal. First, I have something to give you, and second, I have something to tell you. So here is a gift for you in appreciation to a most wonderful time in Antigua." I wasn't surprised. I give the ultimate experience for the ultimate price and it's well worth it. Niggas will pay for this pussy and don't even know it. It was kinda different with him, just kinda though. I said, "Oh, Teron, you don't have to gift me whenever you see me!" I was saying that shit, but I was excited to see what was in the baby-blue Tiffany gift bag. "A yellow diamond tennis bracelet! This is beautiful, Teron. Thank you so much!"

"Chantal, accept the gift and the love I give to you."

"I will, and thank you again."

"You're very welcome, and very worthy." Then he became very serious. He said. "Now, so as not to spoil the evening, I need to tell you something, Chantal." I was getting a little nervous, so I said, "Let's eat first. You can tell me after." Teron was a very spiritual person, so praying over our food was a must. He held both my hands over the meal and blessed it. I never saw the purpose in that, but it was his culture. As always, we enjoyed a most wonderful evening. The news that he wanted to share with me couldn't overshadow the intimacy that we shared. Whatever the news was, I was ready.

"Well, Chan, the other day I called your house and I spoke with your sister. At least that's who she said she was."

Oh, shit. I said, "Yeah, that's my sister, Micha."

"She informed me that you were in the shower and said that you told her to tell me to come on over. Said that you would see me when I got there. I thought was strange but since you had supposedly given the okay, I came. My visit was for the purpose of bringing the blueprints. Well, upon my arrival, Micha invited me in and showed me to the family room. I thought that was odd, but at any rate, I went and had a seat, as instructed. She told me that you were getting dressed and that she was gonna go see if you were ready. I waited maybe twenty minutes, and then there she was, standing in front of me in G-string panties and nothing else. Maybe a pair of your shoes, not sure. She approached me in a very seductive manner. When I tried to get off the couch, she threw herself on top of me, leaving me no choice but to strong-hand her. I threw her to the side and released myself from her grasp. She began screaming and hollering at the top of her lungs, saying she was better than you and I would enjoy her more. She seemed possessed, Chan. My only thought was to get my shit and leave, cause I didn't wanna hurt your sister."

I couldn't believe what Teron was telling me. I asked, "Are you serious, Teron?"

"Yes. I tried to call when I got to the car, but you wouldn't answer. That's why I needed to meet with you today."

I was completely embarrassed. I said, "Wow, I'm speechless, Teron! I apologize for her actions."

"How can you apologize for her, Chantal? She knew exactly what she was doing. She lured me there and I guess tried to rape me." We both thought that was the funniest thing of the day. We enjoyed the laugh and our cocktails. He gently kissed my forehead and escorted me to my car. I wanted to kill this bitch. I had to call Quilla. When she answered, I said, "Quilla, bitch, you ain't gonna believe this shit!" Quilla said, "What's up?"

"Bitch, this little whore done tried Teron. He just told me that the other day, this heffa done tried to rape him!"

"Girl, what the hell?"

"Yeah, he came over to drop off the blueprints, and she comes downstairs half-naked. He said she was screaming like the exorcist had taken control of her ass. Some shit about she better than me and all kinds of fuck shit. I don't know what's wrong with her, but I do know that she's a manipulating, lying-ass little slut. I thought that I would be able to bond with this bitch, but she on a whole nuther level. Those group homes and shit distorted her fucking brain!"

Quilla said, "Chantal, it ain't gonna get no better from here, so what you going to do?"

"I don't know. I'm on my way home now."

"Okay. Call me when you get there. I'm gonna get up and come over."

"Okay, I'll call you later. Let me go deal with this shit first." I hung the phone up and drove home as fast as I could so I could deal with this slut of a sister.

When I returned home that evening, no one was there. The next morning, I was awakened by the phone ringing. I hadn't sleep very well. Jah didn't come home until 4:30 and he slept downstairs. By the time I awoke, he was gone.

"Chantal! Chantal!" Why is this girl hollering at the top of her lungs? I could barely get downstairs fast enough. "What is it, Micha? Damn! And why are you yelling like that?"

"Hey, Sis. I'm so excited! I was wondering if I could have a little company?"

"And when is this going to happen, Micha?"

"This weekend."

"Yeah, okay, Micha. Whatever. Just clean up after they leave, okay?"

"Can I use your car to go and picked them up?"

"My car? How many coming? When you say 'them', is it just one or many?"

"Just one, Chan."

"I see we're gonna have to buy you a car cause you using any of mine is not something I'm comfortable with. I guess you can drive the Range make sure you fill the tank when you're done, okay?"

"But I don't have any cash. Can you give me some money?"

"Here's $200. That should be enough for gas and dinner. Jah is out of town on business and I won't be home until late tomorrow evening. Please lock up the house when you leave and set the alarm, okay?"

"I will. What time did you say that you'll be home?" Sneaky lil bitch. I said, "I didn't say cause I don't know what time. Just make sure you take care of the house and be careful in my vehicle, okay?"

Micha picked up Kenzo from the airport. Micha thought, "I gotta ask this bitch for my money, and then she give me $200 talking bout her cars and her money and whatnot. I got something for this bitch... Oh, I got something for this bitch." Aloud, she said, "Hey, Kenzo. Welcome to California."

"Irrah, mon. It feels like a fresh Jamaican breeze here in California."

"The weather here is wonderful. That's the best thing about this place."

"Ya, mon. You don't like it here?"

"It's okay. It's mostly business for me, so it's cool for the moment."

"So, mon, you must be living in the sky with the stars? You sho nuff riding good." Kenzo looked all over the Range Rover's interior.

"Yeah, this my sister's shit." As they drove up to the house, Kenzo was utterly impressed. "Damn, mon, is this where we laying? It's a palace fit for a king!" Micha thought that was funny. She loved the way he winded when he talked with that Caribbean drawl. "Yes indeed, Kenzo. Welcome."

"Yeah, mon. So, what's in store for us?"

Micha thought about it for minute and smirked. She said, "We're gonna fuck in every room."

"No shit, mon? I'm with that for sure, lovely!"

When I got home, I thought the house was empty. "Micha? I'm home, Micha. Where are you?" I entered my home and looked around at her surroundings. Damn, why was every light and the TV on? Oh, hell no! The kitchen was a mess! And what's that smell? I guess she told Rosa not to come again. I'm sick of this li'l bitch, for real!

"Micha, where the hell are you?" There were clothes, shoes, socks, and all kinds of mess all over the living room.

I approached Micha's bedroom door. I could smell the sex in the air. I know damn well this girl is not in my house fucking! As the bedroom door swung open, there she was riding the dick of some African muthafucka! "Micha, have you gone damn crazy? Who is this in my house?"

"Damn, Chan! I told you that I was having company!"

"Company? Look like this muthafucka done moved in! He got luggage and shit! Come here. Let me talk to you. And you..." I pointed at the dude in the bed. "You get dressed and get the fuck outta my house!"

"Chan, why you tripping?"

"What you mean, why am I tripping? You fucking a stranger in my house, and you tired to rape one of my friends!"

"He's not a stranger, Chantal. He's my boyfriend and your friend lying on me."

"Hold up. Your boyfriend?"

"Well, I didn't think it was that important to you who he was."

"Why would you think that he wouldn't be of importance when he was gonna be in my house fucking my little sister? You're not grown, Micha."

"You might not think so, but I been on my own my whole fucking life, Chantal. Neither you nor anybody else gave a fuck about me, so fuck you!"

"Fuck me? Look, Micha, you can get the fuck outta my house. You and this broke-ass nigga!" I had enough of this bitch, sister or not.

Micha said, "This between you and me, Chantal. Leave him out of this."

"As soon as he get the fuck outta my house, I'll leave him out of this!"

"He can't just leave. He lives in Atlanta."

"Atlanta? Well, he need to make him some reservations to get his ass back."

"Chan, he ain't got no money."

What the fuck? "What you mean, he ain't got no money? If that ain't a bitch! You not only got a strange-ass nigga in my house, but he a broke ass-nigga, too! Micha, you need to tighten up, little girl. I'm gonna give you five minutes to figure out a plan to get this broke-ass nigga outta my house!"

"Chan, can you give me $500 so I can get him a ticket back home?"

"Hell, naw! I don't pay broke ass-niggas, they pay me. You got me fucked up! I'm only going to say this once: get his ass home the best way you can. He can walk, for all I care!"

"Damn, mon! Why your sista tripping like dat?"

"She just a hateful bitch. Don't mind her. If you can't leave, you can't leave. What she going to do, put you out?"

"Mon, I don't want to be in the middle of you and your sista's controversy."

"Just chill, Kenzo. I got this. She ain't nothing to worry about, trust me. I got this. Sister, please, can I talk to you?"

"Hell no! I want him out of my house ASAP!"

"But he can't get home right now. He don't have no money."

"Look, Micha, this is against everything I believe in. I'm gonna give you money for a bus ticket cause I want him out of my fucking house."

"The bus?" Micha had the nerve to look like I was the crazy one.

"Hell yeah! He better be grateful that I'm giving his broke ass a bus ticket! Now, get the fuck outta my face, Micha! I can't stand you right now! And clean my house before either one of you leaves, and I mean it! I want this motherfucker spotless! I'm going out, and when I get back, I wanna see myself in the granite!"

Kenzo said, "Damn, mon. Why your sista act like she don't want you to be happy?"

Micha was unfazed and said, "Fuck her! Let's go get something to eat."

I came back home after going out to get myself together. This little bitch got me so twisted! I wanted to take flight on her ass, but that woulda been ugly. I decided to go upstairs, make love to Jah, and try to get a good night's rest. "Hey, baby." I greeted Jah as I entered the bedroom. "I am so burnt out and horny."

"Chantal, who was that African muthafucka?"

"I don't know. Some dude Micha knew from Atlanta."

"You mean you don't even know who this nigga is and he all up in the house?"

"Baby, I really don't wanna go through this shit. She told me she wanted to have a little company. Next thing I know, this muthafucka done spent the weekend."

Jah kept pressing the issue. He said, "So you telling me you don't know what's going on in our house for three days? Where the fuck they doing that at, Chan?"

"It wasn't like that, Jah."

"Well, how the fuck was it? You been slipping lately, ma. You ain't focused, and your game slippin'! A trick-ass nigga rang the doorbell the other day saying he looking for Micha. You letting this little girl come in here and fuck shit up, and you ain't even checking that shit?"

"What nigga at the door?"

"I don't know, don't care. Something like Freeway or Eno or some shit. And not only that, Chan you don't spend no time with me, I mean none! It gets lonely up in this big muthafucka. That's why I stay gone, and you don't even give a fuck how long I'm gone. I smash for like days and you don't call. Don't even have a problem with it. That sends a message that you don't give a fuck."

"Jah, that's not true! I care about you. I just feel like everybody needs their space. I don't try to crowd you. I let you have your space, cause that's how I want you to treat me. I need my space, too. Don't get it fucked up. I love you, but sometimes I don't wanna be bothered. It don't got nothing to do with you, it's just how it is. Hold up, did that nigga say his name was Freeno?"

"I don't give a fuck about that, Chan! I'm trying to tell you how I feel, and you worried about a fucking nigga at the door. I wonder sometimes if you would prefer I wasn't here."

"No, Jah. I appreciate you being here." Damn, this nigga is straight trippin!

"You *appreciate* me being here? There you go! Wanna play the word game? I ain't playing, Chan! I'm actually tired of this shit!"

"You tired of what, Jah? Huh? You the most comfortable muthafucka I know. You ain't got to do shit but wake up. Everything you need and want is at your disposal."

"Well kept? Is that what I am to you, Chan? A well kept nigga? Bitch, you can't keep no nigga that don't wanna be kept!" Jah stood up as if he was ready for battle.

"Jah, I don't wanna have this conversation."

"I know that's right! Well, if you don't start showing me a little more respect around this muthafucka, I'ma leave."

"Leave? Where you gonna go? Sit your ass down and get ready! I'm gonna go in here and take a shower. When I get out, I wanna see my dick at attention." I started towards the bathroom.

Jah said, "Is that right?"

"Yes, that's right!"

Then Jah dropped a bomb on me. He said, "Shit, how you know it's your dick?"

"It better be or there's a problem. Shit, as much I done paid fo' a muthafucka... another bitch wouldn't be able to afford yo' ass!"

"Chan, that's the shit I be talking about. Like you bought me. Bitch, I'm a man! I'll slap the shit outta yo' ass!"

"Shut up, Jah. And stop calling me a bitch with your drunk ass!" It seems that ever since Jah came home, all he does is drink and smoke blunts. He ain't about no paper, no business. He a safe haven-ass nigga. I know damn well I ain't supposed to be kicking it in this manner with this broke-ass nigga. For some reason, I feel I have an obligation to him. I think he came into this lifestyle and settled to be nothing. If I didn't feel this loyalty for a muthafucka, I would let his ass go. I guess my obligation has turned into pity. He said, "Fuck you, Chantal!"

"Yeah, nigga. Just be ready when I get out this shower, or there will be hell to pay." I headed towards the bathroom. While I was in the shower, Jah made a phone call. "Hey girl, this Jah. What's up?"

"Nothing. You coming over?"

"I was thinking about."

"Oh yeah? So where is wifey?"

"She in the shower."

"I'm surprised she gonna let you out the house."

Jah, still angry from he and Chantal's exchange, said, "Shit, she don't care if I leave. She ain't gonna miss a nigga."

"Well, come on over here and get some of this pussy. Let me massage your neck and all the rest of your shit."

"That sounds like a plan. I'm on my way." Jah was leaving when Micha brushed passed him. She said, "Hey, Jah!"

"Sup, Micha. Where you going?"

"To handle my business, which is none of yours. You drunk as fuck! Maybe you shouldn't drive."

"I'm good. I'll holla, okay?"

"You want me to let Chan know something?"

"Naw, just tell her I left."

"Don't run into a tree and kill your stupid ass."

When I stepped out of the shower, Jah wasn't in the bed. Damn, where he at? "Jah, stop playing. Where you at?" Just then, Micha came in my room and said, "He left, Chan. He went out about ten minutes ago."

I was too done. "Did he say where he was going?"

"Naw, he just said he was cool and left. Is everything okay?"

"Yeah, yeah, it's good." The truth is, I couldn't believe that he left like that. Where did he go, and what kinda of fucking shit is that? Did this nigga just get the fuck up and leave without telling me? I called his phone.

"What's up?" he answered.

"Where you at?"

"I'll be back. I went to handle something. Why?"

"You need to handle some business here at home. Wasn't we about to fuck, Jah?"

"Naw, *you* was about to fuck. I wasn't getting ready to do shit."

Who is he talking to? "Oh, that shit is messed up! You just leave without telling me?"

"Shit. It's like you say, I'm grown. I didn't know I had to report to nobody. Ain't that how you say it, Chan? You wanna get what you give, right?"

"Jah, don't patronize me. Hurry up and come home."

"Chan, don't wait up."

"What's that supposed to mean?"

"Just what I said. Look, I gotta go." Click! No this muthafucka didn't just hang up in my face! I called him right back.

"What's up?"

"What's up is you just hung up in my face! I don't know what game you playin' but it's not gonna work."

"So now you feel like I don't care, right? Okay, I'll be home later. Don't call the phone back, you hear me? Okay? Bye."

"Okay? No, Jah, it's not okay! Please don't make me disconnect the phone."

"What did you just say?"

"You heard me!"

He said, "I'll talk to you when I get home."
Then he hung up the phone. All I could do was look
at the receiver as if it was actually him. Was he
really thinking that whatever he is doing is gonna
be acceptable? His ass is right. If he tired then he
need to go, cause I ain't the one for this shit. I
done bent over for this nigga long enough, and at
the first sign - and I do mean the first sign of this
nigga fucking around, he gotta go! It's just the
excuse I need to get him outta my house. I don't
need him, and I definitely don't need his shit!
When he comes home, he can just lay on the
couch and think about this pussy. He will be the
dumbest muthafucka in the world to let this go. He
better have a good reason for being disrespectful!
Then again, ain't no reason. All this is bullshit!

I wish I could talk to Teron. He has taken
his ass back to Africa for a couple months. He said
he needed to help his family get back on their feet
from the recent tragedy they sustained. I should
have taken that invitation to go with him, if only
for a little while. Going through all this bullshit got
me super stressed so I decided to give Quilla a call
and invite her to a spa day. When she answered I
said, "Hey, Quilla. You wanna meet me at the spa?
My treat."

"Hell yeah! I can't turn that kinda offer
down!"

"Okay, great. Meet me at Rejuvenation."
Quilla showed up right on time. She said, "Hey,

Sis. You look good. Is that the new Chanel? Love it! How you doing?"

"Not good, girl. I'm fucking stressed out. My chest hurting and shit. I feel like just going away and not coming back. Just running away from it all, you know what I'm saying?"

Quilla said, "Yeah, but you gotta get your shit together, Chan. You're at the brink of a nervous breakdown, and that's not good for those involved."

"See, Qui, that's the point. Those involved are the problem. Do you know your brother left in the middle of sex?"

"What you mean?"

"Well, not in the middle of the fuck. I was in the shower and he left. I haven't seen him since."

"You and Jah really need to sit down and listen to each other. You're feeling a certain way, he's feeling a certain way.

"Quilla, sometimes, I think he's cheating on me. The trust I have in him outweighs that thought but I can't understand where he goes every night and stays gone all night. I never question him cause I do my shit too, so I ease off his ass and let him do him. He says by me not saying nothing, I don't care."

Quilla asked, "Do you Chan?"

"Do I what? Care? Of course I do, Qui."

"My brother is all I got. And you my best friend, so I love both of you."

"I know, Qui. I love you too, but this little heifer, Micha... I can't stand her ass! I'm trying to put up with her, but it is challenging. She is so disrespectful. Fucking with these broke ass niggas, disrespecting my house. She don't give a fuck! Bitch, do you know she spits on my shit? She going through my shit. She found my personal business in my office, some stock and bonds. I had to take that shit to the safe deposit box. She trifling, Quilla! I'm so ready for her to get outta my house, but she don't have nowhere to go. I feel sorry for her ass. I've tried talking to her. I've tried hollering at her. Nothing works. I can't understand this little girl. She act like she got a problem. She needs therapy to solve some of her issues. I'm even willing to go with her to do that. There has to be a solution to this drama. She my sister and my dad would have wanted me to try and help her. But damn sis, how much a bitch gotta take?

Chapter 19

Early the next morning, Micha was going to see Joyce. It had been over five years since the last time she visited with her. She said, "Chantal, I'm going to see Mama in the morning. You wanna go?"

"Hell naw, Micha. What for?"

She said, "Cause she your moms, and I'm sure she wanna see you."

"That's your mommy, Micha. Joyce don't give a fuck about me. Hell, she don't give a fuck about you, and as soon as you realize that, you're gonna be able to move past her bullshit. She's a manipulating, selfish bitch, and I would advise you to stay clear of her."

"Damn, Chan! She is our mother, and being in jail, I know she needs us. She loves us."

"Yeah? So why the fuck did she kill our father then, huh? Left us to do this shit by ourselves."

"Come on, Chan. You and I both know why Mama is in jail. If you so busy fucking my daddy, she wouldn't have killed him that night. You know you wrong for that shit."

"What do you mean *your* daddy? He was just as much my dad as he was yours."

"No he wasn't! He would have never had sex with his own daughter! He was a pimp"

"What? You didn't even know him, Micha."

"Yeah, and that's the sad part. But had I known him, I can guarantee he would not have fucked me. He would not have run his dick up my ass. But you wanted that shit, didn't you, Chantal? That's why you let him do it, huh?"

"Look, Micha, I'm not having this conversation with you."

"Why not, Chan? The last time I mentioned it, you ran from it. Is it that the truth hurts?"

"No, Micha. The fact that you think this was all my fault, that hurts. I didn't do anything to daddy, and he didn't do anything to me, okay? Let's leave it right there."

"It's not okay, Chan. Do you realize what you did to our family? I want you to understand how you hurt everybody. How you fucked up everything!"

"Okay, Micha. Stop yelling in my house and get yourself together. I've told you, I didn't do anything."

Micha screamed, "Get out of denial, bitch!"

"Micha, how dare you call me outta my name!"

"Chan, I'm so sick of hearing 'your this' and 'your that'. All this is mine, bitch! Don't you get it? I'm here to get what's mine, and I called you a bitch cause that's what you act like."

What the fuck was happening? I said, "I'm not having this conversation or dealing with this disrespect. I'm gonna go take me a shower and tomorrow we're gonna sit down and figure out where you can move to, cause this right here ain't working. Ain't no use in trying to bond with someone that clearly don't like you. That's a losing battle."

"Oh, you putting me out, Chan?"

"No, you're putting yourself out, Micha."

"Ha! Now ain't that a bitch!"

Later, Micha was visiting with Joyce. Micha said, "I know, but I just want her to feel my pain first." Joyce said, "She gonna feel your pain when you take all her shit. Hell, that's all yours! Maine's inheritance goes to his sole living heir, and that's you! That bitch ain't his daughter."

"That's crazy, Ma! She really thinks she is. She be walking around talking 'bout 'Chantal Laine this' and 'Chantal Laine that'. And prissy-ass Auntie Jackie don't even like me, and I'm her blood, not this bitch! What's her real daddy's name, Ma?"

"Antonio Milton, the one Maine killed in the ice cream shop."

"So her last name is Milton? Who signed the birth certificate?"

"Nobody."

"Why didn't Maine sign?"

"I wouldn't let him."

"Did he know she wasn't his?"

Joyce thought for a moment, and then said, "No. But I always thought he did, but I never told him. And the only other person that knew was Tiffany, my best friend and Chantal's godmother. She hated Maine, so she never would tell him anything. Hell, she didn't even speak to him."

Micha said, "Anyway, time is of the essence. I found some papers when I was going through her stuff the other day. It says that she got five CDs that were given to her from Daddy. Four of them are worth a million dollars and they've all matured, except one that's worth five million. Are those mine?"

Joyce tried to give Micha advice. Coaching her, she said, "Tell Chantal you got a place lined up, but it's gonna take at least two weeks to move out. This will buy you some time."

"Yeah, then I can fuck with her a little more. Oh, excuse me for cussing, ma."

"It's good, baby." Micha and Joyce thought that was real funny. Their visitation was over. The time seemed to pass so fast! She really loved her moms. Micha said, "Ma, before I go, you should know that she called you a manipulating, selfish bitch."

"Fuck her, Micha. That hoe done called me worse than that. Handle your business! I love you. Write me."

"Okay, Ma. I love you." Micha left the prison, excited about her and Joyce's plans. She thought the drive home would be boring until Freeno called. She answered the phone and thought he sounded so good. "Hey, little mama. I been thinkin' bout you."

"Is that right? And what have you been thinking?"

"That maybe you could help me celebrate my birthday. I mean, unless you got other plans?"

"We can definitely work something out. So what have you been doing since the last time I saw you?"

"Nothing. I'm leaving the prison. I was sitting with my moms."

Freeno asked, "Where she at?"

"Brandshaw Women's Correctional. Yep, she killed my dad."

"Oh. I did hear something like that years ago."

"Yea, she coming home soon, though. She got a date to go to the board, so fingers are crossed."

"That's cool, man. That must be tough. I know you miss her." Freeno was playing her. He knew the whole story of Joyce and her prison sentence.

Micha asked, "So, what about your mom?"

"She passed away three years ago from cancer. My dad died when I was young."

Micha said, "Damn, I thought my story was bad! So who is Black?"

"He's like a dad to me. He used to fuck around with my moms back in the day. He just always kept me around. Looked out for me cause Pops was gone, you know what I'm saying?"

"It's a good thing you had him."

"Yeah, he kept a nigga outta trouble."

Micha said, "I didn't have anyone. I was born in that prison. I grew up in foster care."

"What about your sister? Why didn't you come live with her?"

"Until now, she never knew about me. Chantal says that after moms killed our dad, she and my dad's family hated my mom. Hated everything about her. They didn't know she was pregnant when she went to jail."

"Wow. So you're Jermaine's daughter?"

"Yep, and I never knew him."

"I never knew my dad either, so we got a lot in common."

Micha pulled into the driveway and ended her call with Freeno. She came in the house, making so much noise. I came downstairs to see what was going on. She looked cute, if I must say so. Her visit with Joyce must have went well. She had a smile on her face. She said, "'Sup, Chan?"

"Hey, you're back from your visit, I see."

"Yeah and mama said hi." So what? I didn't feel like talking about that bitch, so I changed the subject. "Micha, did you bring in the newspaper?"

"No, I didn't, but I'll get it. No problem."

"That's okay. I'll get it." I opened the door and was startled. "Shit! What the fuck?"

"I apologize. I didn't mean to scare you." I didn't have a clue as to who this nigga was, standing in my doorway. I said, "How may I help you?"

"Chantal, you don't remember me? I'm Freeno."

I looked him up and down and said, "Can't say that I do."

"Well, is your sister home?"

"My sister? How do you know my sister?"

"From the block."

What the hell was this nigga talkin bout? I said, "What block?"

"I met her the other day."

"Is that right? Well look, Freeno. I would appreciate it if you called before you come to my house. As a matter of fact, I would appreciate it if you didn't come to my house at all. Call Micha on her phone if you wanna see or speak to her. Ya'll meet somewhere else. Can you get off my property now?" As I was closing my door, he said loudly, "I see you're still a rude bitch."

"Okay, that's it. Leave please."

"Fuck you, bitch! Stuck up-ass bitch! I'ma leave this muthafucka before I hurt your ass! Raggedy bitch!"

Oh hell, no! "Micha! Don't ever let this muthafucka in my yard, house, cars, or anywhere around me!"

"What happened? What's going on?" Micha rushed to the porch.

Before I could answer, that rude ass nigga said, "This bitch is stuck up. Fuck her! You want to know what happened? I just knocked on the fucking door and asked for you, and this bitch..."

"Oh, okay, okay. Freeno, I'ma call you baby. Okay?"

I slammed the door in Freeno's face. "Micha, I don't like the fact that you got all kinds of niggas in and out my house and all on my property. You're gonna have to make a decision. Respect this structure or you're gonna have to go.

And I need to know what you're gonna do now, cause this shit gotta cease. Right now! It's out of hand."

"Yeah, I know. It's just that I been so bored. I been trying to find a friend to keep me company."

"So how is it that you know that nigga at the door?"

"Oh, I was walking and I met him. He said he know you."

"That muthafucka don't know me!"

"Well, he said that his Uncle Black knew Daddy and Mama."

"Oh yeah. That's where that nigga came from. I remember a couple of years ago he and Black showed up to a party that I was having and I threw them the fuck off the property."

"Chan, I apologize. I didn't think it would be a problem. I didn't know I had to ask you to have company."

"Micha, I would like to know who is in my house at all times. Now I need to be able to trust you when I'm not home."

"You can trust me, I promise."

"Sounds good. Let's try that and see how it works out."

"Okay, sis. By the way, mama said she would like to see you."

"Yeah, whatever. I waved her off nonchalantly. "If Jah comes home, tell him I'm at the spa de-stressing and I need to talk to him. Tell him to turn on his fucking phone. I mean, don't say it like that, Micha, but tell him to turn it on and call me."

"Will do, Chan. Enjoy your massage."

"I will. You should come with me."

"Naw, I ain't into all that boujie shit. You know what I mean, sis. Just go and enjoy yourself. Don't worry about home, I got this.

Back at the house, Jah and Micha were kickin it. Micha walked in on Jah sitting on the lanai. Micha said, "Hey, Jah. You been gone all day?" He didn't answer. "Chan say turn your fucking phone on and call her." Maybe he would pay attention to her now.

"What?" Yep, that got his attention.

"You heard me! She said..." Micha tried to clown with Jah, putting her hands on her hips and rolling her neck. He wasn't having it.

"Shut up, Micha. I ain't trying to hear that!"

"What's wrong with you?"

"Nothing. I just don't wanna hear what your sister got to say. She don't give a fuck about what I say."

"Yeah, she don't care, period. She wanna kick me out, but I belong here. You wanna smoke a blunt?"

"Yeah, give me a minute. I'm gonna go take a shower."

"Okay. I'll be right here." Micha could hear the water beating on the 'European travertine' as Chantal calls it. He was so vulnerable right now. Maybe he wouldn't reject her this time like he did before. She slowly opened the bathroom door and got undressed. She could see his shadow in the mirror. She startled him as she closed the door. He yelled out, "Who that?"

"Oh, it's just me. I was getting some soap."

Jah opened the shower door. He stood there in shock. Micha was standing there naked. She walked over to him and gently put her finger over his lips as she climbed into the shower. He hesitated, resisting her again, but this time it was different. She could tell that he wanted her just as much as she wanted him. The flesh cannot reject the flesh. She knew if she could just get this moment in time, she would show him that she was so much better than Chantal Milton. The hoe wasn't even who she thought she was, fake ass bitch! She hated her sister for what she thought she did to her life. Revenge is the best antidote, so she thought.

Jah said, "Micha, what you doing?"

"Jah, you know what this is. Don't fight it." Micha begin kissing on his neck and whispering in his ear. She said, "Let me suck it, baby. Please!" She slid down his wet body and he didn't resist. She put his dick in her mouth and sucked it like a lollipop. Jah gave in and said, "Damn, girl. Yeah. Just like that."

Micha slurped his dick in and out of her mouth. He couldn't resist that shit. When she stopped, he pressed her head to continue. Micha wouldn't let him cum. She needed him to last. The revenge in her heart was gonna be best served with DNA in her vagina. If she could prove it, she would win. Micha wondered why Chantal never asked her about the shit she was doing she wasn't there, but that didn't stop her. She continued to fuck this nigga and do the most scandalous shit she could think of. Micha bent over so that he could stick his dick in, then she squeezed it with every muscle in her pussy. She knew it was driving him crazy, the way he held her ass open so that he could hit it. Jah was losing control. He needed to bust and tried to pull out. Micha wasn't gonna let that happen. She needed her proof, but Jah must have known something was up, cause he busted all over her ass, wasting the evidence in a big way. She was mad as hell!

Jah said, "Oh shit, baby! I didn't know you knew how to work it like that!

"Yeah, and your dick is hella big! No wonder Chan be tripping bout you!"

"Yeah, right. Now move, girl."

Micha said wasn't going to give up so easily. She said, "Hold up, Jah. Let me suck on it some more. That muthafucka taste good as fuck!"

"Hell naw, Micha! We shouldn't have did what we just did. Chan can never know."

"Come on, Jah! She ain't gonna be home for a couple more hours. Come on. You know you want this. Tell me I can suck that dick some more." Micha was not above begging this muthafuckas to get what she wanted.

"You fire wit' it, bitch, but you ain't gonna never suck on this dick again. And keep your mouth shut. That shit was nothing. You hear me?"

Micha started laughing. She said, "Come on. Just a little more. I promise I'll be quick." She grabbed his dick and started again. Jah couldn't resist.

"Oh shit, Micha! Damn girl, hold up. Hold up!" Micha looked up at him and said, "For what? Don't you like it?"

"Hell yeah! That's the problem!"

"Well then, relax. I want you to stick your dick in my ass, Jah."

"What?" Jah couldn't believe this shit.

"You heard me. Come on, baby. Just put the head in." Jah wanted this bitch real bad now. He inserted his dick in her ass with so much passion. He hadn't fucked Chantal like that in a long time. He grabbed Micha's ass and separated her cheeks. Slowly at first, then faster and harder, he slammed his dick in and then pulled it out. Over and over and over again. He was kissing the back of her neck. He stuck his finger in her pussy and finger fucked the hell outta her while simultaneously sticking his dick back and forth in her ass. He flipped her over and sucked on her pussy. Jah was so aggressive, flipping her like a rag doll. He popped her on his dick and made her jump up and down.

When he busted that nut, he realized what he had done wrong. Stupid muthafucker, the damage was done. He said, "Move, girl. Get the fuck away from me." Micha got up and laughed at this dumb nigga. She had the DNA now. Jah was mad and disappointed that he had let this little girl play with his emotions. Micha said, "Aww, Jah. Don't be mad. That shit felt good."

"Shut the fuck up, Micha."

Micha laughed and said, "Yeah, whatever. Let's see how that bitch, Chantal gonna deal with this! Karma is a bitch! I'm so much better than that hoe could ever be! I am Jermicha Junice Laine! And yo bitch? She's an imposter!

To be continued...

CPSIA information can be obtained
at www.ICGtesting.com
Printed in the USA
LVOW04s2245030616
491182LV00005B/5/P